Hello all,

My name is Jo Thomas. First, a little bit about me. I worked for many years as a reporter and producer, for BBC Wales Radio 5, before moving on to Radio 2's *The Steve Wright Show*. I wrote my debut novel, *The Oyster Catcher*, in 2014 and it was a runaway bestseller in ebook, winning the 2014 RNA Joan Hessayon Award and the 2014 Festival of Romance Best Ebook Award. My novels since then include *The Olive Branch*, *Late Summer in the Vineyard*, *The Honey Farm on the Hill*, *Sunset over the Cherry Orchard*, *A Winter Beneath the Stars* and *My Lemon Grove Summer*.

If you've read my other books, you know you're in for a story about food and love, with a splash of sun, a dollop of fun stirred in and a cast of characters I hope you'll fall in love with. If you're new to my world, you're very welcome. I hope you're here to stay!

I was once at one of my favourite restaurants in Puglia, Southern Italy, where I wrote my second book *The Olive Branch*. The owner brought around a bottle of limoncello, a wonderful Italian lemon liqueur, at the end of the meal with glasses for us all. As he pulled up a chair, he asked what kind of books I wrote. He didn't speak any English and I didn't speak much Italian, but I explained that my books were about food and love, because I have always felt that the two are intertwined. He told me that for him, life was all about the food that he and his family grew on the land, cooked in the kitchen and served on the table. He held out his arm to the olive grove surrounding us, gestured to the *forno* in the kitchen, where the burning wood was glowing orange and merrily pumping smoke out of the chimney, and slapped his hand down on the scrubbed wooden table, *la tavola*. 'For the ones we love,' he told me as he held his hand to his chest over his heart. And this is exactly the kind of book I like to write: about the food we grow to cook and put on the tabl̶e̶ ̶f̶o̶r̶ ̶t̶h̶e̶ ̶o̶n̶e̶s̶ ̶w̶e̶ ̶l̶o̶v̶e̶ ny table.

Love Jo

'Romantic, fun and full of heart, reading a Jo Thomas novel feels like being on holiday without even leaving the house'
A J Pearce

'Warm and witty . . . Well worth a read'
Carole Matthews

'An utterly charming read full of rustic romance and adventure'
Woman

'Jo's trademark warmth and wit sing from the page'
Cathy Bramley

'Perfect for those who dream of a new life in the sun'
My Weekly

'Sun, good food and romance, what more could you want?'
Heat

'Perfect summer read'
Liz Fenwick

'A warm summer breeze of a story that's full of atmosphere and romance'
S Magazine

By Jo Thomas

The Oyster Catcher
The Olive Branch
Late Summer in the Vineyard
The Honey Farm on the Hill
Sunset over the Cherry Orchard
A Winter Beneath the Stars
My Lemon Grove Summer

Digital Novellas
The Chestnut Tree
The Red Sky at Night
Notes from the Northern Lights

Jo Thomas

Coming Home to Winter Island

REVIEW

First published as an ebook in 2019 by Headline Review
An imprint of HEADLINE PUBLISHING GROUP

First published in paperback in 2019 by Headline Review
An imprint of HEADLINE PUBLISHING GROUP

1

Cataloguing in Publication Data is available from the British Library

ISBN 978 1 4722 4602 8

Typeset in Caslon by Avon DataSet Ltd, Bidford-on-Avon, Warwickshire

Printed and bound in Great Britain by Clays Ltd, Elcograf S.p.A.

MIX
Paper from
responsible sources
FSC® C104740

HEADLINE PUBLISHING GROUP
An Hachette UK Company
Carmelite House
50 Victoria Embankment
London EC4Y 0DZ

www.headline.co.uk
www.hachette.co.uk

To Ali Shone, a music teacher like no other.
For inspiring me with your work with the stroke choir and
dementia suffers and for being so much more than a music
teacher. For all the help and support you gave by being there,
helping and healing with song.

And to Anita Burgh, for telling me I could write in the
first place and for her love of gin! Thank Annie for setting
me on this path.

Hello all!

Welcome back, or if you're new to my books, welcome!

Now then, who doesn't love a gin and tonic? Come six o'clock I love the sound of the ice as it hits the glass and swirls in the bowl; the fresh smell of lemon as it's sliced and dropped in; the gin measured out and the fizz of the tonic topping up the glass. And then, that first sip at the end of a long day, as dinner cooks on the stove, bringing relaxing joy.

I've always loved a gin and tonic, as did my Mum before me, but it hasn't always been as fashionable as it is now. But wow, hasn't gin had a rise in popularity over the past few years? And the explosion of small batch gin distilleries has been incredible, as has the rise in gin bars and extensive gin menus in pubs and restaurants. Gin is most definitely on the menu all over the country at the moment and if you're anything like me, I've often been overwhelmed by the choice.

But I have taken my research for this book very seriously! I had a fabulous time visiting Sibling Gin in Cheltenham with Katie Fforde. The story of these four sibling's entrepreneurial spirit is inspiring in itself. But I also learnt about the process of gin making, the dried spices and botanicals added to make their delicious gin. What I have come to understand is how the taste of gin can tell the story of its origins. It has a story to tell. It's fascinating. So when you're next trying to decide which gin to drink, think about where you want to be – by the sea, in the mountains, or in the sun on a Mediterranean island – and let the gin take you there!

I have been so inspired by the distilleries creating their own spirits, telling the story of their terroir, particularly those from the islands, and telling their story of island life through it.

I have also been inspired by how memories can be unlocked by music and stored in our hearts. I hope you enjoy the story of Winter Island and the island's song. Life is for living in the here and now, creating memories along the way. Enjoy it, with a gin in your hand at the end of a long day, and take time to count your blessings. I know I will be!

Love
Jo
x

He who sings frightens away his ills.

Miguel de Cervantes

Prologue

'Breathe,' I tell myself firmly. 'Breathe from your butt!' I clench my buttocks and drag the air in through my nose, then let it out long and slow from my mouth, not allowing even a flicker of nerves in. 'Just breathe!' In. And out. In. And out. *Phuuuffffffff!* My buttocks lift, followed by my hips and then my diaphragm. 'Breathe from your butt!' I repeat, and count, pressing each finger into my thumb, chasing off doubt and jitters, taking control. I focus my mind on the counting and not on any last-minute nerves that might be trying to creep in. This is what I've learnt to do. I begin to smile: this is it! Finally! I've waited for today for a long time and I want to drink in every bit of this performance and remember it.

I can still taste the honey and lemon from the hot drink on my tongue. I look over at Jess, my best friend and band manager. She's way more nervous than me. Jess writes new songs, which we mix into the set with covers in my country/blues/jazzy singing style. I turn to look briefly at the rest of the band and flash them a reassuring smile. There's Moira on drums, looking relaxed as ever, dragging her hands through her short spiky hair. Gwilym on keyboards, nervously running his fingers over the keys and then staring up lovingly at the oblivious Moira, waiting to take his lead from her. Ali on double bass, as tall and impressive as her instrument, with a really high quiff, making her look even more imposing, which is why men are always terrified of her and she can't understand why no one ever wants to ask her out. She plays bass guitar too.

Our two backing singers are Lulu and Pixie Rose, who doubles up on trumpet and saxophone. We don't hang out with them so much. They turn up when they're needed and do their job. And they do it really well. Both want their own careers, of course, but this goes some way to getting a foot in the door. And then of course there's Jess herself, in a smart black trouser suit, on lead guitar and sometimes the mandolin, holding us all together like a shepherd with her flock. She's incredible. She gives me a nod, and the briefest of winks.

We all know how important this gig is. It could change everything, for all of us. I know how much they're depending on me to do the very best I can. I look up. Today I need to knock this performance right out of the park. We've been preparing for this day since we first came together as a band and talked about our dreams of going all the way. For Jess and me, that was right back when we met at an open mic night nearly twenty years ago. We hit it off straight away and started writing songs and performing, adding to the band since then. Obviously we've all done our own stuff too, to make money. I do solo singing in a piano bar, and Jess creates samples for an online music company; but we've kept the band going, adding to the family, growing all the time. It's been a long journey, but hopefully tonight is when we'll all get there together.

And then of course there's Joe, sitting out in the audience, probably as nervous as the rest of us, maybe more so. There's a lot resting on this for him too. Gorgeous, smart, funny Joe, who has been my biggest supporter from the day I met him at a televised battle of the bands competition. His band crashed out in the early rounds and Jess and I went on to win that day, before getting knocked out prior to the show going on air. Joe gave up playing guitar after that; it was just a hobby, he said. Him and some mates from work had entered for a laugh, hoping to be the latest Take That, 'one for the mums'. None of them could actually sing or dance, but they looked gorgeous. He abandoned the idea of instant fame and instead told me exactly how he could help take my career to the top with his marketing ideas. It took years for me to finally give in to his requests for a date. But his persistence paid off and we've been together for coming up to four years now.

I breathe deeply and count on my fingers again. I feel excited, like it's Christmas morning and there's a stack of presents under the tree to be unwrapped, waiting to see people's faces when they see what you've bought them. In Joe's case, one present in particular. The ring that has been sitting in its box for nearly a year now. The one I've promised to put on when everything is sorted. When the deal here is done. When I've got my recording contract. As soon as I can move on to the next chapter in my life, I'll be ready to set a date.

After nearly four years together, life was finally starting to come together for me and Joe. After tonight, life will be sorted. It's our time. And he wants it for me as much as I do.

He's supported me through all the times when I've sung to a handful of people, when shows have been cancelled, and when they've been packed out and we've floated home on a high. He's always had faith in me, even when I've been tempted to give up. He has kept me going, believing in myself and that this day would come. He's been happy standing in the wings, so to speak, and I want him to enjoy this as much as me. I know he will. He's out there now, in the audience. He'll have the champagne ready and on ice. He's even invited his family along.

Joe loves to make a big deal of things. He'll be telling everyone how great I am, and organising photo opportunities for any groupies. He thinks I'm going to be the next big female voice. I hate thinking about things like that. I like to just do the best I can. Joe takes control of all the publicity, and I'm happy to let him, even if I do find his enthusiasm for me a little embarrassing at times. I'm not the big name he tells people I am, not yet. But as he works in PR, he knows how to put on a splash, and if it makes a great marketing opportunity too, well why not? He tells me we have to create the buzz and the crowds will follow. Which is why tonight is so important to us both. This gig – a night of singers and bands performing their favourite Christmas songs the week before Christmas, with an A&R manager here to see us, here in this theatre in our home city – feels just perfect. Perfect for finally putting down some roots. And I know Joe feels it too. He wants me to succeed, he tells me all the time.

The smell of the dry ice sets my adrenalin racing as I breathe in . . . and out, focusing on the finish line, like a long-distance runner. I've spent years putting in the hours, the training and the small events. This is my race today, and I'm going to do it with everything I've trained for. I'm going to sing my heart out. My buttocks clench and release in time with my breathing as the smoke curls around my ankles. I'm totally focused on the job I've got to do here. There's an A&R person in that audience with a contract ready for signing, and a producer at a record company already interested in us. This is it. Our time: the band's; mine and Jess's, mine and Joe's. Finally. And I'm ready.

I look at Jess on lead guitar. She holds my gaze, steady and reassuring, telling me she won't let me fall, and I return it. We're there for each other. We know each other so well; we understand exactly how the other works and how to support them. Then she nods and turns to Moira, who stops fiddling with her spiky hair and lifts her sticks, suddenly very focused as she waits for Jess to give the signal. Jess does one last check around the band. All eyes are on her. I clench my buttocks as tightly as I can beneath my Spandex pants. She nods to Moira, and the band fall into step behind her as she clicks her sticks together. One, two, three . . .

The music starts; the curtain rises. I follow it with my eyes, and the bright lights suddenly shut out all other sights and sounds. I focus really hard on the finish line, right at the back of the auditorium. Somewhere out in that audience is the person who is going to change our lives forever, finally giving us the break we've been working towards all these years: slaving away in cafés and bars, scraping together the money for rent and singing lessons whilst holding on to the dream of finally signing a recording contract. Rushing from shifts to rehearsals with the band and sacrificing every-thing else for paid gigs. It's Joe who's helped me hang on to that dream. Finally the record industry are interested in us. All those years of working and promoting the band has paid off. This is it.

The intro builds to a crescendo. I lift my head, drop my shoulders and relax my buttocks, ready to let my voice do the work. I smile as I slip into my comfort zone. This is what I do. This is what I've always been able to do. And now it's time to make it my everything. Briefly, a light flashes, from a camera or phone, and suddenly, without warning, my brain flicks up an image of my dad, the blue lights, the hospital sign. Not now! I can't think about that now! I shove it as hard as I can from my mind and clench my buttocks really tight, blowing out a big breath, letting the bluesy, jazzy sound wash over me.

Fully focused again, I go to slip into the first note. But though my mouth widens, nothing comes out. No sound. I falter. I dig deeper, and then recoil when something in my throat pops and all that comes out is a croak. I'm suddenly gripped with fear, tight fingers around my throat strangling me. I turn to Jess, who looks at me wide-eyed. She doesn't need to say what she's thinking. I'm thinking it too! What the hell is going on? Where's my voice gone?!

As the band plays on, I slowly step back into the smoke, into the shadows of backstage, silent, hot tears rolling down my cheeks, my moment in the spotlight gone, disappointment hanging heavy in the air.

Chapter One

'Rest!' the doctor orders the next morning in her surgery. 'Your voice needs rest.'

And then what? I scribble furiously on the pad in front of me, making an indentation on the page with my question mark. I look frantically between Joe and the doctor. The smell of cleaning fluids in the shiny consulting room turns my stomach. I hate doctors' surgeries, just like I hate hospitals. Too many bad memories. The smell brings it all back.

'Like I say, try not to talk too much. No singing.'

'No s—' My voice cracks again and cuts me off mid word. *No singing?* I scribble.

'None. Not for a couple of weeks. And then we'll see,' says the doctor, her Christmas earrings swinging cheerfully.

See what? I write. She doesn't reply, but looks up from the page straight at me.

When will I sing again? I write quickly. *Is it nodules?*

'When will her voice come back? How long?' Joe says rather more abruptly than I would have liked, but I know he's as anxious as me. He reaches over and places his hand on mine, squeezing it tightly, reassuring. Taking control of the situation as my whole life feels like it's about to spiral out of control.

'Vocal lesions – nodules – are fairly common,' the doctor says, looking between us. 'But it doesn't appear to be that. There are no obvious signs.'

'Then what?' Joe demands.

She takes a deep breath. 'Vocal cord stress can come about if you've overused your voice or been under stress yourself.'

I frown and go to answer; she holds up a hand to stop me and points to the pencil and paper.

'Try not to speak too much. Drink plenty of water, get lots of sleep; relax, maybe do some yoga and then some voice therapy. Don't strain your voice by trying to cough to clear it. Your speaking voice should be fine after some rest.'

'And her singing voice?' Joe frowns deeply. 'This is her livelihood. She's on the verge of making it big, y'know.'

The doctor smiles and nods patiently. 'Your singing voice?' She looks at me and then shakes her head slightly. 'I can't say, sorry. It may come back, or . . .' She lifts her shoulders, knowing how painful her words are. 'Only time will tell.'

'You don't know?!' Joe lets go of my hand and runs his fingers through his hair, showing his widow's peak. 'But this is everything! This could be disastrous!'

I feel myself sliding deeper and deeper into a dark hole.

'Like I say, only time will tell,' she repeats.

Time is the one thing I don't have. We have gigs booked all over Christmas and New Year. And an A&R person who needs to see what we can do!

'Get some rest,' she tells me, letting me know our ten-minute slot is up. 'Enjoy your Christmas and try to relax.'

Easy enough for her to say, I think, standing and feeling

dazed. Joe doesn't thank the doctor, but marches out. I'd like to apologise for him. He's not usually rude; in fact he's the opposite, quite the charmer usually. All the band love Joe. He's funny, and even flirtatious. But I can't explain all that on this little notepad he's bought me from the newsagent's, and so instead I nod my thanks and she smiles a tired smile, like she's seen it all before.

'Try not to worry,' she says as I leave the room. But worrying is exactly what I'm doing. My whole life is in the balance here. Mine and the band's, mine and Joe's. We had it all planned. A quiet Christmas Day to celebrate our engagement, fitted in around gigs, and then a party once the busy Christmas and New Year party season is out of the way, when there's nothing else going on. Make a big splash and tell the world.

I walk out of the surgery, tinsel and cheap baubles hanging from every available space and on a tree outside, blowing in the damp, grey December day. I look down at my phone, thoughts crashing through my mind. Get some rest, she said. Enjoy your Christmas.

'I'll message Jess,' says Joe, who's standing in the entrance with his coat collar turned up. He pulls out his phone, once again taking control, while I stand there numbly listening to the Christmas tunes on the radio in the waiting room and staring at the soggy tinsel on the tree. There is a draught every time someone comes in or leaves and the double doors whoosh open and close. Despite the heater blowing warm air from above, it's freezing and I'm shivering. I'm not sure if it's shock or cold.

We had a stack of gigs lined up over Christmas that Jess

is now going to have to cancel – unless she can find a stand-in singer. And I can't even bring myself to ask about the A&R woman.

I look down at my phone, but can't think who I should text apart from Jess, and Joe is already doing that. She'll tell the band. I just feel I've let them all down.

'It'll be fine.' Joe turns to me and takes hold of my shoulders. I look up at him and just wish I felt as convinced as he sounds. 'Look, the doctor's right,' he says firmly. 'You need to rest your voice. Do exactly as she says. Jess'll keep things going with the band.' He looks back down at his phone. 'I'll talk to Lulu about taking your place while you're away. Here, let me grab her number.'

He takes my phone and scrolls through my contacts. I feel a bubble of panic rise up in me, like I'm trying to hold on to everything I've worked for. I don't want someone else stepping into my shoes.

He looks up. 'She's just keeping your seat warm,' he says, as if reading my mind. He knows me so well. 'We'll keep it low profile,' he adds, ever the PR consultant.

A message pings through on his phone. 'Jess thinks the band can still hold on to the gigs,' he says. He attempts a smile. 'I think she's right to carry on. The band can't let people down this close to Christmas by cancelling gigs at the last minute.'

I go to argue that I might be fine in a couple of days. 'I could . . .' I croak.

'Shh . . .' He pulls me close and silences me. 'Remember what the doctor said.' He nods down to the notepad in my hand. I'm already beginning to resent it. It stands between me and everything I have known nearly all my life: singing. I pull back.

I could mime, with backing tracks, I write.

'It's a thought,' Joe says. 'But if the A&R woman comes back, she'd know.' He shakes his head. 'We need your voice to come back. The doctor said to rest. Take Christmas off. The band will be fine. I'll make sure of it.' He smiles and kisses me. 'I'll keep an eye on everything until your voice is back,' he adds, with only the merest glimmer of panic on his face.

I look at him. Handsome Joe. I love that he's as invested in my career as I am.

'And then, when you're well . . . let's hope there's still a shot at that recording contract.' His disappointment is creeping in. He lifts my chin with his finger. 'Then maybe we can start celebrating being us. We could still get engaged y'know, if you want. We don't have to wait.'

But I want to wait. I want us to have a contract, to feel we have some sort of solid foundation to build the rest of our lives on. I shake my head and I know he understands.

'I agree. It will be wonderful to get the recording contract and then really celebrate. So, okay, get yourself booked somewhere nice. Maybe go and stay with your mother . . . or perhaps that's not such a good idea.' He smiles. 'You need to get away, somewhere you can rest. Away from the band so you're not feeling you've got to go back before you're ready. I've told you I'll keep an eye on things here.' He kisses me again. 'It'll be fine, Rubes. You're destined for great things. This is just a little hiccup. We'll get engaged next year. You'll be right back on form.'

11

But will it really be fine? I slowly let go of his hands and we walk in separate directions to our parked vehicles. Joe's right. I can't just sit in the flat doing nothing; it would drive me mad. I could go and stay with my mother in Spain like he suggested. At least I think that's where she still is. My mother likes to live in the moment and goes to visit friends old and new with amazing frequency. It's always been the same. She's never liked staying put for long.

I push the key into the lock of the van door – yes, I still have a vehicle that needs you to actually put the key in to unlock it – then climb up and sit in the driver's seat. The damp drizzle gathers on the windscreen, almost obliterating the view. I look down at my phone. At least it would be hot and sunny if I went to visit my mum. But on the other hand, it wouldn't really be a rest. Mum doesn't do resting. She loves to socialise. It would be back-to-back drinks parties and introducing me to new friends. Really not restful at all.

My fingers hover over the keyboard, but instead of texting my mum, I find myself googling warm and relaxing getaways . . . and avoid the word Christmas! In no time at all, I've found it. A three-week winter special, a vocal retreat with yoga in Tenerife. Sun, silence, relaxation. Just what the doctor ordered, I think. When I see the price, though, I gasp. It would use up all the savings I've put aside for the engagement party. But if I don't get my voice back to where it was, then none of the rest of the stuff will happen anyway.

I chew my lip. I need this, I think, then quickly, before I have a chance to change my mind, I enter my personal information and card details and press send. I watch as the circle whizzes round, processing my credit card, and then, finally, the screen tells me that my transaction is complete. Phew! I breathe a sigh of relief. Thankfully I don't have many Christmas presents to buy: just Joe, something to send to my mum, usually a bottle of something, and then Jess and the rest of the band. I'll get them all something really lovely from Tenerife, I decide, and text Jess to tell her my plans.

When an email confirmation comes in from the vocal retreat, I can actually feel my spirits lifting. I imagine the warmth of the sun on my face, the sea air opening my chest as I join in the early-morning stretches. This is exactly what I need to escape a Christmas at home, where I'd be trapped with a pile of selection boxes and the whole of *The Bodyguard* and *Killing Eve* to catch up on, stressing about not being able to perform.

I turn the key in the ignition and the radio comes on. It's the soon-to-be Christmas number one, this year's *X Factor* winner. I quickly switch the radio off. It's not that I don't wish them all the luck in the world. I do. And they'll need a lot of luck. But it's about hard work too. And somehow that song reminds me of everything I've just missed out on, how my luck has run out on me. I open my mouth and try and let out a note, just to see if my voice really has gone and isn't simply playing tricks on me . . . Nothing. Yup, it's gone. Let's hope it's just on a little winter break and the Tenerife retreat is all it needs to bring it back to life.

I text Joe and Jess and tell them my plan.

Go! Jess replies. *Go and relax. You never relax any more!*

She could be right. I don't have time to relax, what with juggling two part-time jobs, my evening gigs with the band

and my solo night at the piano bar. I text both my bosses and tell them I'm away. Neither is happy, to say the least.

Do it! Joe insists. *Doctor's orders!*

You have to, types Jess. *For the band's sake as well as yours!*

She's right. This isn't just about me. I blew last night for all of us. I need to put this right. Tenerife, here I come!

I send a sad-face emoji to the band group chat and tell them I'll be back soon, then scroll through all their messages hoping I'm okay and sending their love. Even Moira tells me that they're missing me already, and to get well soon and get back to where I belong on the stage with them, part of the family, which is way too mushy for her and makes me smile in a teary way.

As I go to put my phone on the seat next to me and start the van, the screen comes to life with another message. It's going to be either Joe or Jess, I think. I could leave it until I get home. On the other hand, it could be the voice retreat, wanting to confirm my arrival times. I feel a little spring of excitement in my tummy. Maybe this could all be fine after all.

I pick the phone up and read the message, then reread it just to check I've got it right. What on earth . . . ?!

Chapter Two

Forty-eight hours later, I'm about as far away from an expensive vocal retreat in sunny Tenerife as I could get. The wind is throwing itself at the sides of the boat and I'm swaying around as though I'm in a tub on the ocean . . . Oh, wait! I *am* in a tub on the ocean and have been for an hour and forty minutes, having flown in to Glasgow airport from Bristol first thing this morning. I came as soon as I could. The sooner I get this sorted out, the better. According to the skipper, Gordan, we still have another half an hour to go, although it could be longer with the weather like this. We've already been delayed leaving, and at this rate, it'll be dark by the time I arrive. A wave slaps itself against the side of the boat and I clutch my sick bag even tighter, hoping, really hoping, I won't have to use it.

'Would you like some tea or cake? There's some short-bread, made on the island,' says the red-haired, pale-faced young woman clutching the back of the seat where I'm sitting, on my own. No one else is making this trip today, and looking out of the window at the dark sky and sea, I don't blame them. I wouldn't be if I didn't have to. I try to shake my head, but any movement is tricky at the moment. She smiles, almost gratefully, I think. 'Give me a shout if you do,' she says, and moves slowly away, bending her knees, moving with the sway of the boat and back to the galley behind the serving hatch.

I look back out of the window as we dip and roll and wonder what on earth I'm doing here. I try and text Joe to let him know I'm on the ferry, but my message won't send. I know he'll be worried. He's been texting me since I left this morning. He's as baffled as I am about why I'm here.

I think back to the telephone conversation I had as I was about to leave the doctor's surgery yesterday. I'd had a message through my Facebook page asking me to ring a number. At first I thought it was a scam, but there was something in the message that rang true. They'd used my full surname for starters, and said they needed to speak to me urgently about Hector Macquarrie. That's my father's father's name. I dialled the number carefully, wondering what it was all about. I don't use my full surname, and I've certainly never had any contact with any of the Macquarries. I don't know anything about them, other than that my father came from an island in Scotland.

The phone was answered by a man with a strong yet soft Scottish accent. 'Gillies Solicitors. Fraser Gillies speaking.'

'Um, my name is Ruby Mac,' I croaked. So much for saving my voice! 'I'm not sure if it's you who sent the message, but I don't think you've got the right person.'

'Ah,' he said, and paused. 'Ruby Macquarrie?'

'Well, I don't use—'

'Your father was Campbell Macquarrie?'

'Yes,' I said cautiously.

'And your grandfather is Hector Macquarrie?'

'Well, I . . .' I hesitated. 'Um, I suppose.'

'Is that a yes?' he said, sounding out every letter in the yes, making it a much longer word than it actually was, the S sitting on the end of his tongue.

'Um, yes,' I said. It's true, I suppose, even if I've never met him.

'Good. I need you to visit your grandfather's home on the Isle of Geamhradh – Winter Island. Your grandfather is in hospital. He's been unwell for some time and this recent fall is a worry.'

I felt like I was in a parallel universe. I don't have a grandfather. Never have. It was always just me, Dad and Mum, even though they were separated.

'I'm sorry to hear that,' I said as politely as I could, 'but I've never met—'

'As I say, your grandfather is unwell; dementia is a cruel thing. And as his next of kin and only relative,' he said slowly and deliberately, 'you'll want to be involved in any plans we make now to get him the care he needs, which may not necessarily be in his own home.'

'I see,' I said, letting the information sink in. How bizarre, I thought, that someone you've never met can be in charge of your future care, just because they're your next of kin. I hoped he wasn't going to ask me to pay for it. I don't have any money! 'I'm sure whatever you plan will be fine.'

'There is a nursing home,' he continued in a slow, almost rhythmic voice, 'where there's a room with a view. Recently vacated, sadly. But of course the house would have to be sold to finance it.'

So he wasn't asking me for money. I heaved a sigh of

17

relief and then felt bad. But really, I don't have any. 'Well, that sounds perfect,' I said, and then, 'Thank you,' because I felt I should.

'So if you could come to the island and meet with me . . .'

'Well I'm just on my way to Tenerife, as it happens. Could we—'

'Excellent. Then you'll be able to fly here first and discuss the matter, and go on from here.'

'Oh, well . . .' My voice had started to thin out, and was barely audible now.

'I'll make all the arrangements this end. I'll let Teach Mhor, the big house, know you're coming. There'll be a room for you there. And you have my number. Ring me when you arrive and we'll arrange to meet at my office.'

'No . . . er . . . wait . . .' but my voice was a whisper, having clearly used up any energy built up overnight in the reserve tanks. Rest was what the doctor had ordered, and it seemed she was right.

'Let me know the moment you arrive,' he said again, then he bid me a cheery goodbye and hung up. And that was it. Somehow, I had agreed to go to a remote island off the west coast of Scotland on my way to Tenerife! Had I not been so shocked by the loss of my voice and the sudden change to my immediate life plans, I might have been able to take control of the situation. I'm not used to not being in control. I like to have a plan and stick to it. But he'd caught me at a low moment, off guard. So now I have to visit this solicitor and sign whatever paperwork needs signing to agree to this care plan before I can be on my way.

Needless to say, Joe was not happy about it.

'What? You don't even know this man! I'll ring the solicitor and get him to send over any paperwork,' he said when I saw him that night.

I shook my head. I'd booked the flight for the next morning. And the ferry. It was just something I had to do, and then I could move on.

'Well just make sure you don't do any talking or singing. Definitely no singing!' Joe instructed, then kissed me and got ready to leave.

'Not staying?' I croaked.

'I said I'd meet Lulu, check she was happy with the song list.' He stopped as he put on his coat. 'You don't mind, do you? I mean, if you do, it's no problem, I won't go. I'll stay here with you.'

I shook my head. Of course he should go. This was my career he was saving here.

He leant in and kissed me. 'Text me as soon as you're on your way to Tenerife. Then we'll have an idea of how long it will be until you're back in the band. And in the meantime, don't worry. We'll keep things ticking over here.'

'Thank you,' I croaked.

'Now get to bed, rest,' he said, and kissed me again, and I couldn't help but feel very sorry for myself, standing in my soft cotton pyjamas covered in musical notes and symbols that matched the little tattoo on the outside edge of my hand of a treble clef, reminding me of the thing I live for: music. Joe gets that. He knows that I live and breathe music. He guided me to bed, tucked me in, and even made me a hot lemon and honey drink before leaving, insisting I text him often and didn't use my voice! I sent the band a picture of my steaming cup of hot lemon and promised I'd be back very soon.

And now I'm here, dipping and swaying as the ferry smacks into the waves, replaying the telephone conversation with Fraser Gillies in my head and wondering how Joe's meet-up with Lulu went. Finally the ferry bobs into the harbour. The young woman reappears from behind the serving hatch, pulls on a woolly hat and a big coat and goes out on deck, presumably to help the passengers – i.e. me – disembark.

I stand slowly and look out of the window. We're here. But where *is* here? The middle of nowhere out at sea, by the looks of it. And why am I here? What exactly does Fraser Gillies want from me? I just need to find out and then get out. I have a vocal retreat in Tenerife to get to!

'It was a rough one, wasn't it? You okay there, missus?' asks a young crew member as I grip the handles by the exit, keen to be off the boat. I don't bother to correct the 'missus'.

'You'll get your land legs back in no time,' says the red-haired woman, standing in the doorway, holding her face to the wind. She looks out at the little harbour and the hills in the distance and starts to smile. 'You here for a holiday?' she asks.

'A holiday? No,' I croak, then shake my head. Why would anyone put themselves through that and call it a holiday? I think to myself, my stomach churning like a washing machine. 'I'm just here . . .' I trail off, because really I have no idea why I'm here, other than a message from a solicitor asking me to come as a matter of urgency. 'Just a bit of business,' I whisper with a smile, hoping that makes sense. The young woman's head tilts as if I've just said a buzz word, sparking her interest. But fortunately the boat bounces and lurches and it's all hands to the deck and my bit of business is forgotten.

I thank the young crew member, Gordan the skipper and the red-haired woman as they finish docking and come to tell me it's fine to go ashore now. I stand looking out at the relentless rain.

'You're lucky we ran it.' Gordan grins and slings his arm around the young woman. 'Even Isla here found the going tough, and she's never without her sea legs.'

'It'll be better next time.' She attempts a smile. 'One thing about this island, you can have four different seasons in a day!' Her freckled face lights up.

'Oh, there won't be a next time,' I croak, ignoring the notepad and pencil I'm supposed to be using; there is no way I'm letting go of the handrail to fish them out of my bag as I'm about to cross from sea to dry land. I say dry land; the puddles forming there are as wet as the sea. 'The only time I'll be travelling back this way is off the island. Do they do a flight, by any chance?' I ask hopefully in my scratchy voice, putting my hand to the scarf around my throat, the rain already soaking through it.

Gordan shakes his head, his arm still slung around his red-headed partner, who is getting a little colour back in her cheeks now.

'Sorry, this is the only way in and out, unless you have access to a helicopter, that is. Like I say, you're lucky we ran. It's pretty bad out there. This time of year, you never know. It could be a couple of days before we run again if the weather stays bad.'

'What?!' I rasp. 'But I have to leave again really soon!' My voice sounds like it belongs to a stranger, like I've been in some kind of *Freaky Friday* body swap, making me feel as though I don't even recognise myself.

'We'll run again as soon as the weather allows,' he smiles. 'In the meantime, enjoy yourself.'

I pull my phone out and go to ring Fraser Gillies, but I can't get a signal.

'Mast has probably been damaged in the wind,' says Gordan. 'It can happen.'

No phone signal! Not only can I not get hold of Fraser Gillies, but how on earth am I going to tell Joe I'm safe and sound . . . well, that I'm on the island at least? It's dark now. I think I'll go straight to the house where I'm staying and message them both first thing in the morning. With any luck, the mast will have been fixed.

'Could you point me in the direction of a taxi?' I ask the woman, Isla, as she stands by the door at the top of the gangplank.

The corners of her mouth turn down. 'No real taxis, so to speak. You could try at the pub. Someone there might be happy to give you a lift. Where are you heading?'

'Um . . . not sure. Teach something?' I think about the note on my phone.

She laughs and raises an eyebrow. 'Could it be Teach Mhor?'

Ah, I realise, so that's how you say the name of the house: Tack More. Not Teach as in teacher and Hoor.

'Yes, that's it,' I say.

'Stop at the pub. They'll point you in the right direction. It's not far. You can't really get lost around here. ' She puts out a hand to steady me as I step shakily out of the door, desperate for dry land and fresh air. The young crew member puts out another helping hand.

'Just watch out for the—'

As I step out, dragging my case on wheels behind me, I am immediately hit by a blast of wind, rain and salty seawater. It feels like a slap in the face from a cold, wet fish.

'The weather!' Isla shouts over the howling gale.

'Okay!' I try and smile and give her a thumbs-up, pulling up the collar of my coat as I make my way down the gangplank onto dry land. I step straight into a dirty great puddle of water and wish I'd worn something more practical than smart, sensible court shoes. They're my only pair. But I'm here for a formal meeting, after all. I thought smart would be appropriate. I didn't expect to be helping Noah build his ark.

I head towards the Portakabin that must be the way out, and the lights in the distance that hopefully mark the pub. The water from both the sky and the waves that intermittently hit the harbour wall and splash over it leaks and seeps into my shoes, slowly filling them. I'm wet and very, very miserable. The sooner I'm out of this place, the better. I can feel Isla's inquisitive eyes following me as I squelch my way miserably down the harbour towards the pub. I put my head down as I walk, and water pours from the top of it like an overflowing gutter.

Eventually I arrive at the front door of the pub, and my

spirits lift ever so slightly from their position lying prostrate on the floor. I just need to get to the house, introduce myself to the carer or whoever, get the paperwork signed and pray that the ferry is running tomorrow so I can get on my way to Tenerife. There is no way I want to be here any longer than I need to be, no matter how friendly Gordan and Isla were. I'm not here to enjoy myself. It's not like this place, Winter Island, has ever been part of my life, and thankfully, it never will be. I shiver as I look around at the dark, bleak island – or maybe it's a shudder.

I push the pub door open, letting in the cold, damp air. There are a few drinkers at the bar. They all turn to look at me.

I go to pull out my notepad from my handbag and it dissolves in my hand, soaked through. Oh sod it! I'll be resting my voice as soon as I get to Tenerife, I think.

'Excuse me, I'm looking for a taxi,' I say huskily.

'Where do ya need taking?' asks the man behind the bar.

I rack my brains to try and remember what Isla said. 'Tack Hoor?' I say tentatively and thinking I've got it wrong. They all look at me, and then the short woman behind the bar laughs.

'You're looking for the big hoose, are ya?' she says.

'Um, yes. Hector Macquarrie's house,' I look down at my phone, which is now dimming and threatening to run out of battery.

'It's no' far,' she says. 'You visiting?' Clearly she's hoping that I'll tell her exactly who I am and what I'm doing here. But frankly, I have barely an idea myself. 'Not seen you here before,' she presses.

'No,' I reply, and don't elaborate. 'Um, a taxi?'

'Sorry. But it's no' far. Just out of the pub, past the shop and café and then the school. After that, it's just a wee way and you'll come to a track on the right. Take that towards the bay and you'll find it. You can't get lost. You'll always end up where you started. A bit like life!' She smiles. 'Let us know if you need anything else. They are expecting you, are they?'

'Oh yes, they're expecting me.' I try and smile.

'Well, there's plenty of room there,' she says with a twinkle in her eye.

They're definitely expecting me, I tell myself; I was asked to come as soon as possible. But if that's the case, why did no one bother to meet me off the ferry? I'm starting to feel a bit put out, though that could just be because I'm cold, tired and very wet . . . and hungry too, now that the seasickness has passed.

Let's hope the woman here is right and there's a warm bedroom and a meal waiting for me when I arrive. Fraser Gillies obviously knows I've come a long way. Yes, they'll definitely be expecting me.

I stand looking up at the old wooden door. It's dark, and it's still pouring with rain. I can barely make out the outline of the house, other than the fact that it is indeed big.

I look at the worn door handle and wonder whether I should feel some sense of connection with the place. This is where my father was born and grew up, after all. But I don't feel anything. This island was never part of my history. It wasn't somewhere my dad talked about either. I realise that I do feel nervous, however. I take a big breath, from the buttocks, and look for a door knocker. I can't see one. I spot a long metal pole and take hold of it with my wet, cold hands, pulling it hard, twice. A bell rings out in the depths of the house.

I am chilled to the bone now. Rain like razor blades is pounding down on me as I wait and wait. There's no reply. I stamp my freezing, painful feet and then pull on the handle again. Still no reply. I have no idea what to do. I have nowhere else to go right now. No other option. I press down on the big metal latch and it clicks, letting me know that the door is unlocked. Well, at least this way I'm going to be out of the pouring rain and the cold, I think. I give the door a little push, then a harder shove, and it opens.

'Hello?' I call out huskily. 'Hello?' My throat feels tight and dry. They're expecting me, I remind myself. I've been asked to come. I push the heavy door wide and step inside.

I can't see a thing in the pitch dark. I pat my hand around and eventually find a light switch and turn it on with a clunk. A dim overhead light comes on in the big hallway. My eyes are immediately drawn up the sweeping dark-wood staircase in front of me. The front door shuts behind me with a bang, making me jump. No wonder no one could hear me. This place is huge! There are spaces on the faded wallpaper above the wood panelling in the wide hall suggesting that pictures might have hung there once. On the floor are threadbare rugs with the remnants of patterns that were probably once bright and vibrant. The blackened fireplace is empty and cold – it might even be colder in here than outside. A single bauble hangs from a stag's antler, suggesting Christmas was once celebrated here, but clearly not now.

'Hello?' I walk down the hall, pushing open doors, hoping to find a light on, a fire lit, the smell of something cooking, waiting for my arrival. There's a big living room with two huge windows overlooking what I assume is the garden, but there's no one in there. I finally arrive at the back of the house, in the big kitchen. But there's no light, no sign of anything cooking. Everywhere just smells musty and damp. The chill in the air tells me that if they are expecting me, there's no warm welcome awaiting me.

Chapter Three

Having checked all the rooms off the long hallway, only to be met by cold, empty darkness, smelling of neglect, I walk back to the foot of the wooden staircase. I look around at the mottled, dusty panelling on the walls. The musty smell of the place is just as strong here, and it tickles the inside of my freezing nose, making me want to sneeze. I take hold of the wobbly newel post and start to walk slowly and hesitantly upstairs. My feet squelch inside my soggy shoes and the stairs creak with every step I take. The wind whistles under the front door and rises up the stairwell to meet the draught coming down it, creating a sort of wind tunnel. The bedroom door handles rattle in the breeze and I shiver with cold. I just want a hot bath and a warm bed. Hopefully a bed has been made up for me. They're expecting me, after all. I just need to find it.

I reach the top of the stairs and feel around for a light switch again. It clunks and fizzles like the one in the hall, and again a dim light comes on. I'm standing on a faded, threadbare rug, and in front of me is a long corridor with doors off it. If downstairs was like a rabbit warren, upstairs is no different. But which door to try first? I sigh.

'Hello?' I call, but my voice is hoarse and shaking. I don't want to scare anyone; I am, after all, wandering around someone's house, even if it does appear totally unlived in; untouched for what looks like years. I'm expecting to see Miss Havisham at any minute, sitting in her wedding dress. I tell myself off for giving myself the heebie-jeebies. I'm cold and tired. There's nothing to be frightened of. I just need to find my room, have that hot bath and get into bed. Tomorrow will be here in no time. At least I'm resting my voice. Feeling a little easier about things, I gently turn the cold brass handles, open the doors and peer into each bedroom in turn.

After finding a few sparsely furnished rooms with barren beds, I push open a door to see a made-up bed and a dim bedside light on. It's a big four-poster with tired, worn curtains. Finally! I step into the room, dragging my case behind me, park it up and start peeling off my sodden gloves. Suddenly I jump back, feeling like blooming Goldilocks, when I realise there's someone in the bed. A curled-up figure under a pile of eiderdowns.

'Mairead, that you?'

Two big black dogs jump to their feet and bark and I back out of the room, shutting the door quickly before they can get me.

'Sorry,' I say through the wood, 'wrong room.'

My heart is thumping with shock. That must be . . . I roll the word around my head . . . my grandfather. Mairead was my grandmother. I never met her, but I do have her name as my middle name. But what's he doing here? I thought he was still in hospital. I think back over my conversation with Fraser Gillies. I still have no idea why he phoned me. He knows I've never met my grandfather. Hector and my father fell out years ago apparently, and he wanted nothing to do with us. That feeling is pretty mutual. I'm not here to try to get to know him and find out why he never wanted to meet me. I just need to sign whatever paperwork needs signing to allow the sale of this house to go ahead, so he can move to the care home. Although looking around at my draughty, damp surroundings, I'm not sure it's worth a huge amount.

I push open the next door and see an empty bed. Another huge dark-wood four-poster. My bones ache with cold. I decide just to take it. Clearly no one has made provision for me. I pull my case in and park it up. This will have to do. It's just for the night, I tell myself.

I look in a cupboard and see an untouched pile of sheets and thin blankets. No warm duvets or eiderdowns! Well, the faster I get it made, the faster I can get into bed and sleep. I wrestle the flat sheets onto the bed, trying to fold the corners under. Then I add all the blankets I can find and spread my beach towel across the top as an extra one.

Once the bed is made up, I look for the bathroom. It's across the hall. There's a huge yellowing metal bath. It would take forever to fill, and that's if there's any hot water in the first place. I use the loo and pull on the long chain. The flush whooshes and then makes a gurgling sound, and I hold my breath, hoping it hasn't disturbed the old man. When I hear no sound other than the ancient plumbing, I have a quick wash, exit the bathroom and dash back across the corridor, shutting the door and hoping I don't have to go to the loo in the night. I put my case in front of the door just for good measure.

I look round at the sparse room, the bare floorboards and worn rug, the peeling wallpaper and lumpy mattress. I've slept in worse conditions, I tell myself, thinking of nights after gigs when we've bedded down in the back of the van to save on hotel bills and woken up early to get on the road before we're moved on from wherever we've parked. But somehow those nights were all part of the adventure of being an apprentice in the music industry. Right now, I think I could sleep standing up.

I glance up at the high ceiling's peeling paintwork and the huge cobweb draped across the seventies light shade. I walk over to the big Georgian window and feel the cold through the panes. No double glazing here! The wind is whistling around the frame like it's playing a tune on a set of old bagpipes. I hold my phone to the window to check for a signal so I can text Joe. But there isn't any. We always text just before bedtime if we're apart, but with no signal, that isn't going to happen tonight. I just hope he realises it's like I've stepped into a different world. The last thing I want is for him to worry about me. As I go to pull the curtains, a rip appears in the thin fabric, disintegrating with age. I don't pull any more, in case they come down altogether.

I hope they manage to find a buyer for this place. It's clearly not got any modern comforts. It will probably cost a fortune to do up. I can't imagine there's much demand for houses this big on a tiny island. But thank goodness that's not something I have to worry about.

I brace myself against the cold I'm about to feel, and then swiftly peel off my wet things, bouncing around on one leg trying to get my woolly tights off. I pull all my clothes from my case and start putting on as many layers as I can, including socks as gloves, seeing as mine are soaking, and three pairs of Lycra yoga leggings. I add my swimsuit over them for extra warmth, then, remembering that you lose most of your body heat through your head, pull on a pair of knee-length Lycra shorts as a hat. I feel ridiculous! But no one is going to see me, I tell myself firmly. And it is freezing. I snap a picture for Joe, just to make him laugh, but still it doesn't send.

I take my wet clothes to the bathroom and hang them over the edge of the bath. Just as I'm coming back into the bedroom, the lights fizzle and go out. I check the switch. Looks like a power cut. I feel my way into bed, clutching my phone, waiting and hoping that signal will return at some point. The bed is hard, lumpy and freezing cold. The wind is still wailing its way through the window frame. I pull the socks up my wrists and the shorts further down onto my head, glad now that I left them on.

I try to text Joe again, hoping it will send as soon as the wind dies down. Not easy with socks on your hands, so I keep it short and sweet: *All fine*, with a kiss, but it ends up not looking anything like that, so I pull off the sock and type quickly, then put the sock back on.

'All fine,' I tell myself firmly. I pull my knees up to my chest, wrap my arms around myself and glance fearfully at the shadows in the corners. The rain is still slamming against the window, the wind still whistling and occasionally howling. I try and edge down in the bed, still holding the phone to me, and hope sleep will come. But as exhausted as I am, it doesn't. I feel totally wired. At home I'd get up and make a hot drink, but here all I can do is lie waiting for morning to come.

It feels like the longest night. Maybe it's because I went to bed really quite early, lulled into a sense of bedtime by the dark and the cold. I've been here for hours now and it's still only eleven. Joe and the band will probably still be out at tonight's gig. I think about Lulu, stepping out from the shadows and into the limelight, and wonder how she got on. I wonder if she was better than me, and shiver. I toss and turn and wrap myself in the bedding like a cocoon, hoping for warmth. It doesn't come.

I close my eyes tightly, and am running songs from our set through my head when suddenly I hear a bang, like a door slamming, making me jump. Must be the wind, I think. It's wild out there. I pull the thin, musty blankets up to meet my ears and screw my eyes tight shut. But then I hear more noises, like a thumping . . . like footsteps. My blood, already cold, suddenly freezes. My eyes ping open. Steady footsteps. And I can't help but think, even though I've never believed in ghosts . . . what if this place is haunted?

I see a light under my bedroom door and I want to scream, but it catches in my throat and no noise comes out. I check my phone again for signal. None! And I'm nearly out of charge, too! I feel a cold draught whistle around the room, and then there are more noises, like chairs being dragged around the floor above my head. Oh God! It is! This place is haunted! I sit bolt upright and bite down on the covers, knowing I'm not going to get a wink of sleep and praying for dawn to come.

I must have fallen asleep at some point, because I wake

with a jolt, my head on one side, neck stiff as anything. It's getting light outside. I try to straighten my neck, making me wince with pain. My eyes are sore and scratchy. I look around, remembering the noises and light from last night, and reach for my phone. Dead! Quickly I push back the covers and, shivering, yank my case onto the bed. I don't want to be here a moment longer than I have to be. I plan to just throw everything in and get the heck out of here. Pretend I was never here in the first place. I'm going to find the solicitor I'm supposed to be meeting, get the papers signed and get out of here. With any luck, the wind will have dropped and the ferry back to the mainland will be running.

I go to the bathroom to get my clothes, knowing there is no way they're going to be dry, and try to work out what to do with them. If I put them in my case, they'll make everything else in there damp. As I step back out into the corridor, I glance around to check the old man isn't about, and my heart suddenly leaps out of my chest.

'Argh!' comes out of my mouth like a scratchy growl, my heart racing at the memory of last night's ghostly footsteps, and I drop the wet clothes at the feet of the dishevelled man who has appeared from nowhere and is standing in front of me.

Chapter Four

'Argh!' shouts the ghost, jumping backwards and dropping a big canvas bag he's carrying. He's standing in front of a doorway that seems to lead to more stairs.

'Argh!' I shout again but hardly any sound comes out.

And another shout comes from the bedroom opposite where we're standing, where the old man was sleeping. Clearly he's now awake.

We stand staring at each other wide-eyed. The ghost has wild light brown curly hair that touches his shoulders, blue-flecked green eyes, a long, straight nose, faint freckles on his cheeks and stubble around his mouth and chin.

'What the . . . ?!' he splutters in a thick Scottish accent. And suddenly he doesn't seem quite so ghost-like any more. He must be a burglar, robbing the place, maybe thinking the old man was still in hospital like I did. He certainly wasn't expecting to see me! And I'm not sure what's shocked him more: my husky, strained shriek or the sight of a woman with socks on her hands and shorts on her head.

'What the . . . ?!' he repeats.

'Who are you?' I blurt out before he can finish his sentence. 'And what are you doing here?' My heart is thump-ing. I mean, you expect to hear about burglars in the city, but out here . . . ? My fear turns quickly to outrage. 'You should be ashamed of yourself! Taking advantage of an old man!'

'Taking advantage?' he repeats with disbelief all over his face. 'And who are you and what are you doing here?'

'I beg . . .' I stop myself. I have no idea who this man is. There's another sound from the old man's room. I go to step forward, to try and explain that I've found an intruder but that everything's okay, when the intruder cuts in front of me and opens the door to where the old man was sleeping.

I open my mouth to speak, but have no idea what I'm going to say. An indignant 'Hey!' is all that comes out.

'It's okay, Hector,' he says into the room. 'Nothing to worry about. Just the wind. Did you sleep okay?'

There's a muffled reply from inside.

'It's Tuesday,' says the wild-haired man. 'How do you fancy kippers for breakfast? I have some in the smokery.' The muffled voice speaks again, and the man smiles. 'Don't forget to put some clothes on. You'll catch your death otherwise. The nurses at the hospital said you're to get dressed; you're too fanciable otherwise! I'll give you a hand downstairs when you're ready. You'll need to use that crutch. You've hurt your ankle.'

The muffled voice asks a question.

'Aye,' replies the wild-haired man. 'You've been in hospital. You fell. You were outside, wandering at dusk again. Looking for something, you said. Bet I know what too. But you're home now. Back at Teach Mhor.'

That was it! That's how it's said. I remember Isla on the ferry saying it now! Tack More. Not Tack Hore, which probably sounded incredibly rude when I said it in the pub. No wonder they laughed!

The wild-haired man looks round at me, and I feel a wave of stupidity washing over me. So not an intruder then, and certainly not a ghost. Suddenly he narrows his eyes at me, raises an eyebrow and tilts his head, a teasing smile twinkling in his eyes and tugging at the corners of mouth.

'You have a visitor too, it seems,' he tells the old man as if he's actually teasing me. 'A young lady to see you.'

'Oh no.' I hold up a hand. 'I'm not staying. I'm just . . . I'm just here to sign some paperwork. We don't know each other, you see . . .'

'Yes, Tuesday,' repeats the long-haired man, not listening to me. 'And don't forget to get dressed!'

'Hurt my ankle, y'say?' I hear the voice more clearly this time. A gruff voice from behind the door; my grandfather's voice. Not that I think of him as my grandfather. Grandfathers are there at Christmas, handing out presents and falling asleep after dinner, saving toffees for the grandchildren. I've seen the adverts. Judging from that gruff voice, my father's father isn't like that. He's just as Dad described him. A man he never got on with.

They didn't have anything to do with each other once they went their separate ways. Not that I minded not having any grandparents; I mean, you don't miss what you don't know, do you? It was just me and Dad and Mum, and then me and Mum and her constant stream of new friends, many of them boyfriends. Well, I say that, but I actually lived with my dad until I was twelve. They decided it was for the best when they split, not long after I was born. Mum's life wasn't what you might call stable. She was pursuing her music career and moving around, and so they decided it was better for me to stay with Dad. And I loved it. We were happy. Mum visited when she could. Life was settled.

Things were never the same after I went to live with my mum. I never stopped missing my dad. He was just . . . well, he made everything happen. My mum, on the other hand, couldn't organise her own life, let alone a child's, which was why me living with Dad had been for the best. But everything changed when he died. Although she never said it, I could tell Mum couldn't wait for me to finish school and leave home so that she was free to move again. Don't get me wrong, she was proud of everything I did; she just didn't always remember to turn up – concerts, parents' evenings. She was too busy living her own life, still singing, still hoping the big break would come, wherever that might be. Once I left home, cruise ships were her biggest earner. She stays in touch through Facebook and messages all the time, sending pictures of her with friends I've never met but who she speaks of as if I've known them all my life, and expecting me to keep up. She's staying with friends in Spain at the moment, in between cruises.

The two big black dogs bark when they see me, and run towards me. I reel back, much like I did last night. They stop and sniff around me.

'I'll take the dogs and feed them,' says the wild-haired man. 'They're not used to guests,' he says pointedly. 'Looks like you're not used to dogs either.'

I take a deep breath. 'Actually, I grew up with one!' I retort croakily, then bend to pat the dogs.

'He doesn't like being far from them. Or they from him.' The man looks down at the two dogs, one clearly older than the other, as they give me a thorough sniffing. Then he shuts the bedroom door, telling the old man again not to forget to get dressed.

'Really, I'm just going to find out where I need to sign these papers and then I'll get off. I—'

'So it's true, then.' He looks me up and down. 'Fraser said the hospital had suggested contacting you. You came then? . . . Finally.'

I bristle, then suddenly remember that I'm wearing a pair of shorts on my head. I take them off, then remove the socks from my hands. I swear I see him smirk, laugh even, making me bristle even more.

'Like I say, I'm just here to sign some papers,' I say.

'What? You'd run off without introducing yerself to your grandfather?' His eyebrows are raised, suggesting that the very idea of it is unbelievable.

'No.' I feel a rush of shame and my cheeks burn with embarrassment. He's right. That does sound terrible. I take another deep breath and try and explain. 'But we don't know each other. He's not my grandfather in that sense. Just . . . my father's father. They didn't have any contact. I'm not sure why I'm here really. From what my father said, he . . . well, I don't think I'd be very welcome.'

'So . . . not back for a piece of the ol' pile then?' He raises an eyebrow again, seemingly having made his mind up about me already.

'The what?' I look at the doorway he appeared from earlier. 'Um, sorry, those stairs. So there's another floor?'

'Uh huh. The attic rooms. Servants' quarters,' he says drily and starts to make his way downstairs.

39

'So does that make you . . . ?' I follow him down. I have to take the steps at speed to keep up with him, trying to make sure I don't trip on the threadbare carpet. At the bottom, he disappears into a huge pantry and the dogs wag their tails excitedly as he opens cupboards and puts down bowls. Once they are happily eating, he pulls a big cream kettle onto the stove.

'He'll be wanting tea now he's awake.'

'Sorry, excuse me.' I need to work out what's going on. 'Are you, um, family?' It feels weird saying it. He stops what he's doing and stares at me, clearly disliking me on sight.

'I'm a friend,' he says steadily, and I feel he's being deliberately evasive. 'Just helping out,' he adds, as if he's enjoying making me feel uncomfortable. 'Someone had to.'

My eyes widen and I stare at him, as if he's just slapped me in the face.

Ouch!

'Look, um, I don't know who you are—' I say quietly, but he cuts me off.

'Like I said, a friend of the family. Lachlan,' he adds by way of introduction.

'And like *I* said,' I repeat firmly, determined not to be toyed with, 'I've never met Hector Macquarrie before. The only thing we have in common is a surname.' And even then I usually shorten mine to just Mac. Ruby Mac is how I'm known.

'And a bloodline!' he says bluntly.

'Sorry?'

'The only thing you share is a surname and a bloodline. You are his son's daughter, yes? His granddaughter?'

I'm flustered. I didn't expect any of this. 'Look, I'm sorry but you know nothing about me or my family.'

'No. But neither do you, it seems, and you weren't here to find out,' he says, and turns to the range, opening the door to check if it's on. I stand and shiver. It's clearly not.

'I just got a message from a solicitor. The hospital contacted him, said Hector was no longer able to look after himself. They've recommended his house be sold so that he can go and live in a care home. I'm presuming they need my signature as next of kin. I mean, even though we're not actually . . .' I trail off. 'So can you please tell me where I need to go to do that?'

'Tell you where to go?' He raises an eyebrow, his eyes dancing with laughter again whilst the rest of his face remains deadpan. 'I can.' And I don't know if he's being very polite or very rude, but I think it's the second. Everything about this man is making my hackles rise.

'I have to sign the papers and then . . . I have somewhere to be.' I swallow, rubbing my thumb and forefinger up and down my neck.

'Bad throat?' he asks.

'Something like that.' I'm not going to explain. Two can play at that game.

He holds my gaze. 'And then you'll be on your way? Once you've been to the solicitor?'

'I will,' I say with a firm nod. I don't want to be here any longer than I have to, or any longer than he wants me here.

'Fraser Gillies, solicitor for Geamhradh,' he looks at me and possibly my blank expression and then translates with a roll of his eyes, 'Winter Island,' he says flatly. 'Just go to the pub, and it's the big house next door.'

'Thank you,' I say as politely as I can. I take a deep breath and turn to go. Then I stop and turn back. 'Just one thing I'm confused about. I thought Hector was still at the hospital, going straight to the care home?'

He looks at me steadily. 'Well, some of us think he would be better off at home. He loves this place.'

'Well . . .' I let out a slow breath, 'I think that's probably for the professionals to decide, don't you?'

'Like I say, someone needed to do what was best for him. He wanted to come home. You weren't here. I was. Someone has to look out for him.'

Suddenly I can't hold my tongue any longer. I'm not going to be made to feel guilty about a man I've never met, and who has never made any effort to contact me.

'Well, clearly you're not doing a very good job, otherwise he wouldn't have been wandering around in his dressing gown and fallen!' I say, then bite my lip. This isn't my business. I'm not involved. 'Sorry, ignore me. Very tired. Not much sleep. Bad throat. Thought there were . . .' I stop short of mentioning the ghosts. 'I should just go. I'll get my bag.' I turn to leave.

'Ah, there you are, Hector! You made it down the stairs. I'd've helped!'

I turn to see an old man in worn but clean pyjamas, a nightcap, and a threadbare brocade dressing gown with a cord tie barely done up around his middle. He's standing in the doorway, waving a crutch in our direction.

'I've buggered my bloody foot. Cannae quite remember how. But must have been a bloody good ceilidh! Ha!'

I stand and stare. I have no idea what to say or do. I don't know what I was expecting, but this man does have a look of my father about him, and yet he is a complete stranger. I want to leave. This is just too strange and I'm feeling all stirred up inside. I look at my dad's father. He clearly has no idea who I am.

'I . . . Nice to meet you.' My words tumble over each other and my voice is huskier than ever. I can feel Lachlan watching me, and my cheeks flush. I look at the old man, taking in one last snapshot of what my dad might have looked like if he'd got to grow old. Then I remind myself that just because this man looks like my dad, it doesn't mean he *is* my dad. He's nothing like my dad from what I know. I look back at Lachlan.

'I'll see myself out,' I say, and head for the door as the old man starts opening cupboards and pulling out papers and small pots of dried herbs and spices as if he's looking for something very specific.

'I'll get us some breakfast in a minute, Hector. There's some bread from yesterday. I'll toast it once I can get the Rayburn lit again. If your foot hurts, there's a wheelchair in the front room.'

'A wheelchair?' Hector carries on taking pots out of the cupboards.

'He does this every day,' says Lachlan with a gentle sigh. 'Yes, a wheelchair. For your foot.'

'Who's hurt their foot?'

Lachlan smiles and shakes his head.

'I'd go if you're going; this could take a while,' he says to me, and I turn and hurry up the stairs.

I gather my things together, then come back down the wooden staircase and stand in the hall. I could just leave, but somehow it feels wrong. I can hear voices from the kitchen. I should go back and say goodbye, wish them both well. We won't be meeting again, so it seems the least I can do.

Lachlan is putting a big cast-iron pan on top of the range. 'Bloomin' thing,' he says, looking to see if the Rayburn is still alight. 'More fickle than—'

'I just came to say goodbye,' I croak.

He stands and turns to look at me.

'Ah, Mairead, there you are!' The old man is waving his crutch in my direction. 'Hurt m'foot! Cannae remember how! Must have been a great do. What happened?'

'Oh, I'm not Mairead.' My throat is so tight I can barely hear myself.

'Wassat? Speak up, woman. I can hardly hear you!' he barks, then limps to the big carver chair at the end of the long kitchen table and collapses on to its flattened cushions with an 'Oomph!' The cupboards have clearly been turned out, and there are papers and clear glass jars everywhere.

I clear my throat. Just what the doctor told me not to do!

'I said, I'm not Mairead.'

'What?' He looks bemused. 'Don't be ridiculous, woman!'

'It's best just to go with it,' says Lachlan, over the sizzle from his pan, as he starts to stir what smells like melting butter. My stomach rumbles and I hope no one hears it. 'Tea, Mairead?' He holds up the teapot, smiling broadly, his eyes crinkling at the corners. The old man visibly relaxes and closes his eyes.

Lachlan pours the dark brown liquid from the big pot into a waiting mug. 'There's milk in the jug.' He points.

'Thank you,' I say, grateful that he's helped me out and briefly wondering if I look like my grandmother. I push the thought out of my mind. Hector's just a confused old man, I remind myself.

I haven't thought about my grandparents in a long time. There was a time when I wanted to know all about my past and where I came from, but my mum always told me that it wasn't where you'd come from that mattered, but where you were going. I seem to have lived my life by that maxim ever since. And right now, I'm going to Tenerife, to get things back on track!

I walk over to Lachlan standing by the range. The sight of the kippers sizzling in the pan is making my mouth water. I watch as he puts crusty bread into a wire rack to toast on another hot plate. The smell takes me right back to school mornings, when my dad always insisted on tea and toast to set me up for the day. He'd put a pot on the table, just like now, and a jug of milk, even though it was only the two of us. Once I went to live with my mum, there was never any milk and the bread had mould growing on it. I made do with a Mars bar from the corner shop, not the happiest of starts to the day.

I suddenly feel I need to get things straight with Lachlan.

'Look, let me just clear this up,' I say. 'I'm not here to suddenly lay claim to this place. I'm here because the solicitor called me. Once the paperwork is all sorted out, Hector can move into the retirement home. Probably be a lot more comfortable there, with heating and hot water and all the mod cons.' I try to be as friendly as I can.

Lachlan puts down a plate of gorgeous-smelling kippers, and a basket of golden toast with yellow butter melting over the top. Then he raises an eyebrow at me, though this time his eyes aren't dancing. This time he's deadly serious.

'Away from the island he loves? A two-hour ferry ride away, on the mainland? Maybe round here we just have a better sense of belonging and loyalty.'

My stomach suddenly roars loudly. I swallow. Clearly Hector is well looked after here. I bite my tongue. I'm going to be gone very soon. I don't need to argue with this man. This place is nothing to me. I'm not part of it.

'Just so you know . . . I'm really not here to claim any of this,' I repeat, and sip at my tea.

'If you say so,' says Lachlan with a nod that tells me he's not convinced, and I'm infuriated all over again. 'Now eat up.' He puts a plate down in front of me. 'My own smoked kippers,' he says, wiping his hands on a tea towel. 'You should never travel on an empty stomach.'

I look from the plate to him. I want to convince him, to tell him that I'm here to do the best for Hector, but my throat feels like there is a vice tightening around it, and my treacherous stomach roars in appreciation as he pushes the plate of food towards me.

'Eat up, Mairead,' says Hector. 'Mrs Broidy will be here any time.' He picks up his knife and fork. 'There's a lot to do before our guests arrive,' he adds, and Lachlan smiles and shakes his head, letting me know there are no guests arriving, and I feel a prickle run over my skin, like I've just had a visit from the ghost of Christmas past, a glimpse of how life used to be here.

Chapter Five

'So you're Hector Macquarrie's granddaughter,' says Fraser Gillies.

He's sitting in a high-backed chair in front of a cheerful fire in his front room. I saw Isla from the ferry coming out of the little shop clutching packets of ginger nuts and bottles of Irn-Bru and asked her where Fraser lived. I could tell she was dying to find out why I wanted to see him, but luckily Gordan, smiling good morning to me, tugged her away before she could ask. The two women behind the counter of the shop were straining their necks to get a good look at me too, but the less I have to tell people who I am and try and explain things, the better. Because I can't really explain what I don't know.

'I . . . I suppose I am,' I say nervously, perching on the edge of my chair. I should be conducting this conversation via my notebook, I know, but I'm not expecting to have to say very much. What is there to say? 'I'm sorry this couldn't be done yesterday. I was delayed by the weather, and when I did get here, the phones were down.'

'Ah yes, they're working on the mast now. Hopefully we'll be back in touch with the outside world shortly.'

I think of Joe, worrying about where I am and wondering

why I haven't been in touch. But I'll be leaving shortly, and I'll message him once I'm back on the mainland.

'So . . .' Fraser puts his fingers together and pauses, clearly not in any rush to get this meeting over and done with. 'I gather you are Hector's only remaining relative.' His soft, rolling accent is like the gentle hills around the island that I can see now it's stopped raining. He smiles, looking down at the paperwork on his lap.

'So I believe.' I give a little cough as I suddenly realise I have no idea if I have any other relatives. This morning, for one brief moment, I thought Lachlan and I might have been related. Thankfully, we're not, as I'm pretty sure we have nothing in common.

Fraser looks at me. His moustache twitches and his cheerful waistcoat strains as he leans in to offer me a shortbread biscuit, and although they look delicious, I put up my hand. I'm still full from the toast and kippers, the smokiest, tastiest kippers I have ever eaten.

'A shame we haven't seen you here before,' he says taking a biscuit for himself and brushing away the crumbs as he bites into it.

I squirm, not knowing how to respond. How do I say I didn't even know until yesterday that my grandfather was still alive? We'd never met, and now it seems it's too late anyway.

'No,' I say. 'I've never been to Winter Island. This is my first visit.' And my last, I think, contemplating the ferry journey back and not looking forward to it one bit.

'Well.' He looks at me. 'I hope you enjoy your stay with us. Take in the island. Enjoy Christmas. If you and your grandfather have nothing else planned, you'd be very welcome to join us here. There's always the full works on.'

'Thank you. But I'm afraid I won't be staying. I have a flight to catch.'

'Not staying for Christmas? But it's only three days away.'

Fraser's house is indeed very welcoming and warm. The plate of shortbread on the table in front of us was put there by Mrs Gillies with a welcoming smile. If I was a Christmas person, this is the sort of Christmas I would love.

'Our children and their families will be coming home, so you won't be alone in being the only visiting relative. Lots of families come back for the festive period. This island has a way of drawing you back.' He smiles. 'Once it's in the blood, it never leaves.'

I smile politely and try and push on. I won't be here long enough for the island to have any kind of lasting effect on me. And looking at the lashing rain starting up again against the window, I'm still struggling to see the appeal. I cough, and Mrs Gillies brings me a glass of water, which I take gratefully, my throat as dry as the desert.

'Of course,' Fraser continues, 'when the distillery was still up and running, we'd all go to the big house at Christmas. There'd be whisky and mince pies and gifts for everyone!'

'Oh yes, those were the days!' says Mrs Gillies fondly.

'Then when the distillery was in trouble and your grandfather brought in the gin and saved the place, it was a double celebration for all the workers there who owed him their livelihoods.'

I swallow. This is all news to me. It sounds fascinating,

and part of me wants to ask more, but I know I can't. This isn't my world. Whilst they were celebrating Christmas with whisky and mince pies . . . well, I had no idea any of this was going on. I was on the naughty list, clearly. Uninvited. There wasn't a place for me at the big Christmas table.

I look down. 'I'm sorry, but I really do have to get going,' I say, putting the glass down on the table, my voice getting huskier.

'Of course,' says Fraser. 'So, let me get to the point. I don't want to hold you up.'

I feel bad, but I really do want to get back to the mainland and start Christmas my way, without baubles and tinsel and shortbread. They weren't part of my growing up, not after Dad died. Mum always worked at Christmas, taking singing jobs where she could. Lunch was whatever she could buy from whichever local shop was open when she finally woke up on Christmas morning. It wasn't how it used to be when Dad was alive, when he would cook a turkey and Mum would join us for lunch and board games afterwards. I loved those Christmases. But they're in the past, and right now, sunshine and yoga and getting my voice back is what I need.

'You are Hector's sole remaining relative. However, as he hasn't made a lasting power of attorney, it is up to the courts to rule on who should decide his fate. Stubborn old bugger. I suggested it many times, but he never thought this would happen to him, and what Hector didn't want to think about, he put right out of his mind, trying to ignore the reality of it. So I am acting as deputy power of attorney, so to speak. The court has put me in charge of deciding his welfare. The hospital has suggested that he move into a home, as he is no longer able to care for himself. However, his house will need to be sold to finance that.'

'Yes.' I nod. 'You said on the phone. He did seem rather confused when I met him. I think he'd be better off being cared for.'

'On the mainland,' says the solicitor slowly, looking at me.

'Yes, you said there was a home with a place available if we can act quickly. Are there papers you need me to sign?'

'No, no papers, my dear. I just wanted to check with you that this is what you want for Hector. That this is what we all agree.'

'I'm sure it's for the best,' I say. 'As soon as there's a buyer for the house, he can move into the care home. No more worries about him wandering and hurting himself.' I nod my head at this very practical solution to solving the problem. Although I never knew Hector, and I'm not likely to now, I still want what's best for him. If that's what the hospital recommend, then I agree. I think briefly about the big draughty house. He'll be much better off in a warm home, being looked after properly. I have no idea why Lachlan was at the house, or what he's up to, but he's not responsible for Hector. The old man is on his own. He needs to be safe.

'It's been tough since your grandmother died and the distillery closed down. The farm animals are gone too and the house is falling into disrepair. And clearly his . . . forgetfulness is getting worse.'

I nod again. 'So, everyone is agreed: get the house on the market as soon as you can.'

He sucks air through his teeth and tugs at the bottom of his waistcoat.

'Of course, these days there's no' much market for a falling-down house two hours' ferry ride from the mainland. No one's staying on the island and no one's buying here either.'

'But we can put it on the market and get whatever we can for it?'

'Yes. But it won't be much. No' much change for an inheritance after the home fees have been paid.'

'Oh, but I'm not looking for anything out of this. I have my own life. I'm just happy I can help get things sorted.'

'Are you sure you haven't, well, considered a life for yourself here on Geamhradh?' he says with a kind smile, holding out a hand as if to introduce me to everything the place has to offer. But of course he's joking, and I shake my head good-naturedly, smile and even let out a polite laugh at his little joke.

'I'm a city girl through and through,' I say. I look out of the window at the road leading up from the harbour and continuing on around the island. 'And I have somewhere I need to be,' I add. It'll be good to get back to the outside world.

He nods thoughtfully. 'Of course. So, just to be clear: you agree with the hospital's recommendation? He should go to the care home?'

'Yes, yes, of course, whatever they think is best for him.'

'Okay. And you're happy for the house to be sold.'

'Of course. Like I say, I don't really know my father's side of the family. There's no . . . emotional attachment for me here. I'm just pleased everything will be sorted out.'

He looks at me steadily through his round gold-rimmed glasses. 'I've known Hector for a very long time,' he says slowly. 'All our lives, in fact. I just want to be sure this is right for everyone.' He emphasises the 'everyone' and I don't really know why. Surely it's just Hector that it needs to be right for. That's why we're here, doing the right thing for him.

'It sounds like you have everything in hand brilliantly,' I say, feeling I should thank him. 'Hector is lucky to have someone here looking after his interests.' I think briefly of Lachlan and wonder what he's doing in Hector's house. Is he taking advantage of an old man who doesn't know what day of the week it is? I feel my hackles rise just a little. I may not know Hector, he may not know me or have ever wanted anything to do with me, but I hate to think that that might be the case.

Fraser slides his glasses off. 'As I said, the care home have a place for him. I pulled a few strings; I knew the manager's mother many years ago, when the mainland was still a tempting place to visit. But we need to confirm he's going to take it soon. If not, he'll go back on the waiting list, and it is quite long.'

'Yes, best to get things moving quickly then.' I smile. 'Right, well, if that's everything . . .' I go to stand. 'Hopefully the ferry will be running and I'll make my flight.' I'm relieved everything is sorted, although I'm not really sure why we couldn't have done it over the phone. 'It's been good to meet you, Mr Gillies.' I hold out my hand to him. 'Hope you have a lovely Christmas with the family.'

'And you, Ruby,' he says. 'However, just before you go . . . As you said, best to get the house sold, and then you and Hector can both move on as quickly as possible.'

'Absolutely. I'm sure the sooner he's there, the better.'

'Well.' Fraser looks up at me. 'There is just one problem.'

Chapter Six

'You knew, didn't you?' I croak as loudly as I can. My throat strains as I stand in the kitchen staring at Lachlan, my eyes flashing. The fire in the living room opposite is blazing to match the feeling in my stomach. 'You knew what he was going to say!'

'Well, maybe you should have hung around a bit longer to find out!' he retorts, leaning against the old stove. The kitchen is full of the smell of baking bread. 'You were in quite a rush to get away from here before finding out anything about this place . . . or Hector.'

'Look, I told you, Hector and me . . . He never wanted to meet me. Has never been part of my life.' Suddenly there's a catch in my throat. Dad and his father were estranged, that was the word he used whenever he spoke about it. But that just meant we made our little family the best it could be. Small but mighty, he used to say. He wasn't that demonstrative, but I did know he was always there for me, and when he died . . . well, it left me feeling totally adrift. Abandoned. Alone. There isn't a day goes by when I don't wish he was still here.

'You knew full well why the house can't be put on the market,' I repeat. 'Why this was all a waste of time for me.'

He shrugs. 'Like I say, you should've asked.'

'Well I'm asking now. What exactly are you doing here? How do you know Hector?'

'I told you. I'm a friend of the family. I'm just helping out.'

'Well if you want to help out, move out! The house can't be sold with a sitting tenant, apparently. That's you! You're living in the attic! The servants' quarters! That's why you were here last night. And every night, by the looks of it. I have no idea what you're up to, or why you won't tell me, but I'm asking now. Will you please move out so the house can be put on the market and . . . Hector . . .' I attempt to say 'my grandfather' for dramatic effect, but it sounds too weird, 'can go into the home he needs.'

'His home is here. Everything he needs is here.' He tosses a piece of bread nonchalantly into his mouth, and I wish he'd missed.

'He needs to be looked after properly.' I glare. This man is just getting in my way now, and it feels like he's doing it on purpose. 'The solicitor needs to go ahead with putting the house on the market and I have to—'

'Yes, yes, I know. You've got a plane to catch!' He waves a hand in my direction.

I sigh, deeply and with relief. He realises, thank goodness. Hopefully this can be sorted out quickly then.

'So in order to sell the house at a "reasonable price" . . .' I quote the solicitor and raise my eyebrows. The figure he mentioned was hardly anything for such a big property. But looking at it now in the clear light of day and in a brief let-up in the rain, I can see just what a neglected state it's in. Apart from the fact that it's a very limited market. Who wants a big, run-down house on an island a two-hour ferry ride from the mainland? How would anyone make a living over here? I certainly couldn't. But it's not going to sell at all with someone living in the attic! '. . . I need you to find somewhere else to live and move out.'

My voice is barely audible, but I have got a pad and pen with me. *You need to move out!* I write and show it to him. He reads it, then goes to the big old fridge and starts pulling out what look like boxes of ready meals and putting them on the side.

'Someone needs to be here with Hector, to keep an eye on him. And clearly it's not going to be you.' He looks at me and raises an eyebrow. 'You've got a plane to catch.'

'Well, clearly someone *is* looking out for him. Look at all those ready meals. Who brings him those?'

'Mrs Broidy, the old housekeeper. She gets them sent over from the mainland.'

'Well, that's great. If Mrs Broidy is making sure he's fed and checking in on him, then you don't need to be here.'

He turns and dumps all the ready meals in the bin. Followed by several packets of biscuits.

'What on earth are you doing? Are you mad?' I exclaim. 'You can't just throw away all his meals! That's abuse. I could report you!'

I rush over to the bin and start fishing out the boxes and putting them on the scrubbed pine work surface. I'm outraged.

'You need to leave! I don't know why you're here, or what you're hoping to get from this, but you need to go. I can't believe you would sabotage an old man like this!'

He watches me as I stack the boxes into piles. Then he steps forward, picks them all up and drops them back in the bin. He dusts off his hands and stares at me.

'All out of date,' he says with a frustrated sigh. 'He forgets to look at the dates on them, and if he eats them, he's sick. And,' he adds, 'he's diabetic. Cakes, biscuits . . . he's mad for them but can't control his sugar levels. I keep telling Mrs Broidy, but she takes no notice. Or maybe she can't remember either.'

I find myself blushing and floundering slightly. 'Right, well, I'm sure the nursing home will be able to look after his diet. So,' I breathe from my buttocks, lift my chin and take control of the situation, 'could you please organise somewhere to live so the house can be sold?'

He stares at me and drops a final ready meal into the bin with a clatter. I look at it and wonder where to get some more, and whether I should contact this Mrs Broidy. I know it's not really my problem, but I do need to make sure the old man is being looked after until he can go into the home. Perhaps we could write the use-by dates on in big marker pen.

'So . . .' I draw in breath again, 'are you going to tell me what you're doing here?' I'm suddenly desperate to find out. Is he just freeloading off a vulnerable old man? In which case, the sooner he's gone the better. But then I think about the kippers that morning at breakfast, caught and smoked by Lachlan, and cooked to perfection. Is he genuinely just here out of the goodness of his heart? He couldn't really be putting his life on hold to help out an old man when there's nothing in it for him, could he? He has to be up to something.

He doesn't reply, and I plough on. 'So, you'll move out and then the house can be sold? It's the right thing for Hector.' I look at him. If he really is doing this out of the goodness of his heart, then he'll want what's best for Hector too.

He stares back at me with his flecked eyes, and I swear there's a tiny smile at the corner of his mouth. 'Yes, I'll do what's right for Hector,' he says. 'And no, I'm not moving out.' He moves away from the kitchen work surface he's been leaning against and picks up his big canvas bag. 'Now if you'll excuse me, I have things to do.'

He walks out, whistling, leaving me standing in the huge high-ceilinged kitchen. What the . . . ? Who is this man, and what is he doing here? And what's in that bag he carries around with him?

I follow him into the living room, where he's stoking the fire. The two black Labs look up at him from their place in front of the hearth. 'I'll just be outside,' he tells Hector, then he walks right past me, raising his eyebrows and nodding his head, and, still whistling, opens the back door and swaggers towards a single-storey red-brick building behind the house.

Of all the arrogant, jumped-up, ignorant freeloaders! I think, fury bubbling up inside me. I have a ferry to catch this afternoon. But there is no way I can leave with this man ensconced here. What on earth am I supposed to do now?

Chapter Seven

'No, wait!' I go to run outside after him, then look down at my feet. I flick off my still soggy shoes and survey the line of wellington boots by the back door. I'm sure no one will mind if I borrow a pair. Who is there to mind? Not Hector, that's for sure, who's emptying the cupboards either side of the fireplace, clearly still looking for something, as he has been since I arrived. The dogs are sitting upright now, as if on guard duty. And I suddenly wonder what's going to happen to them once Hector leaves here and goes to the care home. Will he still get to see them? Maybe I'll ask the solicitor, just so I know they're going to be well cared for, like their master.

I open the back door, which is marked with scratches from dogs' paws over the years. I wonder if Dad's dog – the one he had when I was little, that moved with him when he left the island – made some of them. Outside, it's stopped raining. It's cold, but the air fills my lungs and the breeze gently strokes my face. A big difference from last night. In fact, a lot of things look different from last night, including there not being any ghosts, simply a lodger in the attic.

'Wait!' I call again, but Lachlan holds up a hand and carries on walking towards the red-brick building and the barns beyond it. And beyond *that* is water. Long green grasses edge the sandy shore, where waves are gently lapping, and there are small clusters of rocks at the far reaches of the cove where it opens out into the sea. In the distance I can now see the outlines of the neighbouring islands, silhouetted by the silvery winter sun. I'm suddenly blown away by the spectacular view. It's breathtaking.

As I stand and stare, there's a sudden vibration in my coat pocket. My phone! We must have signal again! I try to pull it out, tying myself in knots in my eagerness to answer it. Finally I release it and sigh with relief. It's Joe.

'Hello? Joe?' I say as I press answer.

'Ruby? Is that you? Where are you? I've been worried sick. No one's heard from you, not Jess, or the band group chat, and the voice retreat say you haven't arrived. What's going on? Are you okay?'

'I'm okay,' I croak, and tears suddenly spring to my eyes.

'Rubes? What's happened? Are you on your way to the airport?'

Just hearing his voice makes me realise quite how far I am from my life and everything I know. Away from Joe, the band, even from performing. Out here I'm not Ruby Mac, the singer. I'm not even Ruby Macquarrie, Hector's grand-daughter. I'm . . . well, nobody.

I have no idea how to tell him I'm not at the airport. That I'm not on the way to Tenerife to find my voice again. That I'm still here, on this remote island, and that, I find myself realising, I can't leave until all this is sorted. I can't just go knowing there's a squatter in the attic and the house can't be sold whilst he's there. I can't walk away leaving that freeloader to live there at Hector's expense and help himself to whatever is left of Hector's home and memories. I may not know Hector, but I do know what's right. And this isn't!

'Rubes, can you hear me? Did you sign the paperwork? Are you on your way to Tenerife?'

I watch Lachlan disappearing. I can't just let him go. I have to sort this. I have to leave. I have a flight to catch this afternoon!

'Yes. All signed and sorted. I'll be leaving shortly. Don't worry, it's all in hand,' I lie with a blush. It's the first time I've ever lied to Joe, I think. Apart from the odd white lie when I've been out with Jess and told him I only had a couple of drinks, because he thinks it's no good for my voice. He's probably right. I should've listened.

'I have to go, love you,' I say into the phone. 'I'll ring when I'm at the airport.'

'Make sure you do,' he replies.

'Oh, how's Lulu doing?'

'Great!' I can hear the smile in his voice, then it suddenly drops. 'I mean, not as great as you. But doing fine. Keeping everything ticking over till you get back.'

'Oh, good,' I say, and suddenly feel a bit teary again, wishing I was home, back with the band. 'Tell them all I'm fine and I'll be in touch soon.'

'Love you,' he says.

After he's hung up, I stare at the phone as if watching my life from inside a glass bottle bobbing about in the ocean. I look back at the swaggering figure of Lachlan. There's only one thing standing between me and getting ashore, and that's him, I think furiously. I ram the phone back into my pocket and start marching after him.

'Hey! Hey!' I shout impulsively, only remembering I shouldn't when my voice cracks and strains. 'Wait!' I wave my arms, but he doesn't respond. The arrogance of the man! I feel myself getting hot with fury. How dare he?

I launch myself forward, stomping after him. I'm not sure if it's my mood that's making me walk like this, or the boots.

'Hey!' I attempt to call again as I march. Thank goodness for the wellies. Much more sturdy than the soggy court shoes. 'Lachlan, wait!' I croak, then break into an unsteady run. I haven't run in years, but it feels really quite good. The blood is pumping round my body and I feel a surge of energy. I jog down the path towards the low buildings. The wind is sharper here. Fresh. There's a spritz of sea salt in the air.

Lachlan turns to me, rolling his eyes. 'Yes?'

It's like I'm some irritation in his life, and I'm infuriated even more. But I take a deep breath of the salty, fresh sea air and swallow to try and get my voice lubricated.

'You have to move out,' I say simply. 'I've told you. I need you to agree to go so the house can be sold. To get Hector into the care home.'

He gazes out across the water at the waves gently breaking on a cluster of rocks. Then he turns back to me and sighs beneath the scarf wound around his neck.

'And I've told you. I'm not moving out. I'm staying.' He looks at the bay. 'I have an agreement with Hector.'

'Yes, the solicitor told me. Hector has said you can stay as long as you need to. Well, now you need to go.'

'I can't go yet. I need to be here.' He looks back out to sea.

'You mean you're freeloading off him!'

He steps towards the big metal door of the red-brick shed and unlocks it.

'Believe what you like. But you don't know anything.' He looks at me with his flecked green eyes, his long hair whipping round his face. Then his expression hardens and he says, 'You haven't been here.'

And that hurts. I don't know why. I barely knew 'here' even existed until I got the call. My father rarely spoke about the place. It was like it was locked away in a box inside him and nothing could unlock it, not properly. He did mention it a few times, like he'd opened the lid just a chink but wasn't brave enough to flip it back completely. My mum never mentioned it either. Only that she'd come here to stay with a friend, a musician who'd found inspiration and was suddenly making a name for herself. Instead, my mum met my dad and got pregnant. The island wasn't part of my world then and it isn't part of my world now. I can't feel guilty about what I didn't know.

My phone vibrates again. It's a text from Joe again, asking if I'm on my way yet. I need to move on and find my voice again. Get my own life straight and see if I can salvage anything of the career I left in tatters on the stage at our last gig.

'I know you're taking advantage of an old man's situation, and it needs to stop!' I say. 'Good job I got the call, by the looks of it.'

'Like I say,' he says slowly, 'you know nothing.' He turns and opens the heavy door into the single-storey building, then stops and turns to me. My spirits lift for a moment. 'But if you're staying around, dinner is at seven.' He steps inside, the lights flicker on and the door closes behind him, ending the conversation with a bang.

'No, wait!' I call after him. 'You have to . . .' But my words are lost on the wind. I'm staring at a big metal door and I have no idea what's behind it or what this man is up to.

Now what? I look down at my phone. One thing's for sure, I'm not going to make my flight this afternoon. I sigh and send an email to the vocal retreat, explaining that I've been held up and need to postpone, just for a day, no more than two. Then I send a message to Joe, explaining that I'm trying to save my voice by texting and that I've been delayed slightly. He replies straight away, asking what's going on and why I'm not on my way to the retreat. I tell him there's been a delay with one of the pieces of paperwork. A hiccup, that's all. Just needs ironing out.

I'm amazed how easily these little white lies seem to be rolling off my keypad. I press send, then tap the phone to my chin. Now what? I repeat to myself, wandering across to the shoreline. Looks like I'm going to have to do something I rarely do: ask my mum for advice.

While I wait for the call to connect, I look out across the moorland to the mountains behind the house, and catch my breath as what I think is a herd of deer run across it. As they disappear, the phone begins to ring.

'Hi, Mum, how's things? How's Spain?'

'You're up early! Spain's glorious! Been having a few days off here with Babs and George. You remember Babs and George. Met them on a cruise I was doing round the Med, years ago. They loved it so much they bought a place out here. If I was the settling-down type, it would be a great place to do it. But I'm about to go back on board in time for

Christmas. So how are you, darling? Don't hear from you much these days. Not thinking about joining me for Christmas, are you? I could get you some gigs. But you're probably back to back with gigs of your own, aren't you?'

'Er, no . . . Actually, Mum, I'm going to be in Tenerife.'

'Tenerife? At Christmas? What are you doing there?'

'Just . . . getting away from it all.'

'With Joe?'

I think about Joe and his last text.

'No, just me.'

'Sounds like there's trouble there . . .'

I think about me and Joe. We're the most solid couple I know. We have joint dreams. We're treading the same path in life. Going the same way. He is invested in what I do.

'Actually, I'm having some specialist voice training,' I lie quickly.

'Over Christmas? But isn't it your busiest time? I mean, even *I'm* in demand! But I bet I could get you on the cruise ships if you needed the work.'

'No, everything's fine.' I decide not to tell her about the problems with my voice. She'd only worry. It's about all she does worry about. My voice and where she's going to be drinking her next gin and tonic.

'Mum, tell me about Hector, Dad's dad.'

'What? Oh, I don't even know if he's still alive. Really, it was such a long time ago. Why do you want to know about him all of sudden? Some things are best left in the past, Ruby. No good ever comes of trying to dig them up. It was all such a long time ago.'

I sigh and wonder whether to tell her where I am. I go to

open my mouth and then my mum says to someone in the background, 'Coming, darling . . . Ruby, I have to go. My lift back to the ship is here.' I think about the cruise liner she's about to board and the ferry I'll be leaving on. 'Look, if you want to join me, you know you can. I'll text you my itinerary for the next month. Bye, darling. Lovely to hear from you!'

I press the end call button and look at a flock of birds coming in to settle on the beach. I have no idea what they are, but I stand and stare at them. It would have been lovely to spend holidays here, I think, learning about birds. And I can't help but wonder why I was never a part of it, why I was never wanted here.

I stop myself in my tracks. That sounds like a dollop of self-pity, Ruby Mac, I tell myself. And I don't have time for that! I give myself a quick talking-to. I have made my own life, and I will continue to do so. It's a good life, and I don't need any of this. But right now, I need to find out what Lachlan is doing here and how to get him to leave. Maybe Hector can throw some light on the matter, I think, and I wander slowly back to the house, breathing deeply with every step, finding the air filling my senses as I do.

'It's in here somewhere,' I can hear Hector saying. 'Got to be in the house somewhere. Got to keep the secret . . .'

I slip out of the boots and back into the soggy shoes with a grimace. One of the dogs barks. I follow the sound of Hector's voice down the hall and into one of the front rooms, clearly unused and not heated. He's still talking, and if I'm not mistaken, it's the dogs he's addressing. There are papers all over the floor, the cupboard doors on one side of the fireplace are flung open and Hector is attempting to climb onto a chair, balancing his crutch in one hand. The dog barks again, letting me know she needs assistance with her charge.

'Hector!' I say. He turns to look at me and nearly topples backwards. I step forward and put out my hands instinctively to steady him.

'Ah, there you are!' he says, and the dogs lie down, happy, it seems, that help is close at hand. I look at his face, finding the similarity to my dad disarming and unsettling.

'What are you doing?' I ask, glancing around at the emptied cupboards.

'Looking!' he says, as if it's the most natural thing in the world.

'Looking for what? Is it something I can help with?'

He regards me blankly, and I get the feeling he's forgotten what he's searching for.

'I'll know it when I find it,' he says finally with sadness in his eyes. 'I know it's here in the house.'

'Why don't you come and sit by the fire?' I say. 'I'll make you a cup of tea.' I wonder suddenly what might have happened if I hadn't come in. What if he had fallen again?

I lead him into the big room at the back of the house and the dogs follow. Once Hector is settled by the window overlooking the bay, I go into the kitchen. On the side is a fresh batch of what look like cheese scones. Lots of them. It seems Lachlan has made himself very much at home here. I remember watching him pull the kettle onto the hot plate, and do the same. I make the tea and spread a cheese scone with butter from the dish on the table.

I can't just leave knowing this guy is here, living rent free, I assume. There's been no mention of any financial arrangement. But then there's been very little mention of anything. I still have no idea what he's doing here. I don't even know his surname. Just that he's a friend of the family and that he's refusing to move out, despite me explaining that it's in Hector's best interests. And what is he doing in that shed? He's clearly got an agenda, and he's not telling me! Until he goes, Hector can't get into the care home. Lachlan needs to find somewhere else to live . . . no matter how good his cheese scones are, I think, picking at the soft yellow crumbs.

Back in the living room, I put the tea and scone on the table next to Hector's chair.

'Hector,' I begin, 'what exactly do you know about Lachlan?'

He looks at me, and once again my heart twists as I see my dad in his eyes.

'Lachlan?'

'Yes,' I say. 'Who is he and what's he doing here?'

Hector picks up the scone and takes a bite. To the dogs' delight, crumbs tumble down his front.

'Lachlan, you say?'

'Yes,' I smile.

'Who's Lachlan?' he asks, and I sigh as realisation washes over me. The house can't be sold until Lachlan leaves. And I can't leave until he does. I have to find out what he's up to, and think of a way of getting him to go.

69

Chapter Eight

Dinner is indeed at seven. And it's absolutely delicious. The smell draws me from the top of the stairs. The big scrubbed pine table in the kitchen is laid at one end, for three. The dogs are happily eating from their bowls in the far corner of the high-ceilinged room, heads down, tails up. Lachlan is ladling the glorious-smelling stew into bowls.

I stand at the door, feeling uncomfortable. On the one hand this man is refusing to leave and is definitely up to something in that shed. On the other hand, here he is creating one of the most welcoming sights and smells I've ever come across.

'Come in if you're staying, sit yourself down. I'll fetch Hector.' He turns to look at me. 'Unless you want to?' He raises a challenging eyebrow.

'I . . .' I'm still very unsure about how to speak to Hector. I haven't met anyone with dementia before, and to be honest, and to my shame, I feel nervous. Nervous of saying the wrong thing, nervous that he might work out who I am and be angry at me being here. I feel ridiculous for even thinking these things, but this is all uncharted waters for me right now and I'm confused. I have no idea why I'm here or what to do for the best. 'Look, I can get something to eat in the village, at the pub,' I say. Sitting down to eat with this man seems too weird. But my stomach rumbles treacherously.

'Up to you, but you'll find the chef's already left.'

'Left? Left to go where?'

'Here!' He gives a little laugh and looks at me. 'I'm the chef. I cook and deliver dishes to the café and the pub. And this,' he ladles stew into the third bowl, 'is the dish of the day. So you can either eat it here, or pay for it at the pub. The locals will certainly be keen to get to know you.'

He's right. The last thing I want is for people to know who I am. They'll all be jumping to the same conclusion as Lachlan – that I've turned up to see what I can get out of Hector – and that couldn't be further from the truth. I don't want anything. It was the solicitor who contacted me, and I'm still trying to work out why. He didn't need my signature, and if he's known Hector all his life, then he knows that I've never had anything to do with my grandfather.

'So . . . you're running a business from here?' I look around at the big cast-iron pots by the sink and the crumb-scattered board with a freshly cut loaf of dark brown bread that he's put on the table next to the butter dish.

'I suppose you could call it that. I catch it, pick it, cook it and deliver it.'

So that's it, I think. 'Is that why you insist on staying here, for the facilities?'

He puts the bowls on the table. 'No, I could do this from anywhere. It just makes it easier if I'm here. To be honest, there are a lot better cookers than this old thing!' He nods at the range with a smile. 'I'll get Hector. Sit if you're staying,' and he walks out of the kitchen.

I look at the stew: tender meat surrounded by soft white potatoes, deep orange carrot chunks and dark green cabbage, sitting in a pool of glistening gravy. My stomach barks at me to sit too. The smell rises from the bowl in front of me and my mouth literally begins to water as the aroma wraps around me, warming me, reminding me of one of my dad's hugs. He was never great with words, but his hugs were amazing. As was his food. A lot like this, I think, looking down at the bowl. I pick up my spoon and, unable to wait, dip it in, lift it to my lips and taste . . . I shut my eyes, imagining myself back there at our little kitchen table. Just him and me. Safe and happy.

'Started already?' Lachlan makes me jump as he comes back into the kitchen, and I drop my spoon with a clatter.

'Sorry, I couldn't . . .' I flush with embarrassment.

'It's fine!' he laughs. 'Glad you like it. It's one of Hector's favourites.'

Hector comes into the kitchen, the cord from his dressing gown hanging low. 'Ah . . . rabbit stew,' he says, and sits and starts to eat.

'Rabbit?' I ask, a little more high-pitched than I meant.

'We like to use what we have here on the island. And we have plenty of rabbits,' says Lachlan. He sits down and hands around the board of bread. 'Tuck in. There's plenty more.'

We eat in relative silence, just the clatter of spoons against the bowls and the contented mopping of juices with chunks of bread. And for a moment I can envisage my dad as a boy, sitting in this big kitchen devouring a Sunday roast. I want to ask Hector about him, but know it's like an itch waiting to be scratched. Once I start, I might not stop, and it'll only make the itch worse in the long run.

'So,' Lachlan says finally when we've finished and he stands to clear away the plates. 'You know what it is that I do; what do *you* do, back on the mainland?' He stacks the bowls by the sink.

'Oh, I'm a singer,' I say, in a voice that doesn't even sound like my own.

'A singer?' he says. 'Me, I'm tone deaf.' He begins to fill the sink with water from the big kettle on the range. 'Can't sing a note.'

I put my hand to my throat. Nor can I right now, I think, and I suddenly wonder if I ever will again. I remind myself not to get too comfortable here, because I need to get off Winter Island and on to Tenerife as soon as possible.

Chapter Nine

When I wake the following morning, I text Joe, telling him I'm hoping to be on my way today and wishing the band luck with the gig tonight. Every bit of me longs to be there with them. I can just picture Lulu stepping up to take my place, and although I know she'll do a great job, I wish she wasn't ten years younger than me with a determination to match mine.

I look at my phone. There's no reply. But then there wouldn't be. It's far too early for Joe. I send a good-luck GIF to the group chat and a text to Jess anyway, and she does reply.

Hey, what's happening? Where are you? You're not in Tenerife?! We've been worried.

Stuck in Scotland on an island called the Isle of Geamhradh, otherwise known as Winter Island! I type back.

Why? Why aren't you at the voice retreat?

Just needed to sort some family stuff here first, I reply.

Family stuff? Your mum's in Scotland?! Is she okay?!

No. It's my dad's side. I try and think how to word what I'm doing here, because I really have no idea myself.

I thought you didn't know your dad's side.

I don't. But they're moving my dad's dad into a care home. Just need to get a few things sorted. I wish her luck again tonight.

Don't worry. It'll be fine. Lulu's been great and Joe's been really supportive too.

I have a twinge of what might be jealousy. I'm not the jealous type. Joe's flirtatious, but like I say, we're solid. He wants what's best for me, for us.

Great, I text back with a smiley face, and just wish I could feel it.

I creep quietly downstairs. Hector is emptying the cupboard by the fire again, the dogs standing guard. Lachlan is in the kitchen. The smell of toast tries to tempt me in, but I resist. I need to know more about this man and how to get him out of the house. Season of goodwill or not, Hector needs to sell up.

The wind and rain may have dropped, but so has the temperature. I walk down the grassy lane towards the road, banked either side by hedgerows. A small stream trickles beside it, clear and busily bustling, as if on its way to meet up with friends. I follow it towards the road and the cluster of shop, pub and café.

As I approach the shop, I see the familiar figure of Fraser Gillies coming out of it.

'Oh, hello, um, excuse me.' I wave, knowing my voice alone isn't going to reach him. He looks up, and my heart lifts. Hopefully he'll have an idea about how to get Lachlan to leave, and that will mean I can too. 'Mr Gillies,' I say, jogging up to meet him.

'Ah, Ruby. How lovely to see you. Glad you've decided to stay on and take in the island.'

'Well, I'm hoping to be on my way soon. Um, tell me, this Lachlan, the one staying at Hector's . . .'

'Ah, Lachlan, he's a good man. Knew you'd get along. Makes a mean rabbit stew. Well, you know where we are if you fancy a Christmas drink. The family are all here and would love to say hello.' He turns to leave with his newspaper under his arm.

'No, wait, Mr Gillies . . .' I catch his arm. 'I mean, Lachlan . . . isn't there any way you can get him to leave?'

''Fraid not. Hector was quite clear that he has a home there as long as he wants it. He has to *want* to leave.'

I look at him in despair. 'But we're just trying to do what's right for Hector. Why can't he see that?'

'Sometimes . . . well, what's the expression about keeping your friends close and your enemies even closer?' He smiles. 'Oh, by the way, I spoke to Flora, the care home manager. She's still holding that place for Hector, but we have to let her know soon if we're going to take it. Her mother and mine used to be on opposing bowls teams. Your grandmother played too.' He smiles, and for a moment I wish I could have seen that. 'They'd take the ferry across to play against each other, bowling bags in hand. Flora's very fond of the island. And the home is in the nearest town on the mainland, so not that far from the island really. He should be able to see it from his room. Anyway, she'll keep the room, but just until Candlemas.'

'Candlemas?'

'February the second, when all payments for the quarter are due.'

'That's just over five weeks away!'

'Indeed. Five weeks. After that, sadly, he will have to go to the bottom of the waiting list. And then who knows how long he'll have to wait to get in there. Five weeks to work out what happens next.'

'Five weeks,' I repeat.

He nods, smiles and wishes me good day. I'm left standing there watching him go, wondering what he means and why he isn't doing more to get Lachlan to leave. Well, if he isn't going to, I'll have to do it myself!

I turn to the shop and duck down through its low white wooden doorway. There are shelves rammed with everything you could think of, from well-worn magazines and tins of food to mud-covered potatoes and carrots. Home-made scones sit under a glass dome on the counter, alongside a humming fridge displaying goat's cheese and ice cream, a selection of whiskies and another of woollen knitwear. As I round the central aisle, I see an opening into the café next door, and standing opposite, in front of the biscuit section, is Isla from the ferry, holding another packet of ginger biscuits and some tea bags. She's staring into space as if deep in thought, and I smile.

'Hi,' I say, and raise a hand, happy to see a friendly face.

'Hi,' she says, snapping out of her trance and forcing a smile onto her face that doesn't quite reach her eyes.

'How's the ferry crossing?' I ask, for want of anything better to say.

'Great! Well, no, actually. It seems to take longer for my stomach to settle after a rough one these days!' She holds up the ginger biscuits. 'How's . . . business?' she asks.

I nod and shake my head at the same time. We stand and

look at each other awkwardly for a moment. I seize the opportunity to ask what she knows about Lachlan.

'Look, I'm sorry, but I was just wondering—'

'Sorry,' she says at the same time, 'did I just hear you mention Lachlan? Lachlan from Teach Mhor?'

We look at each other again. She has pale, soft skin, really pale, the colour of the white foam from the sea, and deep red curly hair.

'Yes.' My eyes widen, realising Isla could be just the ally I need. 'Do you know him?'

I'm suddenly aware of three pairs of eyes staring at me from behind the counter. I look back at them and hold up a hand in greeting. One of the three short, stout people nudges the next, and I can't help but think of the three wise monkeys in a row. They're all wearing matching thick glasses and warm knitted jumpers stretched over their barrel-like bodies.

'I told you,' she says. 'As soon as Isla said there was a guest at the big hoose, I knew it must be a friend of Lachlan's.'

'You said Lachlan must have a new girlfriend,' says the one next to her.

The man on the end by the till nods. 'Lachlan's new girlfriend, y'say.'

'Oh no, I'm not . . .' I hold up a hand and blush, wondering how I'm going to explain my presence at the house without arousing too much interest. 'I'm just . . .' What?! What are you, Ruby? Who are you and why are you here . . . still? I look at the expectant faces. 'I'm here helping Lachlan out for a few days.'

'Helping Lachlan out?' says the middle wise monkey.

From inside the café, a woman in a bobble hat, long padded coat and worn sheepskin boots cranes her neck to get a glimpse of me. I feel like Exhibit A in a courtroom.

'Yes, just helping him out,' I repeat, hoping this leads me to finding out a bit more about what he's up to, particularly in that big red-brick shed.

'You're a friend of Lachlan's then?' says the third wise monkey.

'A friend?' I hesitate. 'Yes, I suppose I am a sort of friend.'

'See, I told you it was Lachlan's new girlfriend,' says the first woman, and they all smile in agreement.

Isla says nothing; just looks at me.

'So, this lovely shop, is it yours?' I ask the three wise monkeys.

'Oh, this is a community shop, we all take our turn here,' says the man.

'Even Lachlan,' says the first woman. 'I expect we'll see you here if you're helping out.'

'Not here,' says the second. 'Up at the hoose, helping out at the hoose.'

'But everyone takes a turn. Here and in the café. Then we split the profits,' says the first. 'We're the Cruickshanks. I'm Lena, this is my sister Lexie and my brother Lyle.'

'Not that there's much profit,' says Lyle, looking down at the old till.

'Same for the café. We don't get many customers these days, though Mrs Broidy is a regular.'

Ah, so that's Mrs Broidy, still trying to get a good look at me. I wonder whether I could join her for a cup of tea, maybe find out more about Lachlan that way.

'You have a look about you,' she says, narrowing her eyes. 'You remind me of someone.'

I turn away quickly.

'I must be going,' says Isla. 'Enjoy your stay,' she adds, sounding a little more reserved. 'How long did you say you were here for? I thought you were just here on business.'

'Yes, some business with Lachlan,' I say quickly, and smile. 'Taking a bit longer than we thought.'

'See!' says Lena, nudging her sister again, making her knock into her brother. I think of Weebles.

Isla turns to leave.

'Oh, maybe we could . . .' I start to say, but she's already gone.

Mrs Broidy is still looking at me with narrowed eyes. I take a sudden interest in the display of knitwear.

'All hand-made,' the three monkeys say together.

I leave the shop with a warm jumper, hat and mittens, and no further in my investigations about Lachlan.

That evening, after a delicious fish pie, Hector retires to bed and Lachlan disappears off to the red-brick shed again.

'What is it you do down there?' I ask as he opens the back door.

'Wouldn't you like to know,' he replies with an infuriating wink, and leaves with a smile.

I decide to stay awake; after I hear him go to bed, I'll investigate the shed. I stare at my phone, wishing I could text the group chat. But the band are all at a gig. I look through the photos they've sent me during the set-up: Moira and Gwilym, heads together, smiling in a selfie; Pixie Rose posing with her saxophone; Lulu looking glamorous; and one of all of them, with a thumbs-up for me. I scroll through more pictures on my phone; most of them are of Joe with the rest of the band. I'm determined to keep myself alert and entertained. I'll stay awake all night if I have to!

Chapter Ten

The following morning is the first Christmas Day I've woken before ten since I was a child. Christmas with my dad always started early, but it all changed once I went to live with Mum. There were none of the rituals and traditions Dad had put in place. I remember waking to feel the weight of the big sock on the end of my bed, with the chocolate Father Christmas in it and a satsuma, always, and find myself smiling. Then it was kippers, just like the ones . . . I lift my head . . . just like the ones Lachlan is cooking now by the smell of it!

Suddenly the memories come crashing in. On Christmas morning, we'd always walk the dog early – our black Lab called Murdo. He was rehomed after Dad died and I never saw him again. I never knew if he was happy, or if he missed my dad as much as I did. A lump rises in my throat. I wish I could have done more, insisted he stay with me. But I was only twelve and my mother hated animals. Then afterwards there was a lunchtime drink at the pub whilst the turkey was cooking, and later, a film and chocolates. I find a big ball rising in my throat and silent tears rolling down the sides of my face. Happy and sad ones all mixed in together. Being here seems to be reminding me of all the things I miss about Dad.

Once I started working as a professional singer – backing vocals to start with, holiday camps and cruises like my mum – Christmas was just another working day. And when I joined the band, it became the day after a big gig and the day before another one; a day to rest the voice and get ready for the big New Year jobs. Joe usually stays at mine, and we can pretty much please ourselves, so we take things at a leisurely pace. Here, though, I'm awake as soon as I hear movement upstairs. And smell those kippers cooking.

I realise that I must have fallen asleep pretty much straight away last night and slept right through. I never do that! I've been a bad sleeper as long as I can remember, not dropping off until the early hours, sometimes even as dawn is breaking. Here, though, last night, I slept just as I did as a child, knowing I was at home, safe . . . It must be the air, I tell myself.

But enough of thinking about Christmases past. I have to get on and find out about Lachlan, or I won't have a future to go to!

I slide out of bed and walk to the window, looking out over the bay as the mist rolls in. The wind seems to have dropped, and with it, so has the temperature. There is a thick frost, making everything white and glistening, like a Christmas card. It's beautiful. I pull on the thick jumper I bought in the shop yesterday, dreading to think what my credit card balance will look like when I'm home. Still, I'm glad I've seen this place, the island where my dad grew up. I can just imagine how he felt here on Christmas morning, waking up to this sight. I only wish I had someone here to share it with me.

I pick up my phone and take a photograph out of the bedroom window, trying to stop the camera shaking as I shiver with the cold permeating through the glass. I pull on my hand-knitted fingerless mittens. I was clearly the best customer they'd had in the shop in a long time, I think, remembering their faces as they totted up my items between them with a pen and paper and rang it into the till with a huge smile. But these gloves and jumper are beautiful. It's a shame more people don't visit to buy them.

I send Joe a text. *Happy Christmas! How was the gig?*

Great! he replies immediately, with smiley faces, and I realise I've probably woken him up and immediately feel bad. I long to be back there. Being on stage with the band feels like home and has done since I joined them. I know where I am, and what I'm doing. It's the one place I have truly felt at home since I lost mine with Dad. The smell of those hot, buttery kippers has certainly stirred up memories I thought were long gone!

My phone pings again. *Lulu did a great job.*

I'm grateful, but I'm also . . . well, if I'm honest, I'm feeling really fed up about it too. She's there, and I'm not. I look out of the window again. I'm not very proud of feeling this way. To make up for it, I send smiley faces and Christmas tree emojis back to Joe and tell him I'm missing him. *What are you doing up so early?* I type, and there's a delay as I wait for him to respond.

Just popped out for a few bits for Christmas, he replies.

On Christmas morning? I think. What could he need and where would he go? I go to ask him, but he sends another message.

So, where are you? By the pool in sunny Tenerife? He adds a kiss.

Leaving soon, I say, and quickly send.

What?!! replies Joe, and I can just imagine his face.

It's fine, I say. *It's all in hand. I'll be on my way soon and back before you know it!*

You need to get to that retreat! The longer you delay, the longer you're putting the band at risk!

I know, I know, I type, feeling bad. He's only saying this because he has my best interests at heart. I send him lots of kisses, but he doesn't reply.

I message Jess and wish her happy Christmas too. I don't expect a reply, but I get one.

You're still there then?

Yes. Hoping to leave soon and still get to Tenerife. Few problems with the paperwork. I find myself rolling out the lie as if it's the truth. Well, what else can I say? I could leave right now, this minute, but I think about Lachlan, walking around as if he owns the place. It's Christmas; why isn't he with family? Doesn't he have anyone else to go to? I can't leave until I know why he's here, what he's up to in that shed. I need to find out and get him to agree to go. And it has to be today.

What are you doing awake? I ask.

Making my way back to my flat. Stayed with a friend I met last night! She adds smiley faces and blushing-cheek ones too.

Jess isn't a one-man woman like me. She enjoys nothing better than life on the road, loving and leaving the next day. I like life on the road too, but I also like the fact that I have

Joe to go home to. I don't need any added complications in my life. I just want to focus on the job in hand, being the best I can be at what I do and getting the recognition from the record companies; signing a deal with a label, finally making it over the finish line. Joe knows that and supports me, which is what I adore about him. He loves the band nearly as much as I do.

My phone pings again.

How's the voice? Jess texts.

I look out through the frosted glass and ponder the question. I've been speaking, which the doctor told me not to do, but it's not like I've seen lots of people. I have absolutely no idea how my singing voice is. In fact, right now, I'm too scared to find out. What if it's still broken? What if . . . what if it never comes back? The lump rises in my throat again. Who am I if I can't be Ruby Mac on stage with the band?

Okay, I lie, and this is becoming a habit. *How's Lulu?*

Lulu's good, but she's not you! Think you'll be home soon? Be great to have you back!!

I smile and type, *Oh yes, back soon, I promise*, and as I press send, I feel the determination rise in me. I have to return home before Lulu gets too comfortable filling my shoes. And there's only one thing standing in my way . . . Lachlan.

I suddenly spot him striding down the path away from the house with his big bag slung across his body. Where's he going? And what's in that bag? I have to get this sorted. I pull on my new hand-knitted hat and run downstairs, straight into the lingering smell of kippers and buttered toast.

Hector is in the kitchen, and just for a moment I catch that resemblance to my dad again and my past comes rushing back to me like a tidal wave, washing over me and then crashing into pieces on the beach. It's not my dad; it's just someone who looks like him. I shake my head, hoping that these moments of my past meeting my present will stop. I don't know this man, I remind myself firmly. He didn't want to be part of our family, or for me to be part of his. It's love that makes a family, not DNA. I know my parents loved me. My dad was always there for me, and even my mum loves me, in her own chaotic way.

'Morning, um, Hector,' I say. He's in his dressing gown as usual. A long, worn robe, loosely held together with a tie around his waist over threadbare pyjamas. He looks up from where he's emptying the dresser cupboards all over again.

'Morning!' he says, before going straight back to the job in hand. 'Must be here somewhere . . .'

Maybe he's hungry, I think. I really do want to go and look for Lachlan, but I can't just leave Hector here like this.

'Can I help you?' I ask. 'Are you looking for something to eat?'

I walk over to the range to see a big pan of home-made soup standing there. There's some cheese on the worktop too, under a netted dome, and freshly baked bread. It's like the elves and the shoemaker. I wonder if this really is all Lachlan's work, or whether Mrs Broidy has been in. I'll have to speak to her and see if she can stay on and look after Hector after Lachlan moves out, just until the house is sold.

'Would you like a cup of tea?' I ask.

'Thank you, Mairead. Cup of tea would be perfect. Just as I like it . . .'

I go to correct him, but he's clearly lost in his own

thoughts, muttering as he sifts through papers from the cupboard.

I make the tea with the big old kettle, and remember that he has diabetes so don't add sugar.

'How about I put it in here, by your chair?' I say.

'Perfect!' he exclaims, and comes and sits by the big living room window, looking out over the lawn to the cove.

'Um, happy Christmas,' I say.

'Christmas?' He looks at me and laughs. 'You're losing your marbles, Mairead. Christmas indeed. If it were Christmas, you'd've had the turkey on hours ago! The drinks'd be laid out and the workers and their families would be here by now! And where are the presents for them all? Christmas indeed.' He laughs and shakes his head, then takes a sip of tea, seemingly oblivious to the drips spilling down the front of his dressing gown. 'You've even forgotten how I like my tea! No sugar in there! You're losing your marbles,' he repeats, then looks back out of the window.

I clear my throat. 'I'm not Mairead. I'm Ruby,' I say, but he's not listening. He's standing up and starting to rummage through the cupboards either side of the fireplace again.

I look around. There is no nod to Christmas in here at all. No wonder he doesn't realise what day it is.

'Shall I get you something to eat?' I ask. 'I think there's some bread that Mrs Broidy made. Or maybe I could find something else.'

'God! If Mrs Broidy made it, we're all in trouble!' He laughs, and the sound echoes around the room. The acoustics in here are amazing. Then he looks out of the window again, frowning, as if trying to remember something.

I think about the solicitor and his wife, and their family arriving to spend Christmas with them. I think about how different Hector's Christmas could have been in the nursing home.

I go back into the kitchen, pick up the old radio and bring it into the living room. I put it on a side table and switch it on. It crackles into life and fills the room with carols from a cathedral choir. I smile. 'In the Bleak Midwinter', one of my favourites, and very apt, I'd say, looking out of the window at the icy scene outside. I close my eyes and let the music calm me. I'm desperate to sing along. But I can't. I can't bear to test my voice out yet. The doctor said to rest it for at least a couple of weeks. It hasn't even been one week yet.

'Good God, woman! What are you doing just standing there?' My eyes ping open and I find myself staring at Hector. He has turned from the window and is frowning at me. He waves his arms. 'We've people coming. It's Christmas! The drinks haven't been laid out. Is the turkey in? Where are the workers' presents? Are they wrapped? Where the hell is the tree?! Come on! We've masses to do! It's Christmas!'

The dogs are on their feet, the older of the two standing unsteadily, just like Hector himself. The younger one barks. My heart starts racing. Is this the bully of a man my father told me about? I step back, knocking the radio off the table, and the room falls back into silence. We stare at each other for a moment or two. He has absolutely no idea who I am, and maybe that's a good thing. Everything that has happened in this house is in the past. We all need to be looking to the future.

'Um, there's a cup of tea for you there,' I say, and Hector

turns and sits down again, his moment of panic over.

'Lovely,' he says. 'And how about some of your shortbread?'

He needs to be in that home, I think. I distract myself and my shaking nerves by putting a couple more logs on the fire. When I stand up again, Hector has closed his eyes and the dogs have settled beside him. I walk out of the room to the back door. I need to find Lachlan. I have to put an end to this once and for all.

Chapter Eleven

I pull on a big coat from the pegs beside the door and look down at the row of wellington boots. Who do they all belong to? I wonder. Judging from the dust and cobwebs, most of them haven't been used for some time. I pick a boot up at random and turn it upside down, banging it for good measure. Obligingly, a dead mouse drops out, making me jump back and shriek . . . but no sound comes out. Just a croak, reminding me that my voice has abandoned me, and making me feel very alone indeed. I feel the familiar ball rise in my throat and wish with all my heart it was my voice coming back to me, but instead it just tightens, and hot, angry tears spring to my eyes.

I brush them away quickly and open the back door, letting in a blast of cold air, which bites at my nose and cheeks. I step into the wellies I wore before, and pull the coat tightly around me, then take a deep breath and head purposefully towards the red-brick building.

I try the door, but it's locked. Then I try looking through one of the windows to see if he's in there, but they're too high up. I check the door again. He's clearly not here. I have to find him. But where to start?

I decide to head into the village, the only route I know

here, and see if he's at the café. I head down the drive and out onto the road. As I walk, I realise there is no one around. No one at all. An idea occurs to me. The best Christmas present I could have is for my voice to return. I wonder if I should just try it, open my mouth and see if anything comes out. Maybe sing a Christmas carol. The doctor did tell me to rest for two weeks, but I need to know. It's as if I'm staring at the pile of presents under the tree as a child and lifting the corner of the wrapping paper to see if I'm going to get what I wished for. Just a tiny peek to see if it's there. Then I'll definitely rest it like the doctor ordered.

I breathe as deeply as I can and attempt a scale, but it comes out as a strangled squawk, scaring me. Did I just make that awful noise?! I hear a rustle from behind me in the trees, and suddenly a huge animal shoots across the road to the rolling open land in front of me. Again I go to shout with fright, but my tight throat doesn't make a sound. I hold my hand around it as I watch the deer run off across the moorland towards the hills on the far side, looking as terrified as I feel.

I wind my scarf tighter around my neck and shove my hands into my pockets. I shouldn't have tried that! I tell myself crossly. Stupid, stupid! Rest, the doctor said! It's not there. It's not coming back! I put my head down and march towards the little cluster of shops and houses that make up the village. The cold makes my nose itch, and I have to keep rubbing it and sniffing. The sooner I'm away from this place the better. As I walk, I run the words of the songs from the band's set in my head to keep me focused and to keep out the anger: anger at my voice for letting me down, for abandoning me; and close behind it, anger that I'm here on an island with a grandparent in a world I was never a part of.

I hear it before I see it. I look up and my heart sinks. Oh no, bad timing! A church bell is ringing out merrily, and everyone is piling out of the village's little church, shaking hands and wishing each other a merry Christmas, just like when I was a child and my father insisted on church on Christmas morning. Of course the church was much bigger than this one, but still, it was the same happy feeling. Everyone I've met so far is there. I think I'll just turn around and go back the other way. The last thing I want is another interrogation about who I am and why I'm here. But it's too late.

'Hey, Ruby! Merry Christmas!' It's one of the sisters from the shop. I turn back slowly and raise a hand.

'Merry Christmas,' I reply.

She beckons me over. I put up a hand, but she's insistent. 'Come and join us!'

My heart sinks. 'Oh no, I have to get back . . .'

But there's no stopping her.

Isla and Gordan are there, and he kisses me and wishes me happy Christmas. She, on the other hand, looks as frosty as the grass on the little triangle of village green. Fraser is there too, with his big family. He invites me to join them in the pub for a drink.

'It's tradition,' he tells me, and I wonder if this is what my father did every Christmas morning with Hector and my grandmother. Was this their tradition? Just like my tradition has become to ignore Christmas altogether.

'Oh no, I have to get back. I'm just looking for Lachlan. Thought he might be in the café.'

'Café's closed today.' He points to the door, with the blind down. 'It's the pub or nothing today.'

'Who's this?' asks a young woman who could be Fraser's daughter.

'This is—'

'I'm a friend of Lachlan's,' I say quickly, looking at Fraser, who nods slowly.

'A friend of Lachlan's,' he repeats.

'Lovely to see another young person!' She smiles warmly. 'Coming to the pub?'

'No, I'd better get back,' I say apologetically.

Fraser nods. 'And Hector?' he asks.

'He's . . . a bit confused,' I say, and he nods again.

'It can be a confusing time of year,' he says thoughtfully.

I look around at the small congregation, which is probably the entire island population. Mrs Broidy is there, but I don't think now is the time to talk to her.

'Lovely organ playing, Mrs Broidy,' Fraser turns to her and she smiles.

'If only there were more reasons to play it,' she says sadly. 'Instead of just Christmas and funerals.'

'Well, I must go,' I say. 'Bye, Fraser, merry Christmas.'

'Are you sure you won't join us?' he asks again.

I shake my head. 'I'm looking for Lachlan. There are things we need to talk about.' I raise a knowing eyebrow and he nods. 'Only trouble is, I'm not sure where else to look for him. I don't know my way around.'

'Follow the burn. You can't get too lost; they all lead back to the sea.' He smiles.

'The burn?' I ask.

'The stream. Follow the stream, it won't steer you wrong.' He smiles again, and his eyes seem to sparkle in the low winter sun. A small child suddenly hugs his legs and he turns away. I look at his family around him, at Fraser lifting his grandchild into the air and the child laughing. The wind makes my eyes sting and burn. At least I think it's the wind.

As the congregation moves off to the pub, I turn to go.

'Bye, Isla,' I call out. 'Happy Christmas,' but I don't think she hears me.

I take one last look at the festive group and just for a second allow myself to wonder what it would feel like to be part of it; like walking into a great big bear hug, I imagine. Singing on stage with the band is the closest I've ever come to that kind of communal experience, and right now, I'm not even welcome there. I have no idea where I belong.

My feet seem to have forgotten how to walk, stumbling over each other, as out of place and at a loss as to what to do as I am. Maybe it's the wellies; I'm not used to them. I need to get back into heels and onto that stage!

I really have no idea where else to look, so decide to head back to the house. Maybe he's in that big shed by now. As I walk, I look out for deer, and if I wasn't so cross that Lachlan was holding me up, this would be a really nice way to spend a Christmas morning. I breathe in deeply as the low winter sun creates patterns with the clouds over the yellow and gold moorland, and the stream gushes and hurries towards the sea. I follow it past the big house, across the sand dunes covered in frosty tufts of grass and what looks to be gorse, until there in front of me in the sandy cove is a lone figure. Whilst everyone else was at church, Lachlan was here at the water's edge, and I wonder why. He seems to be collecting something from the shore. It looks like wood. His hair is being blown up and back off his face. I stand and watch him. He doesn't notice me. He's intent on what he's doing.

The wind whips my hair around too, and I grab hold of it and stuff it into the back of my borrowed coat. I wonder who wore it last. Was it my father's mother? My paternal grand-mother? Then I wonder why that should matter to me. You don't miss what you haven't had. I lift my head to the salty sea air and march down towards Lachlan. It's time to have this out!

'You still here?' He looks up at the sound of my footsteps and drops another piece of wood onto the pile he's already collected.

'Yes. You?' I retort, wishing this man didn't bring out the worst in me. He straightens up. He's wearing a worn waxed jacket, a scarf tied tightly around his neck, and fingerless gloves much like mine. I look at his canvas bag, which is sitting next to the pile of wood, and he follows my stare, then looks straight back at me with a smile tugging at the corner of his mouth and a mischievous glint in his eye.

'It's Christmas,' he says enigmatically, then carries on stacking the wood into a pyramid shape. 'Don't you have somewhere you should be? Family?' he says.

'Don't you?' I reply.

'Everything I need is right here,' he says with one eyebrow raised. He straightens up and gazes out to the water beyond the cove. I turn and look at the big house, and then back at him.

'I'm sure,' I say pointedly.

'Look,' he says, waving a stick at me. I take a step back. This man is freeloading off an old man; who knows what he's capable of? I put my hand on my pocket, checking for my phone and hoping there's signal if I need it. 'Everything I need is right here,' he repeats, pointing with the stick out to sea and around the cove.

'But you're living in my . . . in Hector's house. Rent free, I presume!'

He takes a deep breath and drops the stick.

'Hector and I, we have an agreement.'

'What kind of agreement?'

'An agreement.' And then, with a steely look, he adds, 'And I intend to see it through.'

I find my own eyes narrowing to match his. 'Because you want to stay here, living in the big hoose.' It's a bad imitation, and I cringe at myself and my bad manners.

'Because . . .' he pauses and looks at me once more, 'because I made a promise to your grandfather.' He emphasises the final word, and somehow it stings all over again.

'Look, I don't know you or what you're doing here—'

He cuts across me. 'You wouldn't. You've never been here before.'

I eye the bag suspiciously again.

'You want to know what's in the bag? Want to know if I'm ripping your grandfather off? Taking your inheritance?' He laughs, and I'm rattled even more. 'Fair enough.'

'Look, I'm not here for an inheritance. This place means nothing to me . . . It's not mine to inherit. What's important is using it to get Hector the care he needs. And judging by what I've seen, he does need care. As does the house!'

'He needs to be in the place he's happiest, where his memories are. Where he feels safe,' he comes back at me sharply.

'And how do you . . .' I stop myself.

'Look, Ruby, I saw how scared he was in hospital when I collected him and brought him home. Like I said, we have an arrangement and I intend to keep my promise to him. Loyalty means something to people around here.'

He bends down and takes a box of matches from the canvas bag, then strikes one and puts it to the pyramid of sticks, slowly feeding on more of the wood that he's collected. As I stand and watch, the flames begin to take hold.

'Sit down,' he says, pointing to a large log next to the fire.

'I'm fine. I just came to talk to you, to find out when you're going to leave. I need to make plans.'

'Sit down. It is Christmas Day, after all. Isn't this when we're supposed to call a truce for just one day?' He looks at me with his flecked green eyes, and I sit tentatively on the log and then look out across the water, letting the wind fill my head as I breathe in deeply. I tie my scarf a little tighter in an attempt to protect my damaged vocal cords.

He carries on feeding the fire. His hair is wet and even curlier than usual, like bouncy spirals, and I wonder if he's been swimming. Mad if he has! But then this guy clearly doesn't abide by the rules most of us do.

He points to the bag beside me with that mischievous glint in his eyes again. 'Grab what's inside,' he says as the flames lick higher and higher and the waves rhythmically lap the shingle-covered shore.

I look at him suspiciously. 'What's in there?' I ask. Is this him confessing to taking valuables from the house? Is he going to ask if I want a cut in exchange for my silence, or even offer me a chance to get in on the action? I don't move.

'Just do it!' He throws a hand up. 'For heaven's sake, can't a man do something civil on Christmas morning?' he growls, exasperated. *He's* exasperated?! I'm supposed to be waking up today in Tenerife, watching the sunrise from my yoga mat and getting my life back on track!

'Phffff!' I let out a long sigh, reach into the bag and put my hand on something cold and damp. I pull it out and hold it up. It's a bottle containing a clear liquid, and against the backdrop of the water, the glass seems to have a blue and green hue. I run my hands over it. It's patterned like the waves of the sea, and has an exquisite painting of the island on the front. 'It's beautiful,' I say, staring at it and then at him. 'What is it?'

'Gin,' he says flatly, and then sits on a log on the opposite side of the fire.

I raise an eyebrow, surprised. I don't know what I was expecting, but it wasn't this.

'Will you have a drink with me?'

I think about this.

'It's a bit early, isn't it?'

'It's Christmas. Everything is different at Christmas.'

Not for me, I think. It's much like any other day. Although waking up in Tenerife would definitely have been different.

'How come there's no tree in the house or anything?' I

ask, feeling we've taken a tiny step closer to being civil to each other.

'Hector . . . well, as you've seen, he can get confused and anxious. He lives in the past and becomes upset if there's change.'

I think about the incident with the carols on the radio that morning and feel a stab of guilt.

'It's usually best to go with it, wherever he is in the moment. Contradicting what he's thinking can just cause him stress when he realises he can't remember things.'

He puts out his hand for the bottle. I reach out and pass it to him. He holds it up and narrows his eyes thoughtfully, holding it almost reverently.

'So, you'll join me in a toast?'

'A toast? What to?'

'To Hector's best interests.' He looks at me steadily and I hold his gaze.

'Of course,' I reply with relief. Thank goodness! Maybe now he's realised he needs to go.

'Good,' he says, and stands, casting a dark shadow over me.

'Have you got glasses in that bag of yours too?' I attempt friendly. If he's going, I can stop worrying. I'll ask Mrs Broidy to come in and look after Hector until the house is sold and he can move to the care home. My work here is done! I think with a smile. Nevertheless, something scratches at the back of my brain. Is it regret? Regret that I never got to know this place, that it was never a part of my growing up? But it wasn't, and that's that. I slam the lid down tightly on that thought and look back at Lachlan. I'll happily drink to moving on.

'No, no glasses,' he says.

'Then how are we going to drink, from the bottle?'

'We're not all heathens here, y'know!' he practically growls from the corner of his mouth, and I realise how fragile our truce is. I mustn't do or say anything that will make him change his mind about leaving.

'Hold your hands out and shut your eyes,' he says. We look at each other with mutual mistrust. 'Hold your hands out,' he repeats. 'Or are you scared of what you might find?' That teasing smile appears again at the corner of his mouth.

'I'm not scared,' I say, feeling terrified. Terrified of what will happen if I can't leave this island and find my voice again. I shut my eyes tightly and hold out my hands. Nothing happens.

'Hurry up,' I say, opening my eyes slightly and seeing him reaching into his canvas bag. He turns back to me and I shut my eyes again, keen to get this over and done with.

'Okay. Here. Happy Christmas,' he says in his thick accent, like a low growl.

Suddenly there is something cold and wet in my hands. My eyes spring open and I shriek, but once again no sound comes out. I look down at the round closed shell that I'm holding.

'What is it?' I squint at it.

'Breakfast!' He smiles and pulls out more of the shells from his bag. 'Or maybe brunch where you come from.' He smiles more widely, his eyes dancing, then looks up at the sky. 'Actually, lunch!' He nods. 'You see, I wasn't stealing the family silver after all!' It's as if he's read my mind.

I look down at the shell in my hands.

'What's the matter? You've never had an oyster before?' He gives a deep laugh.

'An oyster! Of course! Of course I have,' although I'm racking my brains to remember when. It's not a regular ingredient in my fridge. To be honest, I live off Super Noodles, cereal and toast most of the time. 'I thought we were having a drink?' I say.

'We are,' he says, and smiles. 'Here.' He pulls out a knife from his bag, and just for a second I blanch. 'Tool of the trade,' he says to reassure me, and takes the oyster gently from my hand. I watch as he places the point of the knife beside the hinge of the closed shell, pushes it in, gives it a twist and slides the blade around. Then slowly he prises the shell apart, revealing the flesh inside.

He hands it back to me, then opens another one expertly and tips it straight into his mouth, shutting his eyes, clearly luxuriating in the flavours. I follow, relishing the feel of the soft flesh, letting the flavours of a wild, windswept shingle shoreline imprint themselves on my memory. When I swallow and slowly open my eyes, he's opening the gin.

'And now, we drink.'

'From what?' I look around.

'From these,' he says, and holds up his oyster shell.

'And are they from the sea round here?' I ask.

He nods. 'I picked them this morning. As fresh as you can get.'

He fills both our shells, then raises his in a toast.

'To Hector and a happy Christmas.'

'To Hector,' I echo, and tip the shell up into my mouth again. This time I get a different taste sensation, but it's still as if I'm drinking in the scenery around me. The gin tastes of the sharp, fresh seashore, of the crisp wind, the clear salt air.

'Wow!' I say, and look at the shell.

'Wow indeed,' he says, opening more oysters.

'This is gin?' I've never drunk gin neat before, or anything as fantastic as this. I never knew it could taste so amazing!

'Uh huh,' he says, lining up the oysters on a wide log. 'Made right here.'

'Here? On Winter Island?'

'At the house. Teach Mhor.' He hands me another oyster.

'This is made here?' I remember now that Fraser, the solicitor, said something about a distillery and gin and whisky and mince pies at Christmas time.

He shakes his head. 'You really don't know anything about this place, do you?'

'No, I told you, I've never been here before.'

'Why not?'

I swallow another oyster and look at him. 'I don't really know. But I'm not some selfish cow who just abandoned her dad's father.'

'Your grandfather,' he corrects, and tops up our shells with gin.

'I don't know him as my grandfather. He and my father never got on, apparently, and so, well, we never met. He didn't want anything to do with my dad or me after I was born. This was never part of my world,' I say, holding out my hand as a flock of birds flies past.

Lachlan tips his gin into his mouth. 'He's not a bad man,' he says. 'He is unwell. But the Hector I know is not a bad man, whatever happened between him and your father.'

I have no idea what to think. According to my dad, his father was a bully and a tyrant and we were better off without him in our lives. I just sort of accepted that. I frown as I process what Lachlan is saying, but it's just too much right now, and too late.

I change the subject. 'What is he looking for all the time?' I ask, as the flames from the fire lick higher and warm my face and hands, while the glorious gin warms me from the inside and makes me feel deliciously refreshed.

'Something he's lost,' says Lachlan, leaning on his knees. 'Something I'm helping him to find.' He looks up at me, his eyes lit by the flames. 'That is, when I'm not foraging.'

I look at him, not quite understanding what he means.

'I live off the land,' he explains, raising his oyster shell.

'Oh, I see.'

He laughs, realising that I probably don't. 'I forage for food, which I cook and sell to the shop and the pub. I also run workshops with the school here, teaching the kids to respect our island but also to work with it and live off it responsibly.'

'Oh, I see,' I repeat.

'It's always been that way out here. But it's dying out. More and more ready meals are making it to the island!' He practically growls again.

'Like the ones in the fridge that you threw out?'

He nods. 'Mrs Broidy thinks she's helping out by bringing them in, but Hector doesn't keep an eye on the eat-by dates. So I try and leave him his dinner every day.'

'And you made the cheese scones?'

He nods again and pokes the fire. 'You thought it was Mrs Broidy?'

'I did. I'm sorry.' I pick up another oyster and look at it.

'Mrs Broidy is a dreadful cook!'

'So Hector said.'

'The ready meals make her feel as though she's done something. I tell her not to worry, but it's her way of looking out for him. We all look out for each other here.'

'Was . . . Did you know my grandmother? Was she a good cook?'

He nods once more. 'She taught me a lot of what I know.'

'You grew up here?'

'I did,' he says shortly. 'And you?'

I laugh. 'City girl. Can't get used to all this great outdoors!' We both laugh, and then he holds up the bottle again.

'Another?'

I'm undecided.

'It is Christmas,' he says, 'and look, just like the Germans and the Brits in World War One when they played football on Christmas Day, we've managed that truce!'

'You're right.' I find myself smiling. Maybe it's the gin, or maybe it's that mischievous grin, which is actually quite infectious now I know he's genuinely trying to help. 'I'm sorry,' I say. 'I may have misjudged you. And . . . well, I suppose I should say thank you, for looking after Hector.'

'You're welcome,' he says, and tops up our oyster shells.

'Here's to new beginnings and safe travels,' I say, feeling happy and warm now that my time here is coming to an end.

'And where's home for you?' he asks.

'Bristol. I live on my own at the moment, but I'm looking at buying a flat with my boyfriend, Joe.'

'Your boyfriend? It's serious, then?'

'Yes,' I say. 'Planning your life and who you spend it with is about as serious as it gets.'

'And what does he think about you celebrating Christmas here on the island with a bunch of strangers?'

What would Joe say if he knew I was sitting on a beach drinking gin instead of going to get my voice fixed in Tenerife? 'He's . . .' I nod, a lot, 'he's fine with it.'

'He's an understanding man,' says Lachlan with a raised eyebrow. Joe *is* understanding, I think. He understands how important my career and singing is to me. He supports me all the way.

'What can you taste?' Lachlan asks, looking at my face and nodding at my oyster shell.

'Well, um . . . gin. And salt . . . Well, it tastes just like here.'

'Go on,' he says, and tops me up.

Buoyed up by the gin, I relax a little and smile. 'Well, it tastes of the wind in my face, clean, crisp . . . like Christmas morning on the beach with a warmth in the background from the fire.' I smile.

'Any particular flavours?'

I put my head down and smell the gin. 'Hmm, not really.' I lift the shell again 'To you; to pastures new,' I say, feeling my spirits lifting.

He raises his own shell, then wipes his mouth with the back of his hand and smiles.

'Oh, I'm not going anywhere.'

'What?' I cough.

'I'm helping Hector. I promised him. I'm not going anywhere until we've found what he's looking for.'

Chapter Twelve

I'm dumbfounded, my dreams of getting on that plane tomorrow suddenly evaporating in front of my eyes.

'And what exactly is it that he's looking for?' I say icily.

Lachlan picks up the gin bottle and looks at it; again it seems to take on the colours of the water, the shore and the grassy banks around it. He takes a deep breath.

'The gin. He's looking for the recipe for the gin. It's somewhere in the house, that's all we know. It's Hector's . . .' He swallows. 'He wants the gin business up and running again. After his wife died and he got ill, the business died too. It's his final wish, to bring Teach Mhor gin back. So that he feels a part of him will always be here.'

'But . . . the care home?'

'He wants to be here,' he says, suddenly gruff again. 'He wants to die at home. He told me.'

He gets to his feet and begins to tidy up, tossing the oyster shells into the water.

'Oh really? And you think he's capable of knowing what's good for him, do you?' Suddenly the peace is shattered and we're back in our trenches.

'I know Hector. And I know what I've promised. I promised to stay until the gin recipe was found and the still was up and running again. Teach Mhor gin is going to be back in business.'

I look around at the big house and the outbuildings. Lachlan begins to walk along the water's edge towards the grassy bank to the left of the cove. I follow him.

'So . . .' I say, my brain turning over. 'You made a promise to help find the recipe and get the gin business up and running.'

'I did,' he says, starting to climb up the bank. Again I follow.

'And you won't move out until it's up and running?'

'Correct. I have an agreement with Hector,' he calls back over his shoulder.

'And we know the house is fairly worthless, being in the condition it's in, here on a remote island. It won't pay for him for long in the care home.'

'Correct again,' he says, still picking his way up the bank, until he reaches the highest point, looking out over the neighbouring sandy cove and across to the islands beyond.

Out of breath, I stand behind him chewing my bottom lip.

'But with an up-and-running gin business, the place would be worth a lot more.'

'It would.'

At that moment, one, two, then three grey heads pop up near the rocks and look around. Seals! I smile in delight, gazing at them as they bob up and down, disappearing under the water then reappearing elsewhere as if playing hide and seek.

'And once the recipe is found and the still is operational,' you'll move out and the house can be sold.'

'Correct. You have my word.' He turns and holds my gaze. The wind whips his hair around his face, but he doesn't react. 'You have to know, going into a care home is not what Hector wants. He wants to stay here as long as he can. And while I'm here, I'll make sure that happens. But I promise I'll leave once the gin business is back up and running; that's what matters most to Hector.' Despite knowing nothing about him, there's something about him that makes me take him at his word.

'In that case . . .' I take a deep breath, look at the seals and then back at Lachlan, 'I'd better help you find the recipe. That way, we all get what we want.'

He stares back at me.

'Just one thing,' I add. 'You do know how to make gin, don't you?'

A smile tugs at the corner of his mouth. 'I haven't a clue.'

Chapter Thirteen

'I know, it's ridiculous!' I'm talking to Joe on video chat, looking at his familiar face, reading exactly how he feels about this. 'But he won't leave until the recipe has been found. I just have to find it and get this still up and running, and then he'll go and the house can be sold!'

'Well, how long is that going to take?' Joe frowns.

'I don't know. A week, maybe. Maybe more.' I really don't have any idea. I've never done anything like this before!

'And what about the vocal retreat? What about your voice?' He sounds really cross. 'This isn't just about you, Ruby.'

'I know, I know. I'll cancel for now and rebook as soon as everything here is sorted.' I'm trying to make the situation sound better, as if it's all in hand. But right now, I can't worry about that. Right now, for some reason, what matters is getting the recipe found and the business up and running so we can all feel we've done the best we can for Hector. I'm not sure why it seems so important. I just know it feels right. And I'm sure it won't take that long. I'll be in that vocal retreat before I know it. This is just a blip, a delay. The quicker I can help find that recipe, the sooner Lachlan will move out.

I look at the screen. Joe is clearly unhappy. He's rolling his lips in on themselves as he does when something's bothering him. I try and distract him by asking about the gig again.

'So Lulu did a good job standing in for me? Not too good, I hope!' I try and joke, but it falls flat, and he sighs loudly.

'It was great!' He sounds really grumpy. Then he says, 'Look, Rubes, I'm not being funny, but Lulu is good, really good.'

I frown.

'I mean, not as good as you,' he says quickly. 'But, well, she's here and doing a decent job. And, well . . .' He sighs again and my heart starts quickening and my mind racing.

'What are you saying? Do you think the band are going to replace me?' My voice tightens and thins.

He says nothing.

'Joe?' I ask anxiously.

'All I'm saying is, the quicker you can get back here the better. Lulu's good and I'd hate for them to think she was more reliable than you. It's your career I'm thinking of, Rubes. You need to get to that vocal retreat as soon as possible.'

I nod. I know he's just thinking of me. 'I will,' I croak.

'So,' he says after a pause, with a hint of disapproval in his voice. 'Will there be turkey and all the trimmings?'

I look around at the bleak, empty house. I'm not here out of choice, I want to tell him.

'No, no turkey and trimmings,' and for some reason, I don't tell him I've just eaten oysters and drunk gin out of their shells by a bonfire on the beach, and I can still smell the woodsmoke on my clothes and taste the clear, fresh spirit in my mouth. Or about the seals we watched playing in the water. I don't want him to think I'm on some kind of jolly holiday. The band need me to get well and back in the saddle! Back to how things were. I don't want them to think I'm having fun, or jeopardising my voice.

'Well, as long as you're keeping warm. Hot drinks, a scarf, and not talking too much, and definitely no singing!' Joe instructs, confirming my decision not to tell him about the oysters and gin. It was quite something, though, an experience I'll never forget. And with different company, it could have been amazing! 'So, no Christmas jollities for you?' Joe breaks into my thoughts.

'No. I'm going to start on the cupboards. The house could probably do with a good sort-out anyway before he goes into the home. It'll save me another trip up here,' I say, looking around. Because once I do leave here, I know I won't be back, no matter how much Fraser Gillies thinks this place can get under your skin.

'So, Scottish island life isn't for you, then?' Joe gives a tight laugh. It's nothing like Lachlan's laugh, which is deep and relaxed and laid-back.

'No! It's cold, wet and a million miles from anywhere!'

'Well, don't waste your voice talking to me. Go and rest it. The more you rest, the quicker we'll get you back. Take care,' Joe says.

'Oh, Joe? Did you hear back from the A&R woman? Will she come and see the band again?'

There's another silence. 'Jess has left messages,' he finally says. And what he doesn't say tells me everything. My spirits plummet into my three pairs of socks. I look out of the window towards the bay and wonder if the seals are still there. Then I hear voices in the background at the other end of the phone.

'Who's there?' I ask, looking at the screen, seeing the minute tree in a pot that I bought for Joe.

'Just the guys, the band. We're having a curry. Bought it last night on the way back from the gig. Just got to heat it up.'

There are gales of laughter, and suddenly they're all there waving at me, wishing me happy Christmas and telling me to get well soon. Even Lulu is there, behind Joe, and she never usually joins in on band get-togethers.

'Don't enjoy yourself too much!' I joke, and just for a moment I wonder if Lulu wants to fill my shoes in Joe's life as well as in the band. Then I scold myself for being overdramatic and ridiculous.

'Okay, nor you!' he jokes back. No chance of that, I think, looking around.

'Happy Christmas. Love you guys,' I say. 'Love you—' But I seem to have been drowned out by the noise at the other end of the phone as they all blow kisses and shout Happy Christmas again. Then the line goes dead and the picture is gone. And suddenly I am very, very homesick. I hold the phone to my lips, hot tears in my eyes, and wish I was there, back in my flat. No, I correct myself. I want to be in Joe's flat. I want to be where Lulu is right now! Actually, I want us to be in *our* flat, the one we plan to buy once I get that recording contract. I want to go home.

I send a quick text to my mum, though I don't let on I'm

in Scotland. She'd only tell me that staying on isn't a good idea. That I should just leave and get on with my own plans. My mum has always supported my career. I tell her I'm on voice rest and that we're hoping an A&R woman will see us in the new year. I don't need her questions right now. I need to make things right here, get off this island, get my voice back and go home!

I rub my nose, blink back the tears and take a deep breath from my butt. I lift my chin as if I was going on stage, then walk out of my bedroom, onto the big landing and down the stairs. At the turn, I stop and find myself adjusting the blue and red tartan curtains there to hide the moth-eaten parts. Then I carry on down, running my hand along the dark wood panelling and brushing the dust off as I go.

Down in the flagstoned hallway, I look around. I have a gin recipe to find. The sooner I find it, the sooner we all get what we want and get out of here.

But where to start?

Chapter Fourteen

I open the door of the front room, wondering if it's warmer outside. My breath looks like clouds in front of my face. I think about Joe and the band and their Indian take-away Christmas dinner and wish even more that I was there. Even though we never make a fuss about Christmas, suddenly being so far away makes me miss our 'no fuss' Christmas.

Joe always says Christmas is just a massive marketing ploy, a way to make people spend money. Then I think about Fraser Gillies and his family going to the pub after church. That isn't about money. It's about spending time with the ones you love, and the community coming together. Those Christmases with my dad weren't about the presents; they were about being together, playing games and sharing music. It might be a marketing ploy in Joe's eyes, but then he doesn't really have much to do with his family, so maybe he can't see it as anything else. His brother's a successful banker with a family of his own. His parents run their own party supplies business, specialising in office parties and baby showers, party decorations and accessories, and it's a busy time for them in the run-up to Christmas, so they always holiday in the Caribbean over the festive period itself. I think it's why Joe is so focused on work: he likes to be able to keep up with his family.

I think again about Fraser Gillies and his family, wondering if that's what Christmas on the island was like for my dad . . . and could have been like for me, if things had been different. I quickly shake the thought and throw myself into the task in hand.

Best to be methodical, I think, rubbing my freezing hands together, letting the cold distract me from my musings about Christmas. I'll start downstairs, working from the front of the house to the back. Then, if I don't find anything, I'll search upstairs. I take a deep breath of air so icy it hurts my lungs, then pull open the cupboard door to one side of the fireplace. Reams of paper, unopened envelopes and photographs tumble and slide over my feet.

'It's here somewhere.'

'Uh huh,' Lachlan is standing in the doorway, one arm across his body, the other hand seeming to touch the corner of his mouth, possibly hiding a smile there, which has lit up his eyes.

I glare back at him. 'Best we make a start then!' I say, nodding to the cupboard on the other side.

'Indeed,' he agrees, but he doesn't seem to be in any rush.

'Come on,' I say. 'It'll be quicker with two of us looking. Though if someone had given him a hand before now . . .'

'Yes, if someone had been here to help out . . .' he retorts, and I bite my tongue, knowing he's right. It wasn't his job to do it, but then I'm not sure it was mine either. 'In fact,' he continues, bending to pick up a pile of papers and starting to go through them, stacking them in piles and throwing the rubbish into the empty fireplace, 'where have you been? What do you even do for a job?'

'I told you, I'm a singer, a full-time singer.'

'A singer?' He nods, impressed. 'And where do you . . . sing?' I detect a hint of scepticism in his voice. But then that seems to be a fairly common tone when he's speaking to me.

'Wherever I can. I mean . . . I don't just stand up and sing. I'm a professional.' I cringe at my own words. 'I'm in a band. We play gigs, and hopefully we'll land a record deal and tour really soon. And then I do a bit of solo stuff, lounge singing at a big restaurant and hotel, and sometimes weddings. Though once we sign to a label, I won't have to do that.'

'Aren't you . . . well, isn't that for youngsters? I mean, I don't want to be rude, but wouldn't it have happened by now if it was going to happen?'

I stop sorting through papers and stare at him. 'You don't have to be young to be a performer. I've been doing this all my life. You don't just decide to sit down one day to be a pianist, for instance, and immediately play Mozart. You have to work at these things. I've been working at this for years. It's my time.'

We fall into silence and go back to working our way through the papers, scrunching up anything that looks redundant – old envelopes, out-of-date bills . . . way out of date. It looks like the distillery struggled for some time, judging by the red reminders. We're kneeling either side of the fireplace on the threadbare rug, the cold, hard flagstones beneath digging into our knees. I grab an old tapestry cushion, as worn and faded as the rug, but it helps a little. I can see my own breath in front of me, and despite my thick fingerless gloves, my hands are freezing.

After a while, Lachlan gets up and leaves the room.

Typical! I think scratchily. Leaving me with all these papers. But it has to be here somewhere. It must be. Everything else is! I tug at a box stuck at the back of the cupboard and pull it out, spilling papers everywhere. When I open it, I see that it's full of photos. I flick through them and see pictures of my dad, and of Hector. There are some of the distillery too, with the workers standing in front of the red-brick building. Tears fill my eyes. The family I never knew, and the father who isn't here.

I look through the photographs of my dad. There's one of him down on the beach, the beach where we ate oysters and drank gin this morning. One of him in school uniform. No doubt the start of term, just like he used to take a photograph of me every September in my new uniform. And another of Christmas, beside a huge tree in the hall here, the whole family dressed in their smart clothes. Hector has his hand on Dad's shoulder. What happened? How have these memories been forgotten? What would it have been like to have a place like this to visit, with grandparents holding open their arms in welcome? To come back here with my dad?

What would Dad have made of Joe? I find myself wondering. Would he have been pleased about our relationship? What would it have been like to bring Joe here? Then I think about Joe's collection of expensive shoes, and his smart wool coat, and smile at the thought of the dogs greeting him. Joe likes five-star hotels and thinks that's what we should be aiming for in life. I don't think he would have warmed to

Teach Mhor as the family home. I smile again at the thought of him trying to drink gin from an oyster shell and asking for the nearest hotel. Joe is much happier in a chic city bar than somewhere like here. He likes comfort. He even bought me Egyptian cotton sheets for my birthday one year, because he likes to sleep in the best he can. I'm not sure that he would ever have fitted in here.

I quickly put the lid on the box of photographs and on the thoughts they're raking up, and try to run through some songs in my head, just to keep on top of the set. Suddenly Lachlan reappears with an armful of logs and smaller pieces of wood and drops them by the hearth. Then, without a word, he lays up the fire, kindling first, and sets light to the paper, slowly feeding on the bigger logs until the fire is roaring. The heat makes me feel better. He leaves the room again and returns with a plate of sandwiches and two glasses of wine.

'I've made some for Hector, too. We'll eat properly later. You're welcome to join us,' he says crisply.

The door opens and in walks one of the Labradors, the younger of the two, come to see what's going on. He jumps up onto the big sagging sofa and settles down to watch us work. I reach over and help myself to one of the sandwiches, biting into the thick home-made brown bread. Inside is soft smoked salmon with a crunch of black pepper. It's heaven. I sip my wine.

'How's the salmon?' Lachlan asks.

'Gorgeous,' I say, my hand over my full mouth.

'Caught and smoked myself.' He nods towards the back of the house, and I have to say, I'm impressed. I've never tasted anything like it. Then he tosses another log on the fire and looks straight at me. 'So, you're a singer,' he says, and I sense a little devilment in his tone. 'How come you're not singing? I'd've thought it was a busy time of year.' He tosses more papers onto the fire. 'Oh, there are some photographs here. You might like them,' he says, and puts them to one side.

I swallow and look at the pile of photographs, not sure if I want to see any more of the life that shut me out.

'I'm . . . I just need to rest my voice. I'm on my way to a healing centre in Tenerife. As soon as I finish here. Then I can get back to my band. We're hoping that things are about to happen. There's been an A&R woman interested in us.' I fall silent. I hope she's still interested. And then the bigger fear surges up in me again, like a monster waking from its one-eye-open sleep and rising to its full, scary height with a roar: I hope I can still sing.

'What about you?' I try and clear my throat, and take a sip of wine, which seems to help. 'How come you're here, foraging? Haven't you ever wanted to leave the island?'

'I did,' he says flatly. 'Thought there was something better out there.'

'And was there?' I ask.

'No,' he says flatly. 'So I came back and realised everything I'd ever wanted had been here all along.' He sighs heavily. 'But I'd left it too late.'

'Too late?' I frown.

'Shh!' he says, putting a finger to his lips. 'Voice rest, remember, no talking.'

I ignore him. 'But now that the house is going on the

market, you can go wherever you like. Surely you must have plans.'

'No, nothing like that. There's an old expression: if you want to make God laugh, tell him your plans!' He gives a derisory laugh. 'I thought I had a plan, but let's just say it took me a while to make it, and once I had, like I said, it was too late.' He nods, clearly shutting down the conversation.

I don't ask any more, realising he's diclosed all he wants to on the subject.

We wade through piles and piles of paper: magazines, knitting patterns, bills, and shopping lists written on the back of envelopes. Every now and again I think I've found a recipe, but I haven't. Eventually the pages are neatly stacked and the rubbish is burning brightly in the grate.

'Ah! There you are, Mairead.' Hector comes into the room and sits on the sofa, next to the dog. The other dog follows him in and climbs up stiffly to sit on his other side.

'Here, Hector.' Lachlan hands him some of the photographs. He takes them, smiles and nods, but his face shows no sign of recognition. Eventually he falls asleep and snores, sounding exactly like the dogs.

Lachlan stands up stiffly and the dogs follow him with their eyes, looking hopeful that it might be dinner time.

'I'll get the food sorted. Hector won't want to eat too late.'

'Great. Can I help? I'm good with a microwave,' I try and joke.

'It's venison.'

'Venison?' I say. He nods. It's a long way from microwaved takeaway curry. I suddenly remember how Dad always tried to get a piece of venison at Christmas. The butcher would order it in especially.

I pick up the photographs that have fallen from Hector's hand onto the floor. I look down at a picture of my father and his parents standing on the shore, the wind making their hair stand on end. And another of Dad standing next to a new bike, beaming widely. There are an awful lot of memories buried away in the house, by the looks of it. But that's the past. I need to move on, I tell myself. Tomorrow we have to find that recipe. I'm not sure how much longer I can stand being in this big, cold house, or how much longer the healing centre will hold my place. And I don't know whether I will be able to keep my curiosity about my dad's family at bay for much longer. The last thing I want is to start getting emotionally involved; that will only make everything harder.

Chapter Fifteen

I start the following day by texting Joe, who replies that I need to sort myself out. *You really need to think about where your loyalties lie, Rubes. I can only keep things going here for so long. The band are talking. They want to know when you're coming back . . . if you're coming back.*

There's a message too from Jess, checking that I'm okay and saying she misses me, that the band are missing me! She sends it with lots of smiley faces, but I'm worried. I send a silly GIF to the band group chat: a monkey with its hand over its mouth and a surprised look on its face that makes me smile, letting them all know I'm fine and resting my voice. But despite their messages back, laughing and sending me more GIFs, hoping that I get well soon, I can't stop thinking about what Joe has said. What if Jess isn't telling me the whole truth, trying not to worry me? What if the band think I'm not coming back? I think about Lulu standing in the spotlight, standing in my place. I have to get my voice back.

I throw myself into looking for the bloody elusive recipe. There are more cupboards full of papers, boxes of books and toys. Nothing in this house has ever been thrown away, by the looks of it. Who were these toys saved for? A tiny voice at the back of my mind wonders whether they were meant for me. Or is that just wishful thinking? I push the thoughts away.

I pull out another box and open it. Inside are layers of aged yellow tissue paper, and beneath them a beautiful crocheted shawl, along with a pile of knitted baby clothes: cardigans, hats, bootees, all in pristine condition, as though they've never been worn.

'Ah, Mairead!' Hector sees me with a box of toys from under the stairs. 'Good thought. I'll get the bike out of the shed too. Campbell always loved that bike.' I suddenly catch my breath and hold it. Campbell was my dad. 'Bet the wee one will too!' Tears spring to my eyes. He thinks he's getting a visit from his son and . . . me, I realise. Maybe that means he did care, or at the very least that he thought about me. He thinks we're coming for a visit!

'Oh, I'm not . . .' I spot Lachlan down the hall and remember him telling me it's best to go with the flow so as not to cause Hector confusion or distress. He's living in the past, and from what I can see, it looks like quite a nice place to be right now. He's obviously very excited about the prospect of a visit from me and Dad. Why spoil that?

'Yes, I bet she'll like the bike,' I say. She would have done too, I think, and brush away the tears that linger there. She'd've loved to ride the bike and play with the toys here.

When I glance up to where Lachlan was standing, he's gone. I look down again at the unworn baby clothes. Were these for me? I lift a tiny hat out of the box and hold it to my cheek, feeling the soft wool against my skin, breathing in the slightly musty smell, the smell of this place, Teach Mhor. Then I place it back in the tissue paper and put the lid on the box, wondering what on earth to do with the clothes. I can't just throw them out, but I can't take them with me. They obviously meant something to someone; maybe my grandmother, I let myself think. I put them back where I found them for the time being.

Behind the box of toys is a grey case. I reach in, wondering if it's what I think it is. I pull it out. It is! It's a record player. And there behind it is a box of vinyl records. I carry the box into the kitchen and put it on the table, my heart starting to lift at the sight of the beautiful covers. I want to sit and look through them, but I really have to find this recipe first. There are some more photographs tucked into the box, of the buildings behind the house, with workers and big drums beside them, and the shoreline and bay beyond. I leave them on the big scrubbed pine table, worn from years of people sitting around it: my family I think . . . where my family sat.

Lachlan walks into the kitchen.

I put my hands on my hips and try to pretend I wasn't thinking about a life I never knew, and say with more tetchiness than I mean to, 'Where have you been?'

'In the distillery, giving it and the still a good clean,' he says, wiping his hands.

'Have you really no idea where this recipe could be?'

He shakes his head. 'Just that it's somewhere in the house. Hector can't remember.'

'And he's definitely the only one who knows?'

Lachlan nods. 'Yup. His father . . . your great-grandfather, I suppose, ran the distillery.' He spots the photos on the table and walks to them, spreading them out. 'They made whisky and sold it to the mainland. But business was bad, sales were dropping off. It was Hector who came up with the idea of the gin. It's quick to make and it saved the business . . . for a time. But then . . . well, from what I gather, after your grandmother died, things went downhill, and with no one to take over the business, it just shut down.'

'And where were you in all of this?'

He looks at me. 'I grew up on the island. My father was the gillie here. He looked after the hunting and the fishing. He helped out on the farm here too, when needed. There's not much farm work around these parts any more. Nowadays it's mostly wild goats and deer.'

'Wild goats?'

'Local legend has it that there was a shipwreck, an Armada vessel. The goats swam to safety and have lived on the island alongside the deer ever since.'

I smile at the story, then look at the box of records and put my hand in to pull one out. I'd love to sit and go through this lot, but there really isn't time. 'We need to find that recipe, Lachlan,' I say firmly. 'I have to be gone by New Year.'

'Hogmanay,' he says.

'Sorry?'

'It's Hogmanay. New Year.'

'Yes. Then I need to be gone by Hogmanay.'

'It'll turn up,' he says, and nods with a wink and a smile. 'All in good time.'

My stomach flips over and I'm not sure why. Maybe it's the thought of getting to Tenerife, recovering my voice, getting back to where I belong, on stage.

God, this man is so infuriating. We need to work quicker! 'But we don't have time, Lachlan. *I* don't have time.' A

126

thought hits me. Sure, he agreed to move out as soon as we found the recipe and made the gin. But he also said he wanted to keep Hector at home for as long as he could. 'Is it possible that you're stalling for time here? Maybe you don't want to find this recipe at all.' I feel myself frowning. 'After all, once we find it . . .' he ignores me, and heads for the back door, 'once we find it, you'll have to move on too! Maybe you want things to stay as they are!' I shout after him.

'Maybe I do.' He turns to look at me. 'For Hector's sake,' he says, and I smart.

'But he would be better off in the home!'

'Says who? You?' He opens the door. 'Can you keep an eye on Hector while I go to the shed again?'

'Of course,' I reply tightly. I mean, it's not like it's that hard to keep an eye on him. He'll just be sorting through cupboards like he has since I arrived here.

As Lachlan leaves, Hector arrives in the kitchen with the dogs. I pick up the photographs and hand them to him. Maybe, just maybe, they might trigger something in his mind.

'I thought you might like to go through these,' I say. He looks at me as if he has no idea what I'm talking about, then goes to one of the cupboards I've already searched and takes everything out again. Including the bottle of gin that we drank from on Christmas Day.

I look down at the bottles and jars Hector is going through with no idea what he's looking for. I need to speed things up. I look at the bottle of gin again and I'm transported back to Christmas morning. I can smell the clean, salty air and taste the gin on my lips. I roll my bottom lip in as if tasting it all over again. Maybe there is another way.

Chapter Sixteen

Hector is back in the front room, which is now warm and toasty. He has decided to empty the cupboards all over again, looking for the recipe. I sigh. I'll restack the papers later. There's no stopping him once he starts.

While I wait for him to finish his rummaging, unable to resist temptation any more, I take the record player into the living room, where the fire is also lit, and has been every morning since I've been here. Presumably that's Lachlan's doing. I pick out a record, Ella Fitzgerald, one of my dad's favourites, and put it on the turntable. It crackles, and I wait with bated breath; then the music begins to play and the sound of her voice fills the room. It lifts my spirits and my soul, making me feel anything is possible.

I go to the kitchen and pick up the gin bottle and take it back into the living room, where Ella is still singing. I'm desperate to sing along, but I know I can't. I open the gin bottle and smell its contents. It smells like . . . gin. I can't work out what's in it. But I'm hoping someone else might.

'Ah, you must be the new PA.' Hector makes me jump as he comes into the room behind me. 'I'm Hector Macquarrie,' he says, sticking out a hand. 'Thank you for coming over this morning.'

'I, er, yes . . .' I say.

'See you're getting acquainted with the gin!' He picks up the bottle off the table in front of me and studies it. I watch him with interest. Then he looks down at himself – 'Will you excuse me a moment?' – and leaves the room again before I've had a chance to ask him what I wanted to.

I sigh, and turn up the volume on the beautifully crackly record player, drinking in Ella's voice and the peace it brings me, letting it wash over me. I have always loved her singing and I think she definitely influenced my jazzy, bluesy-with-a-hint-of-country style. The track comes to an end and Hector suddenly comes back in . . . dressed! For the first time since I've been here! With a stick instead of his crutch. His buttons are all done up wrong on his cardigan and there's an egg stain down his front, but he's dressed. A tie hangs loosely around his neck.

'There!' he announces. Ella launches into another song, and he doesn't seem to mind, so I leave her playing but turn the volume down a little.

'Um . . . can I help you with that?' I point to the tie.

He looks down and I wonder if he's about to lose it again. But instead he looks at me and smiles.

'That would be very kind. Can never remember how to tie the damn things! I can see you're going to be a great asset. Sorry, what did you say your name was?'

'R . . . Rubes, everyone calls me Rubes.'

'Right, Miss Rubes.' He smiles and lifts his chin for me to tie his tie, just like my dad used to do, and I find myself transported right back there. Dad could never tie a tie properly either, despite insisting on wearing one nearly every day. 'What would I do without you?' he used to say. But it was what I was going to do without him that was the real question. I was lost without him, singing and music the only constant in my life once he'd gone. And if I don't get my voice back, I'll be lost all over again. I'll only have Joe left. I'll message him in a bit. Maybe we shouldn't wait for me to get my recording contract . . . maybe, I think, we should get engaged now. Have the party, celebrate being together. That's what we should do! I think, my spirits lifting as the music fills the room.

'Thank you,' Hector says when I'm finished, stepping back and standing in front of the mottled mirror above the fire. He nods approvingly, then turns to the bottle of gin. 'Ah, I see you've been getting acquainted with the product,' he says.

The track comes to an end, there's a crackle and then the next one begins.

'I was just wondering what's in it,' I say tentatively, desperate not to let this new, lucid Hector slip away from me. This Hector who could actually sort everything out for us right now! I'm on tenterhooks.

'Ah, as do my rivals, dear girl, as do they!' He lets out a deep, hearty laugh. 'It's the recipe that makes it so successful. I only hope my son will realise it and stop this foolish talk of leaving the company and the island.' He frowns and starts to looks stressed. 'He has all the skills to take over from me one day. He has talent. I hope he comes to appreciate what he has here.' He taps the bottle.

'I'm sure he will,' I say quickly, having no idea what I'm talking about, but wanting to keep him in good spirits. I wonder if Dad knew that his father thought he had talent, and how he felt working as a security guard on the front desk of a big office block all those years. Never took a day off sick. Always smartly turned out and polite. He was known by all the employees and he knew each of them by name. It was a secure and steady job and allowed him to be home in time to meet me from school every day. He was always there. But would he rather have been here?

'Well, maybe we should toast your first day with a tot,' Hector says. Leaning on his stick, he makes his way to the kitchen, arriving back with two glasses; clearly he knew exactly where to find them.

'Um, well, yes . . . like I say, if I'm to work for you, it would be good to know the recipe,' I say, growing in confidence. This is it! He can remember! He's going to tell me! Seeing the gin bottle has brought it all back. It looks like we're nearly done here after all, and I'll be in Tenerife way before New Year, back on schedule. And then I intend to tell Joe my new plan . . . for us not to wait, but to seize the day! Enjoy what we have, not what's round the corner. I feel elated that coming here has made me realise that that's the right thing to do, and smile to myself as Hector pours two glasses.

'Have a seat.' He points to the chair next to the fire and I sit in it. It's a lot lower than I was expecting, but once there, it's like sinking into a marshmallow, and I feel like I could stay there all day. But I mustn't let myself get too comfortable. I have work to do. I try to shuffle myself to the edge of the seat as I take the glass of gin that Hector hands me.

'Well, you have all your basic ingredients, which you know,' he says, putting down the bottle.

'I'm not sure I do.'

'That stuff's simple, but you'll need to make sure you keep the orders coming in. The dried ingredients from our suppliers. There's carda—'

'Wait, I'll get a pen and paper.'

'Good idea, you'll need those at all times. First rule of being a good PA. But I'm sure we'll soon lick you into shape!' He laughs deeply again, and I have to shake myself and remind myself it's not my dad I'm hearing. I wish I had the courage to ask Hector what happened between them. Why he played no part in my dad's life . . . or mine, for that matter. 'As I say,' he continues, 'the basics are simple . . .' and he reels off a list of spices. 'Got that?' he asks, standing in front of the fire, the dogs staring up at him with matching profiles.

'Yes!' I say, beaming. 'Wait! I'll be right back!' I need that pen and paper, now! I push myself up out of the sagging seat with an *oomph* and hurry to the door.

'It's the other five that make this special,' he says as the song comes to an end.

'Other five?' I turn and look at him.

'Yes. The basic ingredients are simple, but it's the five special ones that make it . . . well, special. That's what captures the spirit of the island in the bottle.' He looks from the glass to me and I'm transfixed for a moment.

'Just wait there. I'll get that notepad.'

Hector pours himself another large glass. 'Just a small one, to celebrate your first day,' I hear him saying.

'Lachlan! Lachlan!' I call, running to the back door. I quickly grab a coat from the rack, step into some wellies, then open the door. The sharp wind, which I'm getting used to expecting, comes at me and bites me on the nose as I set off towards the red outbuilding, feeling and probably looking like a drunk duck in the oversized boots.

'Lachlan!' I feel my throat tighten and break again. Bugger!

I make it to the outbuilding and pull at the heavy door. This time, it opens. I step inside and look around at the high-ceilinged room. It's huge, and in the middle of it is a big piece of kit that looks like it could be one of Caractacus Potts' inventions from *Chitty Chitty Bang Bang*.

'Hey! What's up?' Lachlan appears from round the back of a huge copper drum, making me jump.

'It's Hector!' I'm out of breath and very croaky, and suddenly feeling wildly excited.

'What?'

'He's . . . well . . .' I can't think what to say.

'He's what?'

'He's . . . He can remember everything! Including the gin recipe!' My smile widens. 'He can remember the gin recipe!' I repeat, and Lachlan runs to the door, clearly keen to see for himself. I follow as fast as a drunken duck can, the wind still nipping at my cheeks and lips. He beats me to the back door and throws himself in through it. I follow, stumbling and tripping, to find him standing in the living room doorway with his back to me.

'See! See what I mean?' I say in hushed tones as I slip out of the boots.

'You said you'd keep an eye on him,' he says, not turning round.

'Yes,' I beam. 'And not only have I done that, but he's . . . well, he's completely back to how he was. Although, of course, I don't know how that was, obviously. But see for yourself. Ask him. He can remember the recipe for the gin . . . the basics and the five special ingredients that "capture the spirit of the island in the bottle".'

Lachlan turns slowly round to face me.

'Hector's gone,' he says flatly.

'What? You're joking, right?'

The look on his face says he's doing anything but.

I elbow my way into the doorway next to him. I can smell woodsmoke on his jacket.

The record player needle is clicking in its groove, signifying that the record has come to an end. But other than that, there is nothing and nobody in the room.

Chapter Seventeen

'We have to find him!' Lachlan's face is etched with worry.

'Oh God! What have I done?' I say quietly to myself.

He turns slowly towards me. 'What exactly do you mean?'

'Well . . . I just thought . . .' I start to roll my hands over each other nervously. My throat tightens. He stares at me, his eyes narrowing. 'I just thought . . .' I'm feeling hot all of a sudden, very hot.

'Quickly! We've got an old man with dementia possibly out in the freezing bloody cold. Anything could happen!' he says angrily, and I feel like crying. But I can't. This is my fault and I have to put it right.

'I'll find him!' I say.

'What . . . did . . . you . . . do?' he says slowly and clearly.

'I just thought . . . maybe if he could smell the gin, taste it like we did on the beach, the recipe would come back to him.'

'And did it?'

'Yes! That's when I came to get you!'

The record player clicks and clicks. I step forward and remove the needle and set it back in its home position.

'And he was drinking gin, you say?'

'Just one . . . or two.' I sniff.

'And where's the bottle now?' He looks around, as do I.

'I don't know. He must have taken it!' I look at Lachlan and he holds his hands to his head, then runs them through his long curly hair.

'We need to find him. He's not well. He's forgetful, and if he's drinking as well . . . The dogs are probably with him, but his balance isn't good even on that crutch—'

'He's not on the crutch . . . he's on a walking stick,' I say, my voice thinning out as my throat tightens with tension.

Lachlan turns to the back door and grabs two torches. He checks they're working, then hands one to me.

'It's going to be getting dark soon. We need to find him. But let's start with the house.' He takes the wide wooden stairs two at a time. I follow. 'I'll do the first floor, you check upstairs! Hector?!' he calls, opening each door in turn.

I turn to the door to the next level and put my hand on the cold latch. I hesitate for a moment, feeling like I'm intruding on Lachlan's private world. But we have to find Hector. This is my fault. I fling back the door and run up the narrow wooden stairs. I stick my head into the room that is clearly Lachlan's bedroom, and catch a glimpse of the amazing views from the window in the sloping ceiling, across the loch and beyond to the sea. Then I check an unused room that seems to be a storeroom, and the bathroom with its big old rolltop bath. Hector isn't here. I run back down the stairs, practically colliding with Lachlan on the landing.

'Sorry.' I jump back, as does he, and shake my head. 'Not there.'

'I'll check the cellar!' he calls, running downstairs. I follow and head to the kitchen and the door I'm presuming is the cellar. He's out of there as soon as I arrive, pushing back his hair. 'We'll check the outbuildings next, and the distillery.'

Again I follow him, down the path to the outbuildings. He pushes open the door where I found him earlier.

'Hector! Hector!' we both shout, and somehow my voice lets me.

'What is this place?' I ask as we move around the big copper drum and into a back room.

'The distillery. Where the gin was made. Well, first whisky, then gin. That's what I was doing when I asked you to keep an eye on Hector. Trying to get the still up and running again and make the wash, the basic clear alcohol.' He sounds cross. I can't reply. 'Why couldn't you just have waited?' he asks. 'We'd've found the recipe!'

'I just thought . . .'

'That you could rush it. Get it sorted and get to your retreat thingy. I know! You have a plan! But there's an old expression: what's meant for you won't pass you by. If we're meant to find that recipe, it'll happen.'

I can't say anything. His words sting. Maybe it's the truth in them that hurts the most. Tears prick my eyes. Hot and embarrassed.

'Let's get in the car,' he says, grabbing keys from the work surface covered with jars and pots and large test tubes of who knows what.

'Maybe you could show me around tomorrow,' I say with a croak. 'I'd like to know more. That's if . . . unless . . .'

Neither of us finishes the sentence. Instead, he leads the way, leaving the door unlocked in case Hector returns, and we both run to the old red Land Rover on the drive.

* * *

'He was here, Lachlan. Not that long ago. He wanted chocolate bars, but he didn't have any money. I've put it on the account.'

'Thank you,' Lachlan says as we stand in the shop. 'Take it from my wages.'

I look at him.

'Lachlan does more than anyone around here, what with his work with the class at the school, and the food he cooks for the café,' says Lena with a proud smile.

'And looking after Hector,' adds Lexie.

'He could've left us a long time ago. It's not been easy for him since—'

I'm not sure if Lachlan's embarrassed by the praise or just worried about Hector. He quickly puts a stop to the conversation.

'Right, well, we'll crack on. Hang on to him if you see him!' he says, moving towards the low door.

The light outside is fading fast. The sky is turning an inky blue.

'I tried to give him a cup of tea,' Lena calls after him, 'but he just got up and left. I was about to ring your mobile.'

'Okay. Call me if he comes back,' Lachlan says over his shoulder. 'We'll take a drive around the island. He can't have got that far.'

'We'll put the word out,' says Lyle.

'And he had the dogs with him. They never say no to a biscuit,' smiles Lexie. 'Nice to meet you again, dear,' she says to me.

'Um, and you.'

'Hope to see you for Hogmanay.'

I don't tell her that I won't be here by then, and hopefully neither will Hector. Well, that might be wishful thinking, but as soon as we can find a buyer, preferably a cash one, he'll be in his nice warm room at the old people's home, and not wandering around the island. We just need to find him and get him back to the house right now, safe and sound. Anything could have happened!

Chapter Eighteen

We jump back in the old Land Rover and it starts with a chug and shake. It's getting cold, really cold now. We need to find him. I know Lachlan is thinking exactly the same.

We drive first to the harbour and then to the church and graveyard. Each time we jump out with our torches and look around and call his name. Then quickly get back in the car.

We drive around by the beach near the house, and past a small croft that looks empty and dark, just on the outskirts of the distillery buildings. We drive from the bay across moorland and towards a small pine woodland nestling between two small hills. But nothing. We pass small cottages and crofts with lights beginning to go on and the smell of peat and woodsmoke in the cold evening air, and a field of small goats, where a short woman with a white bun flags Lachlan down. He gets out of the car and goes to talk to her. After a few minutes, he gets back in the car and starts it.

'She saw him not long ago, heading this way with the dogs,' he says, and veers the Land Rover off the single road we've been travelling along onto an uneven stony track leading up one of the hillsides. We arrive at a clearing and both jump out. I can hear a dog barking, low and gruff and rhythmic, and another yapping more erratically and excitedly.

'It's Rhona and Douglas!' Lachlan says, and breaks into a run.

I follow him through some trees, and then – whoa! I hear it before I see it! The torch lights it up as I swing it around. There in front of me is a waterfall, crashing over big worn rocks, the water swirling in a pool below. Hector is sitting on the edge. The older dog is lying across his lap, no doubt keeping him warm. The other, Douglas, is running around barking, letting us know where to find his master.

'Good boy,' Lachlan tells him. 'Good fella,' and he pats the dog's head. 'We're here to take him home,' he reassures him, and the dog stops barking.

Hector is holding the bottle of gin, his legs swinging over the edge of the rock bowl, and my heart leaps into my mouth and bangs loudly. One false move and he could fall. I don't want to startle him.

'Come on, Hector, let's get you home,' says Lachlan matter-of-factly, even though I know he's feeling anything but. He walks purposefully over the rocky moss-covered ground to where Hector is sitting, and I can hardly look.

'Came here all the time,' Hector says, and he seems to be humming to himself. 'This is the place.' He smiles. 'This is where it starts. The water gathers and then runs all the way across the island, you know that?'

'I do, Hector,' Lachlan says kindly, not rushing the old man.

'Across every bit of terrain and ending at the sea. It's like the main artery, the lifeblood of the island.'

'It is, Hector. Now, pass me the bottle and I'll help you up.'

'Yes, yes,' says Hector. Rhona climbs off his lap and stands stock still at his side.

I have to do something. I step forward to help.

Hector wobbles as he attempts to stand.

'Whoa!' says Lachlan, and grabs hold of him.

'Whoa!' says Hector, thrusting the bottle in my direction.

'Whoa!' I say as I attempt to grab the bottle and it slips through my frozen fingers into the deep pool below.

All three of us stand and stare at it.

'Sorry!' I say, and grimace. 'But there's more, right? And now we know that Hector can remember things when he's tasting the Teach Mhor gin.' I smile. I think I have done some good here today.

Lachlan looks at me and slowly, very slowly, shakes his head.

'That was the last bottle . . . saved for research purposes,' he sighs. 'Come on, Hector, let's get you home.'

He guides Hector back down the stony path to the Land Rover and helps him in. We take off our coats and layer them around and over the old man. Shivering, I get in the back with the dogs, and Lachlan turns the big vehicle around and begins driving back down the hill.

'Lovely day out, Mairead,' Hector says over his shoulder.

'Yes, Hector. Lovely day out.' I sigh. Not only are we back where we started, but we don't even have the gin to help us out any more, and it's all my fault!

Chapter Nineteen

I sit at the kitchen table with the pen and pad I found in the dresser, chewing the end of the pen as I try to remember the list of basic ingredients Hector rattled off when he thought I was his PA, Miss Rubes. Joe has texted me several times wanting to know what's happening. I'll ring him later. Tell him I've decided we shouldn't wait to get engaged. But first I have to try and remember this recipe, try and help put things right here.

Lachlan has taken Hector upstairs. He was leaning heavily on both of us when we came in, and I'm guessing his ankle is playing up. I couldn't feel any worse if I tried. This is all my fault, and to top it off, the last bottle of gin has gone. Now we have no hope of guessing the recipe. I write down what I can remember, then throw down my pen and hold my head in my hands. If it hadn't been for Lachlan, I find myself thinking, tonight could have turned out very differently. My phone beeps again. I know it's Joe, but I ignore it.

'He's in bed.' Lachlan's deep voice jolts me and I lift my head from my hands and the pit of despair. 'He's a bit confused, but he's had a bath of sorts. Takes ages for the water to heat up here.' He drags the big cream kettle onto the hot plate. I'll take him up a hot-water bottle and a cup of tea.'

'I'll do that,' I croak, going to stand.

'Sounds like you could do with a hot drink yourself,' he says, taking down a couple of chunky mugs from the hooks at the side of the range.

'I'll take Hector's up first,' I say, coming to stand beside him. He smells of outside; of the sharp, fresh, salty air. Not like back at home, where outside is full of fumes. I swallow, my throat tight. 'I'm sorry about today.' I look up at him slowly, feeling strangely shivery, even though I'm out of the cold. 'And thank you for what you did out there this evening. I . . .' My voice gives up on me. I want to tell him so much more. I want to thank him for what he's clearly been doing here for a very long time. But also to tell him he needs to be able to get on with his own life. He shouldn't have to wait here, looking after someone who isn't actually a relative. Hector's *my* relative, I think, but a stranger too. And judging from the illness, it looks like it will stay that way. My chance to get to know my grandfather has been and gone.

'No problem,' he says, and turns back to the kettle, which is slowly coming to a whistling, steaming boil.

He makes tea for Hector, and a hot-water bottle, and hands them to me.

'You sure about this? I mean, you're just here to sign the papers and move on, remember?' he says with a twinkle in his eye, and I wince but take it. I *was* just here for that. I didn't expect to get emotionally involved. Of course I care; Hector's an old man who could've died tonight thanks to my stupidity . . . still could! I think with a twist in my stomach. I press the hot-water bottle to it for comfort. But also, I realise, I want to know more before it's too late – about Hector, about this place, about my dad growing up here. And it's only Lachlan who can help me with that now.

'I'm sure,' I say with a nod, and turn to the door, still holding the hot-water bottle to my fizzing tummy. The dogs are in the kitchen now, getting treats from Lachlan, and as I walk out into the wide hall, I can hear him telling them what a great job they did tonight.

I climb the stairs slowly, thinking about the generations who have walked up these stairs before me, and wondering what happened. When did the clocks stop here? Because that's how it feels. Like the clocks just ground to a halt one day and the heart of the house stopped beating. Was it when Hector's wife, my grandmother, died? Or was it before then, when my father left? I think about the baby clothes, knitted but never worn, and the joy on Hector's face when he talked about getting the bike out of the shed for the 'wee one' to play on; clearly my dad's old bike, the one in the picture where he had such a look of pride and joy on his face. Before it all changed.

I stand outside Hector's bedroom door and look at the chips in the paintwork, at the layers of paint – years' worth, generations' worth. Layers and layers beneath the outer coat. I wonder what will happen to it all once the house sells. Everything will be stripped back and any trace of the past will be gone for good. I knock on the door, but there's no reply. I push it open gently, feeling the warmth of the hot-water bottle against me still, tucked into the crook of my arm. Then suddenly the dogs arrive and shove past me, wandering into the room, settling on the blankets on the floor by the bed. Clearly their usual place.

Hector is asleep. I don't want to disturb him. I put the tea by his bed, just in case he wakes and wants it, and then, feeling a little intrusive but doing it anyway, I slip the hot-water bottle into the bottom of the bed and tuck the covers in. As I turn to leave, I take a moment to study him. My father told me Hector was a bully, which is why we never had anything to do with him. Well he's not now, I think. He's just an old man. An old man with no family around him. And I wonder briefly who will be there when I'm old, when my singing days are well and truly over, if they're not already. Will it be Joe? When all the thoughts of recording contracts and record deals are done, will it be just Joe and me, sharing a life together? What will that life be like? And what are the memories I'll hold dear? I think of Hector tonight, remembering the good times, remembering how important the waterfall and the stream have been to his life on the island. What will I remember of my own life? Will it be the day we finally got a recording contract? Or something else? I think again about the seals bobbing up in the water, and drinking gin from oyster shells on a beach on Christmas morning.

I turn to move away and creep out of the room.

'Thank you, Mairead. Goodnight,' Hector says, not opening his eyes.

'Goodnight, Hector,' I say, glad he's safe and well and home.

* * *

Downstairs, Lachlan has put out hot drinks and a plate of cheese and oatcakes for us, home-made by the looks it.

'Hot toddy.' He hands me a mug. 'You look, and sound, like you need one.'

'Thank you,' I croak, and sit at the table. In my head I can hear Joe telling me I shouldn't be drinking alcohol, it'll have an effect on my voice. He read it on the internet. I ignore him and breathe in the hot, alcoholic steam, feeling its restorative powers already.

Lachlan sits down opposite me. 'Here, tuck in,' he says, and hands me a knife and plate. 'Nothing fancy. I expect you're used to much more glamour as a singer, staying in fancy hotels.'

I shake my head and manage a tired smile. 'Nothing could be further from the truth. I might dream of fancy hotels, but that's all it is until I get that record contract. If . . .' I add, and sip the hot drink. 'Whoa! That's powerful!'

'It'll put hairs on your chest.' He laughs, a deep, relaxed laugh now that Hector is safe and all is well at Teach Mhor.

The lighting in the kitchen consists of a dim yellow glow over the table. On the wooden board in front of me is a soft white cheese wrapped in nettles, along with the home-made oatcakes and a jar of deep brown chutney.

'Goat's cheese,' he says with a smile. 'From the goats you saw this evening.'

'The ones that arrived here on the island after the shipwreck,' I say, my smile widening.

'Exactly the same,' he says, popping a piece of oatcake topped with cheese and chutney into his mouth.

I sip the hot toddy and am unsure whether to grimace or

let myself just wallow in its strength. I take another sip and go for the second option. Joe's disapproving voice in my head is practically a whisper now, like he's in another room and I'm shutting the door.

'Just one thing, Lachlan,' I say finally, feeling bolder with the hot toddy.

'Fire away.' He smiles, and actually, as he does so, he looks quite attractive. Must be the lighting, I tell myself, and the relief of the day and gratitude for what he did out there.

'Even if we can find the recipe, how do you plan to actually get the business up and running again? Surely,' I swallow, 'surely that's going to take a fair bit of cash. And I'm presuming that if the house has to be sold, there isn't some slush fund there to help launch it.'

'No. You're right.' He waves a knife, as if to tell me he'll carry on speaking when he finishes his mouthful. Then he picks up the whisky bottle and sloshes some into each of our mugs, neat this time.

'I mean, would it be enough just to find the recipe and make a small batch of the gin? Would you have fulfilled your promise?' I smile hopefully.

He shakes his head. 'I promised Hector I'd get the business going again. I don't run out on a promise.'

I sigh. 'I thought not.' I sip the whisky and blanch. 'So . . .' I say through the fumes and the burning sensation. 'What's the plan?'

'Well, I thought . . . seeing as you're back here now helping out . . .'

'Just until the house goes on the market so Hector can move into the home,' I remind him.

'Just until then,' he confirms, putting more cheese on an oatcake and handing it to me as if it's the most natural thing in the world. I don't think anyone has ever put cheese on an oatcake for me before. I look at it. Joe would just have told me that cheese is no good for my voice, along with the alcohol. It's such a small gesture, but, well, so thoughtful.

'What?' he says. 'You have to eat! Everyone has to eat!'

And it seems that that is exactly what Lachlan is: kind and thoughtful. This is a man who puts others' needs before his own. He's not here to rip Hector off, I know that now. I have to trust him.

'So, I was thinking . . . perhaps you have some money you could put up,' he says flatly.

I look at him. Is that why he's being nice to me? He thinks I have money? I look at the cheese and oatcake. But that wasn't a game; that was just instinct. This guy is not trying to rip me off.

I shake my head. 'Sadly, no. I don't have a bean. I've spent the last of my savings on the retreat in Tenerife!'

'Oh yes, the healing retreat!' He gives a little laugh, and there's a hint of cynicism there.

'What?'

'Healing comes from where you are in here.' He points to his heart and his head. 'Not jetting off to a hot country.'

'Says you. You know about these things, do you?'

He looks at me. 'I know healing can take time. It's about being in the right place, taking time for the things you love.'

I think about this. Where is the right place for me? What is it I love? It's always just been about the singing, and if I don't have that, what do I have? I have Joe, I tell myself.

I must ring him and tell him I think we should get engaged straight away; enjoy what we have rather than waiting for everything to fall into place. I find myself wanting to tell him about today. About this place. I want to tell him about Hector suddenly becoming lucid, thinking I was his PA; talking about the gin. I want to tell him about the deer and goats. The fright we had when Hector went off, and finding him by that amazing waterfall.

Joe is who'll be with me when I'm old. We'll share stories of places we've been and how we got there; the early days with the band, happy times touring, sleeping on friends' floors and in the van. And now this. I want to share this with him too. When Jess and I started out, it felt like we had all the time in the world for our dreams to come true. Now, though, time is running out. I need to grab those dreams with both hands and make them happen.

Lachlan cuts into my thoughts. 'So . . . no money,' he says. 'That's a bummer.'

'If I get my voice sorted and get this record deal that's been on the cards . . . if Joe and I can get a mortgage, then maybe I could help out, a loan perhaps . . .'

'Well, that's a lot of ifs,' he says flatly, hitting the truth on the head again as he seems to have a habit of doing. 'What's the story with you and Joe? Have you been together long? Engaged? You haven't really said much about him.'

I bristle. Why would I tell him about my personal life? We've only just met. And we weren't exactly on friendly terms when we did. But then a small voice in my head says: *Why* haven't *you mentioned him more?*

'Joe's great. Really great. He's really supportive of me.

We're travelling the same path in life. Want the same things. That's what a good relationship is all about, isn't it?' I smile.

'But you're not engaged or married?' he says, knowing he's hit a raw nerve, and that teasing twinkle lights up his eyes once more.

'No,' my voice tightens, as do my lips, 'not engaged yet. But we will be . . . soon.' He raises that eyebrow at me again. 'We're just . . . we were waiting. Have been waiting.' I look down at my plate.

'Waiting for what?' he pushes, still teasing, but interested too. I take a deep breath.

'For the right time,' I say, not expecting the sigh that follows it.

'Take it from me. Waiting is never advisable. Grabbing a good thing when you have it is by far the better option. Just in case you lose it.' He takes a slug of whisky. 'What's he like, this Joe of yours?'

'Joe? Like I say, he's great!' I smile. 'He works in PR and marketing, for a big company. But he also puts loads of time into marketing the band and trying to get us noticed.'

I pick up my phone to show him a photograph, and notice the seven missed calls and the text message from Joe telling me to get in touch and let him know that I've got things sorted. I swallow and scroll through to my photos.

'Wow!' Lachlan says as I show him the screen.

'Oh, not that one. That's me getting ready to go on stage,' I say quickly, and swipe back to one of Joe.

'Very Jessica Rabbit,' he says, and I blush, realising that this man has only ever seen me in knitted jumpers and hats and, at our first meeting, with shorts on my head and socks for gloves!

'And where did you and Joe meet?'

'At an open mic night,' I tell him, putting down my phone. 'He was trying to get a band together, but they realised they didn't really have what it takes. I think they were trying to relive their childhood dreams of being rock stars. They gave up after that.'

'And he started promoting you and your band?' he says, putting more cheese on an oatcake and handing it to me. I bite into the tangy softness and the crumbling oatcake beneath.

'Yes, he's really supportive,' I repeat. 'Always there, always hoping our big break is just round the corner.'

'Sounds like he's hanging off your coat tails,' says Lachlan matter-of-factly.

'What? No!' I exclaim. 'He just wants me to succeed. I've worked hard for this, we all have. That's why I have to get back there.'

'You're right. Sorry. Not my place to comment.'

'It's fine,' I say, putting his bluntness down to tiredness and worry. I can excuse it after what he did today. 'Joe and me are fine. We've been together long enough to know what we both want in life.'

'And what's that?' He lets his oatcake crack in his mouth and part of it falls onto the plate. Crumbs cling to his bottom lip before he licks them away, his eyes smiling.

'Well, we were due to get engaged this Christmas. Once the band had secured the deal with the A&R person who came to see us.'

'Sorry, but you're talking gobbledygook now.'

I start again. 'Basically, we were hoping to settle with a manager, who would sort out a record deal and a producer. Joe and I were waiting for this to happen, and then we planned to get engaged and start looking at a flat together once the contract was sorted. But ... then, well, this happened.' I hold a hand to my throat. 'My voice went, on stage. No sound came out at all. Years of training and it just ... went.'

'Ouch,' says Lachlan. 'That's gotta hurt.'

'Not just me, but the band and Joe too. He had all the marketing lined up and our lives planned.'

Lachlan shrugs. 'Like I say, what's meant for you won't pass you by.' He tops up our mugs again. 'But also, don't put off what you can do today. If this Joe guy is the one for you, why wait?'

I nod. He's right. And I'm going to message Joe and tell him. Tell him it's time to start celebrating. I look at Lachlan and feel a rush of gratitude and affection and ... well, I'm not sure what else, but a real liking for this man. It's like something inside me has shifted. He's just trying to fulfil a promise, I think. Doing something for someone else. He's not thinking about himself in all of this. But why?

I ask the question he's been avoiding telling me the answer to. 'Why did you make the promise to Hector?'

He stops chewing and puts his knife down on the wooden board, then looks at me, thinking.

'Let's just say Hector was there when I needed somebody. When he thought I might fall, he was there to catch me. Anything I've done for him is payback.'

I wait, but I think he's told me all he's going to. What I do know is that he's repaying a kindness, and that whatever Hector did doesn't sound like the actions of a bully to me. Maybe, just maybe, my dad – and my mum for that matter – had this all wrong. What if there is more to the situation? I need to find out. And the only way I can do that is by helping Lachlan set up the gin still.

'I don't know anything about business,' I tell him, 'but I do know about needing money to do the thing you love.'

'And?' He picks up his knife again.

'Well, there was this singer. He had a bit of success and then the record label dropped him.'

He raises an eyebrow; clearly he has no idea what this has to do with the gin.

'So he crowdfunded his next album. Put on a special event for fans who bought it upfront.'

'How does that work then?'

'Crowdfunding? You build the business up with the help of investors. In our case, gin drinkers. You offer them something special in return for putting up money. For pre-ordering.'

He looks at me thoughtfully.

'I mean, what do you need money for?' I ask.

'Well, ingredients, running costs, bottles and packaging. In the past, the bottles were made on the island. A family-run business. But they went under when the gin business did. Isla used to work with her father hand-painting them, but she runs the ferry with her husband now.'

'Oh, I've met Isla,' I say, thinking about how she practically blanked me in the shop and on Christmas Day.

I thought she was lovely when I first met her. I wonder what changed. 'But essentially we need enough money to put down a deposit on the place in the care home, just until the house is sold. Agreed?'

'So you say,' he says. I look at him, and this time it's me who raises an eyebrow. 'Okay,' he says reluctantly. 'So . . . this crowdfunding. How does it work?'

'I'll get my laptop.' I go to stand, and realise the whisky was indeed strong. But when I return with the laptop and put it on the kitchen table and we start to look up crowd-funding pages, Lachlan sploshes more whisky into the mugs and I don't complain, and the deal is sealed.

By the end of the evening, the whisky has taken control of my lips and my legs and indeed my voice too, which seems positively perky. It's clearly time for bed. Feeling happier than I have in a long time, I say goodnight to Lachlan and make my way up to my room, where I find the fire lit and a hot-water bottle in my bed. I photograph the fire and send it to the band, who all want to know where I am and what's happening. I send a smiley face, then look back at the flames, which seem to be warming me from the inside out. It could only have been Lachlan!

Chapter Twenty

The next morning, I think back to the phone call I had with Joe last night before I went to sleep, and cringe. I was trying to tell him about Hector and the gin and the waterfall, but I have no idea what words actually came out. And something about not letting it all pass us by and that we should get engaged straight away, whether my voice came back or not. I can't remember his reply. But I don't remember him cheering for joy. In fact, I seem to remember the call finishing rather abruptly. If only I could remember what I actually said, and what he said, and where he was for that matter. I remember there was loud music.

I ring him again.

'It's very early, Rubes! Especially after your late call last night!' he says grumpily. 'You're supposed to be on voice rest, for goodness' sake, not going out and getting hammered.'

'I know, I know,' I croak, and my head bangs.

'I mean, I've been working hard here to make the best of this situation. I've managed to get a couple of women's magazines and a Sunday supplement interested in your story: "My road to recovery", covering your time at the vocal retreat. If it works, it'll definitely help get a label interested again. I'm going to try and get you on some medical phone-ins.

And it would be good to book a big gig. A comeback event to really give the story some weight.'

Joe's enthusiasm is great, but right now all I can think of is tea. A big mug of tea.

'Won't be long before you're back. Once we get that contract signed, we can start living life like we planned it. We'll be in that plush apartment. I can be the house husband and bring up the kids while you do what you're good at. Just like we talked about.' There's no mention of my suggestion that we get engaged and find somewhere to live straight away, with or without the contract, and I decide it's best not to bring it up again. 'Just need you to get to that retreat,' he says firmly. 'I mean, like I say, I can't do it all, and I'm doing this for us, Rubes. I want to give up working at the office, be your backup team. Maybe take on a few select clients, but nothing that will interfere with what you do. But we need to strike while there's still interest in the band.

'Surely you've done what you need to do there by now? You don't even know this man,' and just for a moment I wonder if he's talking about Lachlan or Hector. 'He's not part of your life. It's not like he was there while you were growing up. You don't owe him anything. Look, tie up any loose ends and tell whoever, the solicitor and the carer bloke, that you have to go.' So I must have told him about Lachlan last night! My cheeks heat up and I have no idea why. 'It's down to them to get more help in if they need it, not you!'

I stare out of the window and don't say anything. I spot a group of deer running across the moorland, and feel a moment of envy for their freedom to roam wherever they like.

'Okay. Good. Don't talk. Keep resting your voice. I'm off to work. Message me later when you're on your way. Love you,' he says in his usual way, and finishes the call.

I think about Joe's plans for our future, with him working part time from home so that I'm freed up for recording sessions and going on tour. It's what I've always wanted too. So why, as I look out over the bay and the mountains towards the low golden sunlight emerging on the skyline, am I thinking about nothing other than the big gin still and how crowdfunding actually works and whether the seals are there again this morning? I lift my phone and snap a picture of the view and send it to the band group chat, and then reply to their concerned messages, telling them I'm fine and hoping to be at the retreat really soon.

I pull on my jumper and hat and follow the cooking smells rising up through the house from the kitchen.

'How's Hector?' I ask, my head thumping with each syllable.

'Alive, and demanding breakfast!' Lachlan laughs, standing by the open door of the big cream range. He turns up the heat, checking the gauge to see if it's responding, and then shuts the door firmly, making my head bang. 'Better than you by the looks of it,' he adds. His curly hair bobs cheerily as he stirs bright yellow soft scrambled eggs. 'From the croft down the road,' he says when he sees me looking. 'She keeps hens. I swapped her a batch of scones for them. Want some?'

My rumbling stomach and watering mouth tell me I would very much like some. 'Yes please. They smell delicious,' and I smile tentatively. At this rate we might even become friends, and my stomach flips happily over and back again at the thought.

He serves up the fluffy eggs beside thick slices of home-made wholemeal bread. I help myself to hand-churned butter from the dish on the table while he takes Hector his breakfast in bed, and I'm suddenly feeling very much better.

'And you're sure Hector is okay?' I ask when he returns, through a mouthful of crunchy brown bread softened by the salty melting butter.

'He's fine. Just thought he should rest his foot. He's happy to stay in bed, which isn't really like him, but he doesn't remember a thing about last night.'

'Which is the problem,' I say gently.

Lachlan stares down at his plate. For a moment neither of us says anything, and I can tell he's worried.

'He really will be warm and safe in that home,' I say. He puts down his knife and fork with a clatter. 'You've done so much for him. But you can't do it all on your own. What if something like that happens again when you're not here?'

'I'm not on my own,' he says. 'You're here. Not that you're much help,' he tries to joke. 'More trouble than you're worth!' He picks up his knife and fork again and begins to eat.

'I'll be leaving as soon as we have the gin sorted, though. Talking of which . . . no more delaying tactics! We need to crack on.' I try and jolly him along, but he's deep in thought. 'This is the right thing to do,' I say, and without thinking, I put my hand on his forearm.

He looks up at me as if considering what I'm saying, then swallows and says evenly, as if trying to keep emotion at bay, 'Even if he wants to die at home?'

'Yes. He could've died last night!' I feel for him, but the care home is the right thing to do.

'Only because you started giving him gin and then wandered off and left him! Hector . . .' He swallows again. 'Hector was there when I needed him. He's been like a father to me. I want to do the right thing by him.' I can tell he's conflicted, on the one hand wanting to do as he promised, and on the other maybe seeing that Hector really would be better off in the home, because he is only going to get worse. 'It's what we all want, isn't it?' he says quietly. 'To be looked after by people who care about us, in a place we love.'

This time it's me who swallows. I've never really thought about it. Never thought about what happens further down the line. I've spent so many years chasing the record label dream, I've never considered what happens when we're old; where we'll be, what we'll be doing. What will I have when my days as a singer are over? Will I be like my mum, never settling? Still looking for gigs on cruise ships, trying to ignore the passing of time until the phone stops ringing and the gigs stop happening. What then? Will I be in a place I love? And who will be there to care for me? Will it be Joe?

'I'll come back and visit,' I say to Lachlan.

'What, for Hector's funeral?' he says with a tilt of his head, and I don't know if he's still cross with me over Hector disappearing last night, or if he's just stating a fact. But the sad part is that he's probably right.

'We need to get this gin made!' I say, clapping my hands, making my head thump again, refocusing on the matter in hand and trying to push out all the other worries, including my phone conversation with Joe and the fact that he thinks

I'm leaving today and I have no idea how to tell him that that isn't going to happen. I wish he would understand that this is something I have to do before I move on.

'You're right,' Lachlan says. 'The still needs to be up and running. Hector needs to see it. I'm sure it will help him . . . stay as well as he can.' I can tell he's worried that Hector seems to be getting worse. 'And I've been working on that. On your laptop. I hope you don't mind?' he says.

I shake my head, surprised. So he really is going to do this. He's not stalling.

'I've been reading up on the basics of making the gin.' He shows me diagrams that are frankly far too confusing for me. 'I'll deal with all of that,' he says. 'Years as an engineer, I can do this side of things.'

'An engineer?'

'Yes. Went off to college on the mainland. Got a good job in an engineering company. Hated every minute of it. But I was too proud to come back. Until . . . well, until I had to and realised everything I'd ever wanted was right here.'

'And was it?'

'Not quite,' he says quietly. 'So,' he moves the conversation on, turning the computer round. 'I've been thinking about the crowdfunding page . . . We need to sell *this* many bottles, at *this* price.' He points to the page, where he's done graphics of bottles of gin. 'We offer everyone who invests the chance to buy a special edition of Teach Mhor gin . . . or better still, six bottles. We describe the gin *here*, and what's in it.'

'And what do they get in return?'

'Well, that's the thing we need to think about. They get the special edition and become stakeholders in the company;

we pay them their annual dividend in gin, rather than money.'

'Great! And we have to sell all that gin for this to work?'

'Uh huh. If we don't make the target, we don't get a penny of the money that's pledged.'

'Maybe we should do something . . . a party or something when we reach the target,' I say. 'A tea party, so people can see the place in daylight, see where the product's made. We can serve them gin and tonics and scones and shortbread!' I add, suddenly warming to the idea.

'I'll get in touch with Isla about the bottles, get some special edition designs maybe. She may still have some of the old artwork, or better still, some of the bottles themselves!'

'The ones that look like the sea?'

He nods.

I think about Isla eating ginger biscuits and looking as sick as I felt after the crossing from the mainland. 'She doesn't seem to like working on the ferry very much,' I say.

'She's always loved it. She loves everything about the island. Been riding that ferry all her life.'

'We could invite her and Gordan over to talk about the design. Or go to the pub,' I say cheerfully. 'Maybe show a picture of it on the crowdfunding page. We could all talk it through if you invite them.'

He shakes his head. 'I'm not sure that's a good idea. I'll see Isla when I go to the village at some point.'

'Not a good idea?' I ask with a frown.

'No,' he says firmly, and I realise he doesn't want to discuss it any more but have no idea why. Is he worried about Hector? But I'm sure Hector wouldn't mind people coming to the house. He might enjoy the company. I don't push it. I don't want the good mood to evaporate.

'Maybe you could put up some pictures of the island on the crowdfunding page. We could go and take some new ones.' I think of the gin and oysters on the beach. 'From what I've seen, it's very . . . atmospheric.'

He laughs. 'Atmospheric! So we haven't sold the beauty of the place to you yet?'

'Let's just say I'm more of a city type. I can see the pleasure in cities. Out here . . . well, it's very remote.'

'Remote . . . wild, you mean. This is the wilderness.' He throws out an arm to the window. Outside, the wind is starting up and the long grasses towards the beach are bent, and the sky and the water are darkening. He looks at me and something in me shivers. 'And once it gets under your skin, you won't want to be parted from it for long . . . Well, that's what they say.'

'I think we can safely say that won't happen to me. And it obviously didn't do it for my father, either.'

'Maybe there were other reasons your father didn't stay.'

I hesitate. A voice inside me says: *Don't ask. You don't need to know.* Out loud I say, 'Do you know about my father? Do you know why he left?'

'I know there was bad feeling between him and Hector.'

'My father said Hector was a bully.' But I'm confused. The Hector I've met is far from a bully. In fact, he seems like someone I would have liked to have known. I try and stop the thought before it comes rushing into my head, but too late . . . Someone I would have liked to have called my grandfather.

Lachlan studies my face and then says slowly, 'I believe . . . in life, there are always two sides to a story.'

I think about what he's said. 'Just too bad it's too late. I'll never get to hear Hector's.' The words hang in the air between us, and this time it's Lachlan who chivvies us into action.

'More tea,' he says, picking up the big pot, 'and then let's get this crowdfunding page sorted out. We're going to get Teach Mhor gin back up and running. Whatever was in the past looks like it's going to stay there. A lot of water has gone under the bridge.'

And briefly I think of Hector sitting at the waterfall last night. It has indeed. Water that I'll never get to know about.

'Wait there!' I stand and go back into the living room, where the fire is lit, as usual, waiting for Hector to sit by it. I pick up the photographs I took in there, then pause and look at the box of records. There are so many I'm dying to play: more Ella, Louis Armstrong, Astrud Gilberto, Billie Holiday, music I remember from my childhood. I always thought it was my mother who gave me my love of music. Looks like my dad had something to do with it too, and maybe Hector before that. There are some other records there that I don't know, titles in what I think is Gaelic, folk songs I'd love to hear. But it will have to wait; first we have to get the gin business sorted. I close the lid on the record player and return to the kitchen carrying the photos.

'Let's put some of these up on the site,' I say, holding up a black and white picture of the distillery, the workers standing outside. 'Give people a sense of the history of the place.'

He takes it from me and looks at some of the others.

'We need to sell the dream!' I say, starting to feel quite excited.

'Often dreams can be a long way from the reality,' he says. 'And then it's time to change the dream.'

I have no idea what he's talking about. Does he mean Winter Island? The idea of it being beautiful as opposed to the harsh reality of living here?

'We need to stand out,' I tell him. 'Look how many gins there are now. We want people to feel they're buying a piece of this place, a piece of the island and life here.'

He's still looking through the photos. 'This is the distillery in its heyday,' he says. 'And there's a lovely one of your dad and Hector and Mairead on the beach. Oh and another of Hector and the dogs.'

I experience that pang again, that feeling of having missed out on visits, trips, Christmases and summer holidays, and suddenly a large tear plops onto one of the photographs. It's not really a sad tear; more a wistful one, at seeing my dad here, knowing where he came from and how happy he was. Lachlan wipes it away and looks up.

'Maybe you're right,' he says thoughtfully. 'It's time we took some new ones. Then and now.'

'Yes, good idea. Nothing stays the same forever. New photos will show we're looking to the future of Teach Mhor gin . . . a legacy for whoever might end up taking it over and taking it forward.' I see Lachlan's shoulders droop as he thinks about the not-so-distant future. 'At least you'll know you did what you promised Hector. He will have left his legacy here. Now all we need to do is find that recipe!'

I sniff quickly and look around, trying to distract myself

by thinking of places I haven't yet searched. And trying to ignore the fact that a voice in my head – Joe's voice – is wondering what time the ferry is. I try and ignore it, because I know for a fact I won't be on the ferry today. Or even tomorrow. But I will be on it soon, and suddenly I feel quite sad. I still have no idea how to tell Joe that I'm staying a bit longer, and judging from our earlier conversation, he's not going to be happy when I do, not happy at all. But instead of feeling guilty as I have been, I'm starting to feel a bit angry about that. I need to do this, with or without his blessing. There is more to life right now than getting to the vocal retreat. Because who knows if I will ever have another chance to find out about my dad's past.

A message pings onto my phone. I look at it, then at Lachlan.

'It's the care home. Fraser must have given them my number.'

'Interfering in other people's business,' Lachlan mutters, and he's back to his grumpy self.

'They want us to go over for a visit. Show Hector round the place.' I look at Lachlan, who is picking out more photographs of the house, the bay, the animals that were once here and laying them on the table. 'I think we should go,' I persist. 'I think it's something you need to think about.'

He finally stops what he's doing and looks at me, then lets out a huge sigh.

'Okay, let's go and visit and see what Hector thinks of it. If he likes it and seems happy there, well . . .' He looks to be struggling to say the words, but finally manages it. 'Maybe you're right. Maybe he would be better off somewhere like that.'

'Last night was a real scare,' I remind us both.

He nods sagely. 'Let's see this care home of yours then!' and tosses the photographs to one side.

I reply to the care home manager, do one last check for messages, then turn my phone off. My cheeks burn with guilt, but it needs to be done, to avoid any further questioning from Joe. I'll message him when everything is sorted, I tell myself . . . just as soon as it's sorted.

Chapter Twenty-one

The ferry journey is not quite as bleak as the one on the way over here. When I thought about doing this journey again, I imagined I'd be leaving and never coming back. Now I'm looking back at the island, cold yet sunny, with clouds making shifting patterns over the gorse-covered wilderness, wondering if I'll ever get away. Like the cloud patterns, everything keeps changing. I certainly didn't expect to be here with Hector, or Lachlan. Hector's hardly spoken since Lachlan persuaded him to get dressed and we left the house for the ferry. Neither has Lachlan, for that matter. He and Isla seem to be swapping looks then studiously ignoring each other. Isla and Gordan just seem to be swapping looks. And Gordan and Lachlan are blanking each other completely.

'He's very quiet,' I say, nodding at Hector, who is looking out of the window at the deep, dark water.

'He is,' Lachlan agrees, then looks concerned, like a worried parent taking a child to visit its new school, knowing it has to be done. He says nothing more, and I find myself looking back at the island and wondering if the seals are there again this morning. I decide to take a walk up there when we get back. I can at least try to get my fitness up, so I can tell Joe I'm working on that.

'You should photograph the seals,' I say, thinking out loud. 'People would like to see them.'

He nods, still preoccupied.

I know this is for the best, I remind myself, for all of us. To get the house sold and for Hector to go into the home and for Lachlan to move on with his life. I wonder where he'll go and why I feel so guilty about trying to make this work. It is the right thing to do, isn't it? And just for a moment, I find myself wondering how my father felt when he left the island for the last time. Then I look at Hector and think about Lachlan's words: *there are always two sides to a story*.

I pull out the pad and pen that I found in the kitchen and go over the ingredients we have so far for the gin. The basic ones that Hector was telling me about. I've shown them to Lachlan and he says that from what he's read on the internet, they make sense. It's the island botanicals that will make the gin different. The five special ingredients. Now all we have to do is work out what they are.

Lachlan watches me as I ponder the list. Then he pulls out his phone and snaps a photograph of the island from our vantage point out at sea.

We spend the rest of the journey in silence, all of us lost in our own thoughts. Hector, Lachlan, me, Isla and Gordan . . . each of us seems to have something on our mind, and I have a feeling it's all to do with the past and the future, as we travel from the island to the mainland; from where we've come from to where we're going.

Chapter Twenty-two

The heat hits me, embracing me and suffocating me at the same time, as I pull at the scarf around my neck and drag my hat off.

'Come in, dears, come in!' says the big-busted lady in the tight floral dress, holding open the door of Island View Care Home for the Elderly. 'Let's keep the cold out!' she laughs, and her whole body wobbles.

I step inside the tropical foyer, and Lachlan ushers in Hector, who still has said nothing. We stand and peel off coats and extra layers, holding them in big bundles in our arms. I feel like I'm having a hot flush. Hector doesn't seem to notice the change in temperature. I wondered whether being in the warm might have raised a bit of a reaction, but it hasn't.

'Come and have a cup of tea and some shortbread,' the woman says, holding out a wobbly arm with a big smile to match her welcome.

'Oh, Hector can't have too much sugar, he's diabetic,' Lachlan tells her.

'No problem, we'll find something else. Come through into the residents' lounge.'

That phrase, 'residents' lounge', makes my heart sink, and

I look at Lachlan, knowing he feels the same. He hates the idea of Hector ending up in a residents' lounge, though at least he would be safe.

We step into the big bright room, looking out over a frost-covered garden, and beyond that, the island.

'I'm Flora, the care home manager. Let's have a cup of tea, and then if you like I can show you the rooms. You'll find you have everything you need here. You can even bring some belongings from home to help you feel, well, at home.'

'Except it isn't,' Lachlan mutters under his breath. But at least he is here and he is taking everything in. So he must realise that as hard as it is, this is the right thing to do.

I wonder what Hector would want to bring from home. His dogs, probably, and that can't happen. Once again I wonder what's going to happen to them, and I know it's something else Lachlan and I need to discuss. I look at Hector. He seems to have aged just being here. His shoulders are rounded and hunched and he still hasn't spoken.

In the residents' lounge, people are sitting looking out. Some are covered in blankets. A man and a woman are playing draughts. There's a television on in the background, with subtitles. Jeremy Kyle is helping to put mismatched families back together in some shape or form. I wonder what he'd say about mine. Probably that it was all too late. We should've talked. I look at Hector. It *is* too late, I think sadly.

Lachlan looks like a caged animal, with his mane of curly hair and his broad shoulders. With his hands behind his back he's pacing up and down by the big windows, gazing out, and I'm not sure if it's the garden outside or the island

171

beyond it that he's hankering after. Hector sits looking at the cup of tea in front of him, and the oatcake turning to soggy mush in the slops in his saucer.

'It's very hot in here, isn't it?' I say to Flora.

'Like summer all the year round,' she says with her wide, happy smile, and I can't help but like her. 'Our residents prefer it that way. Nothing worse than feeling cold.'

Hector won't miss the draughts at Teach Mhor, I think. And then I think about the big, welcoming open fires there, and I know he will miss those.

'We have cinema night once a week,' says Flora. Please God don't say bingo, I think. 'And bingo twice a week, because the residents love it so much. Other than that, well, we're working on trying to bring in some new ideas. But with staffing cuts, it's not easy.' Her smile has become some-what strained. 'Still, with more residents, maybe we'll get a staff member or two back again.'

I look around the lounge. So that's it? They're put in front of a TV and treated to bingo twice a week?

'It's hot in here . . . mind if I get some air?' Lachlan points to the French doors.

'Not at all. Give them a shove. They haven't been opened for a while.' Flora turns to Hector. 'So, when do you think you might like to move in?' He just stares at his teacup and she looks at me.

'Um, just . . . getting the finances in place,' I say.

'Right.' She smiles hopefully. 'Well, I can only keep the room for a while. There are always people wanting to move in. When a place comes up, it's usually snapped up, and there's a waiting list.'

'I understand. We just need to get Hector's house sold.' My mouth is dry.

'Of course. Look,' says Flora, 'I know how important it is to see your granddaddy sorted. But as I told Fraser, I can only hold the room for a while. Just until Candlemas. Then I'll have to let it go and you'll have to go to the back of the queue, I'm afraid.'

'Yes, fine,' I say. 'Candlemas.' I look at Lachlan walking the garden and occasionally glancing out to the island. At least Hector will be able to see it from here, I think, trying to be positive, but it doesn't seem to bring me any comfort.

'We look forward to welcoming him here. Now, let me show you the rooms.' A buzzer goes off. 'Oh, excuse me,' and Flora gets up. 'All our rooms have buzzers for residents if they need us, night or day,' she says, looking flustered but still smiling.

I glance around the room, smiling at some of the residents, though I don't get much reaction. I look out at the garden again. Lachlan has been joined by an old man, and it looks as though they're having a chat about plants. I find myself wondering how much longer we're going to be here. I could do with some fresh air myself. My throat feels dry in the sweltering environment, and I gulp the tea from the cup I'm holding. There's an upright piano against one wall and I find myself drawn to it, lifting its stiff lid and running my fingers over the keys. It reminds me of the piano I learnt to play on as a child. It's the only time I really remember spending quality time with my mum. She would visit us at Dad's house and sing while I played. They were happy times.

I press down on a couple of keys. It's out of tune, but still, the sound makes me smile. I look around. No one seems bothered by me tinkering on the piano. I put my cup on top of the piano and sit down, then let both hands run over the keys.

'Ooh, smashing! The entertainment's here,' says an old man, looking over from the TV. I glance outside. Lachlan has been joined by another resident, a woman this time. He's crouching down, picking some leaves from a plant, holding them up and tasting one, then offering them to the two residents to smell. They're listening intently to what he's saying. It makes me smile.

'Do yer know "The Bonnie Banks o' Loch Lomond"?' asks the old man.

I smile and attempt to remember the notes, singing it through in my head. I'd like to sing out loud, but I know I can't. My voice is tight and dry. If I'm honest, I can't bear the idea that it's deserted me for good after my clumsy attempt on Christmas morning, and I have no idea how I'll tell Joe and the band if it has. But the feel of the keys under my fingers brings me a real sense of happiness, and so I launch into playing the song. When that one's finished, I dredge up some of the songs I learnt in my early days with my piano teacher, and carry on playing as the residents begin to smile, clap and even sing.

As I start playing 'Daisy, Daisy', the room goes suddenly very quiet. I look around, wondering what's happening and whether I should stop playing. Everyone is looking at a frail woman sunk into a chair with a blanket over her legs, and after a moment I realise that she is singing in a thin, wavering voice, moving her head gently from side to side. I play to the end of the song. The room still doesn't make a sound. Flora is standing by the piano now, tears rolling down her big round cheeks.

'Did I do something wrong?' I ask. 'I just thought it would be nice to play . . .'

Flora smiles and shakes her head.

'Quite the opposite,' she says. 'That was wonderful. Agnes hasn't spoken a word since she came here three years ago. That's the first time we've heard her say anything. You've obviously unlocked something in her.' She clasps my hand, her eyes full of happy tears. 'Thank you!' I find myself tearing up too.

'Yes, good work, Miss Rubes.' Hector is suddenly standing behind me, bolt upright, chest pushed out. He turns to Flora. 'It's a lovely place you have here. Please tell me if there is anything else we can do to support your work.' Flora's eyes widen. 'My company likes to help out where it can. Perhaps we could send over a few bottles for the residents to enjoy on their bingo night. Make a note, will you, Miss Rubes? Better still, a visit to the distillery . . . Miss Rubes will organise it. She's new to the job, but really quite efficient!'

'Um, of course.' I pull out the notebook and pretend to make a note.

'Now, I really do think we should make tracks. It's all go at the distillery at this time of year. The still's never off. Great to meet you all. Interesting smell in here . . . pine, I think.'

'It's the disinfectant,' says Flora.

'Like the pine trees by the distillery. We always use pine in the gin. Gives it a unique flavour. Reminds me of my courting days when Mairead and I were teenagers.'

Pine! He just said that they used pine in the gin! It's one of the five special ingredients, I realise.

As I stand and stare at him, it hits me like a brick. It wasn't drinking the gin that brought back his memories yesterday. It was the music! The Ella Fitzgerald record I was playing when I asked him about the recipe must have triggered something in him, taken him back to when he was running the distillery. Just like on Christmas morning, when I put the radio on and he suddenly realised what day it was and panicked that nothing was ready. Oh, stupid me! Of course! I jump up.

'Um . . . thank you so much for our visit,' I say to Flora. 'We need to get the ferry. We'll be in touch soon.'

I run to the French doors.

'Lachlan! We have to go!'

'Why, what's up?'

'It's Hector! He's remembered . . . The pine! He used pine for the gin,' I say, beaming.

'What?'

'It was the music . . . he responds to music.'

Lachlan beams. 'You beauty!' he says, and he picks me up and hugs me, much to my shock and surprise.

'Ah, young love,' says the old woman in the garden.

'Oh, we're not . . .' I point between us. She just smiles dreamily. I remember what Lachlan said about going with the moment, wherever it might be. What does it matter if she thinks we're together? It's making her happy, and we could all do with a bit of happiness in our lives.

'Right, let's get back,' Lachlan says. 'We've got a pine

forest to visit.' He bids goodbye to his two garden companions and promises to come back soon.

'Looks like that music malarkey of yours has some use after all,' he tells me as we head back towards the ferry, all of us, by the looks of it, happier than when we left a few hours ago.

Chapter Twenty-three

'Good trip?' asks Isla as the ferry heads home – or should I say back to the island.

'Very good!' I tell her.

'Good.' She nods a lot, but her smile doesn't quite reach her eyes.

Lachlan keeps his distance from her, and I can't help but think there's some kind of problem here. I wonder if he's spoken to her yet about the bottles.

'So, you're staying on the island?' she says, as if cutting to the chase of what's on her mind.

'Oh no.' I shake my head, wondering why I get the feeling she wants me gone. Suddenly I begin to suspect there's something going on between her and Lachlan, and I quickly glance at Gordan, who seems to be also watching us.

'So, not staying,' she says, nodding again.

'No, just here until . . . Candlemas,' I say, thinking on my feet but once again with no idea of how I'm going to break it to Joe. 'To help with the business,' I add. 'I'm here to help with the gin business,' I repeat, as if trying to make it right in my own head.

'Oh, so you and Lachlan aren't together?' She seems almost relieved, which concerns me even more. Is this what keeps Lachlan here? Are he and Isla having an affair? I glance back at where he is standing looking out towards the island. Are they cheating on Gordan?

The wind stings my face, and I'm not sure if it's that that hurts me more, or the fact that once again, Lachlan is not the man I thought he was.

Chapter Twenty-four

'I can drop you off at the house if you like,' Lachlan says as we drive off the ferry. I emerge from my musings about him and Isla and realise I'm enjoying the familiarity of being back on the island. He's watching me in the rear-view mirror and seems to understand that I have things on my mind. 'I want to see if Hector can remember where they foraged for the pine, although I have a fairly good idea.'

'The what?' says Hector from the passenger seat.

'The pine you use in the gin, Hector,' I say over the rattle and shake of the old red Land Rover.

'Pine,' he repeats, the memory seeming to evaporate in front of our eyes.

'Yes, you remember, Hector.' Lachlan is looking from Hector to the road and back again as we swing and sway our way up the single track around the island. 'The pine in the gin. Teach Mhor gin!' Even he is getting frustrated now.

The sun is low in the sky, casting a bright light over the island as we drive up through the village. To the right is the water's edge, with white horses riding the little waves, and to the left, the distant mountains. Suddenly the herd of deer are running almost parallel with the Land Rover over the rolling moorland, as if welcoming us home, glad that the travellers are back in the fold, making me feel I can breathe again after the claustrophobic heat of the nursing home.

'Pine,' Hector says vaguely again, shaking his head, and the memory is almost out of reach now.

'You know . . .' Lachlan waves one hand, keeping the other on the wheel, 'Daisy, Daisy . . .' He looks at me, urging me to help.

'What? Oh, I can't . . . My . . .' I hold my throat.

'It's not the effing Albert Hall. I'm just looking for a bit of support here!' he growls. 'Do you want to get this distillery up and running so you can go to your healing retreat or not?'

I swallow. He's right, of course. I open my mouth, but can't quite seem to take the step to see if I can let out the first few notes.

'No.' Hector shakes his head. 'Can't remember any pine.'

'Daisy, Daisy, give me your answer do . . .' I suddenly blurt out, no idea whether it's in tune or not, and not even caring. 'I'm half crazy, all for the love of you . . .' I'm nodding, and so is Lachlan, who sings along, roughly but boldly. And then we both smile as Hector joins in merrily.

We look at his beaming face at the end of the song.

'So the pine forest . . . where you collect it for the gin?' Lachlan asks, and we hold our breath.

'Ah yes, used to go there all the time when I was courting Mairead. Proposed there! Well, proposed lots of times actually, until she finally gave in.' He chortles. 'It's just up the way. Best pine ever. Brilliant idea to put it in the gin. Gives it a real wintry, fresh flavour.'

And as we both breathe a palpable sigh of relief, he points

us towards the part of the forest he and Mairead used to come to.

'Course, gin originated in the Netherlands,' he says informatively. 'Known as genever. Was invented as a cure-all; anything from stomach upsets to the plague!' He laughs heartily. 'Then of course it was given to English soldiers fighting the Anglo-Dutch wars. That's why it's called Dutch courage, didn't you know?'

When we arrive at the forest, Hector is still humming the tune of 'Daisy, Daisy' over and over. We all get out of the Land Rover and walk towards the trees as the sun starts setting across the vast expanse of sky. As we step onto the needle-strewn floor, I breathe in deeply. I can taste the gin on my lips again, the taste of the pine forest.

Hector suddenly stops walking and humming.

'You okay, Hector? Is this it? Is this where you come for the pine?' I ask.

He's looking straight ahead, then he holds out a hand and steps forward to a tree trunk. We both look to where he's reaching. There in the trunk is a heart, with two initials gouged into it.

'This is the place,' he says quietly. 'This is where she said yes!' His eyes fill with watery tears, and the most contented smile I have ever seen sits on his lips as his fingers trace the heart carved into the trunk. That, I think, is enduring love. Will that be me and Joe one day? Will there be somewhere that reminds us of the moment our lives became intertwined? Tears spring to my eyes. What will be the memory I will hold on to? But to my frustration, I can't think of anything. I can't think of a time when our lives together haven't been about the band and my career. Will they be the only memories I have of us being together? Isn't there anything else to our relationship?

I try and think of one thing we've done together, one romantic gesture that hasn't been about the success of the band. And suddenly I feel very empty inside. I love that Joe is so supportive, that he wants me to succeed. And then, just for a moment, I wonder . . . Is it me he loves, or is it my career? Is it so he can hold his own with his family, his successful parents and brother? What would happen if my voice never came back? Would he leave me? Is that why he's so keen for me to go to Tenerife?

I shake my head to try and dispel the nagging voice of doubt, and find myself looking over at Lachlan, who seems to be brushing something from his eyes too. And I wonder who his tears are for.

'We'll gather the pine from here, Hector,' he says with a catch in his throat, and pats the tree as if reassuring it that a little bit of the love that Hector and Mairead shared will be in there in the special edition gin. 'Best we come back in the morning,' he adds. 'Looks like a two-man job. Pine can be tricky to get at.' He points up to the treetops. 'We'd better get you kitted out properly!' He nods to me and I go to protest, but close my mouth, suddenly finding myself wanting to be part of the pine picking, and to be here, close to the family I've never known. 'We'll bring a ladder!'

'Come on, Hector, let's get you home. Soup, bread and cheese do you for supper?'

'Hmm, lovely,' Hector says, and lets Lachlan lead him back to the Land Rover.

As we drive back to the house, dusk draws in, and the huge expanse of sky turns purple and pink with the setting sun. Something in me shifts. These are memories I will take with me forever. These are things I want to remember when I'm old.

There's a smell of peat smoke in the air as we climb out of the Land Rover. We guide Hector to the wooden front door.

'Looks like we'd better launch that crowdfunding page,' Lachlan says with a slight smile at the corner of his mouth. 'Teach Mhor gin is going to be back in action. The recipe was in the house all along . . . in Hector's head. Now that we have the key, we just have to unlock it.'

And I can't help but feel that something inside me has been unlocked too; an empty box that is now filling with memories.

Chapter Twenty-five

'Well, if you're going to come collecting pine needles, we'd better find you something more suitable to wear!' Lachlan says with a smile the next morning.

Last night we uploaded photographs old and new to the crowdfunding page. 'We can give the history of the place.' I pointed to the screen. 'You'd better do that. I have no idea about it.' I listened in fascination as he told me all about Winter Island, the people, the local legends, the flora and fauna.

Afterwards, we toasted the project with another tot of whisky, after hot soup, fresh bread and more of the creamy goat's cheese beside the huge fire in the living room, with Hector in his favourite chair and the dogs on the floor beside him.

I briefly turned my phone on to find a number of more and more frustrated, even cross, messages from Joe asking why I hadn't been in touch. Was I on the way to the vocal retreat? I messaged back and told him I was fine. Then – and I can't believe I did it – I told him I was finally on my way, and that I'd been informed there were no phones allowed at the retreat, so I wouldn't be in touch for a while. I quickly shoved my phone away, feeling a sense of light-headed relief and, well, freedom.

I feel bad lying, but I know the truth really doesn't make much sense. I was brought here to agree to a care plan for a relative I'd never met, and now I seem to be involved in crowdfunding a project to safeguard his future. I know I could leave at any time, but there's something stopping me. I have to see this through. Not to mention the fact that I want to find out more about this place, about my dad and the family he left behind. It's never bothered me before, but the island has started to work its way under my skin. I want to find the piece that seems to be missing in the jigsaw of my life.

I also texted the vocal retreat to tell them I'd been held up, and they cancelled my booking, telling me to rebook when I was ready. There was a text from Flora too, who said how much she'd enjoyed meeting us and that she hoped Hector would be able to take up his place by Candlemas, gently reminding me that she'd have to let it go to someone else if not. It didn't seem the right time, in amongst the fun of preparing the crowdfunding page to ask Lachlan what was going on between him and Isla. Seeing Hector in the forest had been a very special moment, and I wanted to savour it.

This morning, Hector has emptied the kitchen cupboards of herbs and spices and is now sitting in the big living room at the back of the house with a cup of tea and the dogs at his feet, watching a flock of black and white birds with long orange beaks on the sandy bay shore. For a moment I picture the nursing home and its small, well-tended garden, and think how different Hector's outlook will be there.

'Here!' says Lachlan, handing me a coat and boots he's found in the newly tidied cupboard under the stairs. 'You'll be fine in these. You look to be your grandmother's size.' It takes me a moment to realise he's talking about Mairead. My grandmother. I roll the word over in my head. 'Now let's go and pick some pine,' I say, hoisting up the step ladder leaning against the wall and carrying it out to the car.

We drive out towards the forest where we were last night, with Hector wrapped up against the cold in the back seat with the dogs. Lachlan and I agreed it's best we have him with us to keep an eye on him.

'You have to be careful what kind of pine you pick,' Lachlan tells me, as if teaching a group of students, and I don't think I've seen him look this alive since I arrived. 'The right sort can add great flavour, but the wrong type . . .' He shakes his head. 'Really we'd be better leaving it a bit, until the spring and the new growth, but . . .' He looks sideways at me.

'We have a deadline,' I say firmly. 'Candlemas. We need to complete the crowdfunding by then and put down a deposit to secure the room. That means finding the recipe and making the special edition bottles.'

He harrumphs, but good-naturedly, I think, making me smile as I turn away and look out of the window at the passing hedgerows and moorland, which is covered in a white frosting. The long grasses at the edges of the stream we're following are coated in frosted patterns like crystals. Across the golden glen deer are running, and once more it takes my breath away. Lachlan glances at me as we bounce along the single-track road.

'There are more deer than people on the island, you know,' he tells me, and again his face is lit up.

'And goats . . .' I add, and he laughs.

'Look up there,' he says suddenly, and points up to the sky. I peer up at what looks to be a lone dark cloud in the sky, and then realise it isn't a cloud.

'Whoa! What's that?!'

'A sea eagle. They completely died out but were reintroduced in the seventies. We have a couple of nesting pairs here.'

'Wow,' I say, watching the huge bird circling above us in the cold, clear air.

I feel the car slow down.

'Oh no . . .' says Lachlan.

'What's the matter?' I look away from the eagle. Lachlan is pulling on the handbrake.

'There.' He points up towards a rise on the glen. Two deer are facing off, and then start to lunge at each other with their antlers, like jousters. 'Mating season is over, but those two just keep goading each other.'

'Why are they fighting?'

'They're father and son. They've locked horns many a time and it's a heck of a job to untangle them, I can tell you! They're stubborn. Won't let each other be. There'll be no winner here.' He looks at me, and then at Hector, wrapped up warmly in blankets in the back of the Land Rover with the dogs lying over him. 'No good will come of it,' says Lachlan. 'Someone will get hurt, unless one of them gives in.'

He puts his hand on the car horn and holds it there in a

long blast. Then he does it again, and the two stags finally jump away from each other and run off in different directions, dipping their heads, shaking them, and then lifting their heads and their front legs high. Neither has bowed to the other. They have both saved face.

Lachlan winds down the window. 'Get over it, fellas!' he calls, watching the two stags strut off proudly across the golden moorland. He shakes his head and puts the Land Rover into gear. 'It's really not worth it in the long run,' he says quietly, looking back at Hector in the rear-view mirror.

'Right, time to go and find some pine needles. And let's hope they're less prickly than the locals!' He's made a joke, I think, and smile widely. An actual joke! Relations must be thawing!

Hector walks slowly through the forest with the dogs, leaning heavily on his stick. He's looking more sprightly than I have seen him since I've been here, I think.

'So at this rate,' says Lachlan, picking out a tree near the one with the engraving on it, 'we'll soon have all the ingredients for the gin and you'll be on your way. He places the ladder against the trunk of the tree, just below the first of the branches. 'Like I say, this would be better done in the spring, but no, some of us can't wait until then. Need to be on your way. Have everything done and dusted and neatly tied up by the end of the month.' He looks at me and I know he's teasing, but still I respond.

'I can't stay here until the spring. I need to get back to work!'

'Well hopefully this will be good enough for the first

batch. But it's always better to pick when there's plenty of new growth around. And not take too much from any particular area. Leave enough so it will grow back.'

He looks up, his big canvas bag slung across his body. His swag bag, as I like to think of it. Only now I know he's not stealing from the house, but foraging from the woods and grounds. I'm fascinated watching him. He takes so much pride in collecting and cooking food from the island, and I really admire his skill, though I know that when I get home it'll probably be back to packet soup, pasta and toast.

'And when it's done and Hector's place at the care home is secured, you'll be free to move on too,' I say tentatively, wondering if he'll tell me about Isla. 'Where will you go?'

He shrugs, giving nothing away. 'Look around for jobs on the mainland, I suppose,' he says. 'Hold the ladder, will you?' I step forward. He tests it against the tree to check it's firm and then I reach around him and hold it as he climbs up and into the lower branches of the tree. 'I'll take anything as long as it's working outdoors. Couldn't bear to be inside again all day. But just being away from here will be enough.'

'So you want to go?' I ask, curious.

'Can't wait! It's time I moved on,' he says, making me wonder anew about what happened. 'There's nothing for me here now.' I'm surprised. I thought he wanted to stay. To my shame, I thought he was freeloading. But I realise he's doing this just for Hector.

Hector is sitting on a fallen tree trunk, the dogs by his side keeping him warm and safe, and looking into the forest in deep, contented thought.

'And what happens at this retreat of yours that you're on

your way to? What magic powers will they have . . . what special spells?' Lachlan laughs as he climbs higher into the tree, then reaches out and cuts a sprig of pine with his penknife.

'Err . . .' I put my hands on my hips. 'It's a healing retreat. We'll spend time outdoors, getting in touch with nature, away from the outside world.'

'Bit like here then really!' He reaches up for another deep green shiny sprig and puts it in his bag. 'I'll take some from another tree now,' he says, climbing and then jumping down.

'Well, no . . . it's different,' I tell him, stepping back as he lands on both feet in front of me.

He studies me for a moment. 'Of course, what would I know? I'm just some forager bloke, living off your grandfather, hiding away from the world,' he teases, and yet there's a glint of challenge in his eyes, like the stags staring each other out. He turns and moves the ladder and starts to climb a neighbouring tree, then stops and looks down at me. 'Come up!' he says with a nod of his head.

'Oh no, it's fine. I'm okay here.' I wave a gloved hand.

'Come on,' he says. 'We're making this gin together, remember.' He holds out his hand to me, challenging me once again, and I can't walk away. But I have no idea when I last climbed a tree . . . if ever, in fact! There weren't many trees to climb where I grew up.

'Um . . . I don't think . . . I haven't climbed a tree before,' I confess.

'You haven't climbed a tree?! Jeez, no wonder you're as het up as you are! What, never? Even as a child?'

'No,' I say flatly. 'I didn't have somewhere like this to grow up and run around in, remember?'

'Come on . . . climbing a tree is something everyone should do at least once in their life.'

I look at the hand stretched out towards me. Then I look up at his face. He tilts his head. He's right. Maybe climbing a tree *is* something everyone should try once. I stand on the bottom rung of the ladder, and look at his outstretched hand. Then I start to climb until I reach his hand and take it and grab a low branch with the other and follow his instructions and I pull myself off the ladder, and move up the tree. Until I can't.

'I'm stuck!' I say.

'You're not,' he says calmly. 'You just think you are, and that's made you panic and freeze.'

I hold on to the branch for dear life. 'I can't move!'

'You can. Don't look down, or up. Just look out. Take in the other branches, the trees. Breathe them in. Don't over-think it. Go with your instincts.'

I take a deep breath, and the smell is just, well, glorious. It reminds me of Christmas. It's making me feel reinvigorated. Free. I close my eyes and focus on the smell again, and remember those Christmases when Mum and Dad would get together and make it a brilliant day not just for me, but for all of us. They stayed great friends after they separated. They just weren't right for each other when it came to marriage. Neither of them married again. Mum had various partners, but Dad stayed single until he died. A heart attack. Went to bed feeling unwell one night. And I was left with a huge Dad-shaped space in my life.

But in the early days, I had the best Christmases. There would always be music in the house. Carols on the radio, or my dad's record player, just like Hector's. Or even Mum singing when she was in the mood, and me too. It's where I started to sing in front of an audience. Well, that and school concerts. Mum and Dad always came together. I loved those concerts. I loved the looks on their faces when I sang. I think that's why I went on to be a singer.

I take another deep breath of the clear, crisp, pine-filled air. I move one foot, then a hand, and feel my way slowly up the tree to where Lachlan is sitting.

'Okay?' he asks.

'Okay.' I nod and smile, then follow his gaze as he looks around the forest from our treetop vantage point.

'Here.' He hands me a sprig of pine, and I take it and instinctively put it to my nose, letting its scent fill my senses and my head fill with carols all over again, lifting my spirits, my shoulders and my head. I breathe in deeply.

'You could sing here if you wanted. No one would hear,' he says. 'Only me and Hector. But I'm tone deaf and wouldn't know a good tune from a bad one, and . . .' he looks down through the boughs, 'and I think Hector's asleep.'

I look at him. Part of me wants to open my mouth and sing as loudly and joyously as I can. But part of me doesn't want to even attempt it, just in case I open my mouth and nothing but a few crackly notes comes out.

'You sang in the car, remember. Daisy, Daisy . . .' He nods his head from side to side and I laugh.

'And you growled!'

'But you sang.' He smiles.

'That was . . . different,' I say. And a voice says: *You didn't have to think about it.*

I close my eyes and breathe in again, this time from my buttocks, so the smell and the feeling fill my whole body. But just as my lips begin to part, my eyes ping open, and once again I am full of fear. It's like getting stuck in the tree, only this time there's no one to tell me how to get out of it. Not like at the healing retreat. They'll be able to tell me how, I know it.

'Okay, well, if we're not singing, let's get these pine needles back,' Lachlan says briskly. 'We'll freeze these until we've got the other ingredients. I've started making trial batches of the mash, the clear spirit, and I've looked up the measurements of the dried ingredients online. So once we have the rest, we can get started.'

'Yes, and now we know that Hector can remember them, we should be up and running in no time.'

'Agreed,' he says. 'Teach Mhor gin is on its way back!' and he nods at me.

'I couldn't have worked out how to use the still,' I say. 'You did that.'

'But you worked out how to find the recipe,' he says.

'And Hector had it all along.'

'Teamwork. You, me and Hector.' He smiles.

'Teamwork.' I find myself smiling back. 'Hang on,' I say, and I pull out my phone and photograph him in the tree. Then I photograph the other treetops and a sprig of pine in Lachlan's big hand. 'We'll put it on the crowdfunding page.'

'Okay, come on then, lots to do.' He starts to climb down the tree. 'Need a hand?' he calls up.

'No, I think I'm okay,' I say, and smile, and then miss a branch and bounce off the next two. 'I'm fine. Really fine.'

I may have misjudged it and bounced a bit, but I am fine, I think, and kick myself for not having attempted to sing when I felt I could at the top of the tree. It might have been a bit croaky, but like Lachlan said, who was there to hear it? Maybe I just need to remember the scent of the pine trees a little more often.

We gather up Hector from where he's been dozing, and pile him and the dogs back into the Land Rover, fired up to find the rest of the ingredients. Teach Mhor gin is back on!

Chapter Twenty-six

'Ready to go live?' I ask.

'Yup! Ready as I'll ever be,' Lachlan says with raised eyebrows.

This is it. We're bringing Teach Mhor gin back to the big hoose. And something inside me is suddenly really excited at the prospect. We've spent the last three days, getting set up to 'go live'; together we've written the copy for the crowd-funding page and Lachlan has worked down at the distillery, getting the mash right, the basic clear alcohol to add the ingredients to and checking we have all the dried ingredients that Hector listed. And Lachlan has apparently seen Isla and Gordan at the café and talked to them about bottles and labels for the gin. Why we couldn't have gone to the pub all together I have no idea!

'Let's just run over what we've got here,' I say, sitting at the kitchen table with my back to the range, which is slowly warming me. The overhead lighting is weak this evening.

'Hang on,' says Lachlan. He puts a large storm candle on the table and lights it. The kitchen suddenly feels as welcoming and warm as anywhere I've been. Like it's put its arms around me in a huge hug. I look at the screen again and try and concentrate on the job in hand.

'"Have your own piece of Scottish history! We need investors to bring back Teach Mhor gin. You get an exclusive edition bottle of gin and an invitation to a special tea party on Winter Island to celebrate reaching our target",' I read from the screen. 'You sure about this?'

'Why not?' He shrugs. 'Invite them here. We'll lay on scones and shortbread, like we discussed, and gin from the distillery to celebrate getting the financing we need to get the still up and running and the first batch out. After that, well, it's up to the new owners how they run things.'

'Okay, so a distillery tour and tea party here on the island. We need the funds to secure Hector's place, so we should aim for Candlemas,' I say, chewing my bottom lip. I need to leave here. We all do.

'Candlemas it is!' says Lachlan with gusto.

'Are you sure we can do this? We need to find the other ingredients, make test batches and get it all made and bottled before then.'

'Well if I'm not mistaken, you've not got a lot else going on, have you? Other than going to your healing retreat at some point.'

'No,' I say. 'I've nothing else on.' I take a deep breath. 'Everyone back home thinks I'm at the retreat right now, on voice rest and with no electronic devices.'

'Let's hope you get your money back,' he says.

'And my singing voice. If I can't sing again, I don't know what I'll do. I'll have lost the lot.'

'Not necessarily,' says Lachlan. 'Maybe what you need is some time not thinking about singing. Take the opportunity to look around you and enjoy what's right in front of you.'

I go to protest, but something stops me. It's about the most I've heard him say in one go. Not right, but still, at least we're talking and getting along.

'So, Candlemas,' he says, and nods. 'Agreed?'

'Agreed,' I say. 'But what if we don't manage to do it; what if we don't find the ingredients?'

'We don't have a choice. We can't fail. We have to pull this off, otherwise we're all stuck here. None of us will be able to move on.'

I nod. We have to do this. We look at each other, and then I press the button, sending the crowdfunding page live.

'Oh, and Ruby?'

I look at him.

'Happy Hogmanay!' he says.

It's New Year's Eve, I realise.

'Happy New Year, Lachlan.'

'Let's hope we all get what we want.'

And we raise our glasses over the table, the glow from the candle lighting up the amber liquid. 'Here's to Candlemas!' A smile spreads across both our faces and I feel a bubble of excitement rise in me that I haven't felt in a long time, and I have no idea why.

Chapter Twenty-seven

The next morning I wake early and look out on the mist rolling in off the sea and almost obscuring the neighbouring islands in the distance. Something in me just wants to get outside on this first day of the new year, and without giving it too much thought, I pull on my yoga leggings, a couple of layers on the top half, gloves, trainers and a hat and make my way down the stairs through the sleeping house to the back door.

Outside, I take a deep breath and do something I haven't done in a very long time. I put one foot in front of the other and begin to run, breathing in deeply as I do. I head down the path towards the loch and then up to the outreach of rocks. I follow the cliff edge for a while, then stop for a moment and catch my breath. Hands on hips, I breathe in deeply, and within no time, I'm rewarded for my efforts by three little black heads, with huge black watery eyes, bobbing up to say good morning, making me smile. Feeling revived, I decide to run on, following the burn. After all, didn't Fraser say I couldn't get lost if I followed the burn? I turn and head for the road, and spot the little croft there. I slow down as I pass it. It looks totally abandoned; no sign of life there at all. Such a shame.

Jo Thomas

I put my head down and carry on alongside the crystal-clear water, tumbling and hurrying to its destination over rocks and stones. As my feet pound along the single-track road, I can't help looking around. Behind me the bay and the sea, around me open moorland, in front of me the hills, and in front of them, the forest of pine trees where I climbed my first tree. And now here I am . . . running! I take deep gulps of the air, filling my lungs with its cool freshness and a hint of sharp saltiness, reminding me of the gin we drank on the beach.

Very quickly the sky starts to darken and spots of rain begin to fall. As I've realised here, the weather can change in an instant. I slow up and look around as the rain suddenly gets heavier. I'm halfway to the village. In front of me I can see the herd of deer, and if I'm not mistaken, the two stags in the road, having a stand-off. I look at the stags, then back at the lonely-looking croft. The rain is getting heavier, hitting my face. It's ahead to the stags or run back to the croft and see if I can just sit it out. If there's anyone there, I'll just ask if I can shelter by the front door.

I turn and run back. I open the little picket gate and run up to the front door.

'Hello!' I knock loudly, the rain now pelting down. 'Hello!' I call again, but there's no reply. I try the latch, and it opens. I gently push the door. 'Hello,' I say, more quietly, not wanting to scare anyone. But I can see the place is empty, and by the looks of it has been for some time.

The open fire at one end is full of embers. On the table, melted wax from half-burnt candles has dripped down and made hard puddles. It looks like someone has just shut the door on this place. A bit like the big house, like the clock has just stopped ticking. Time has stood still. I walk around the table as the rain throws itself against the small square windows. I wonder how long it will last. On the table are two plates, knives and forks and glasses, an unopened bottle and a small jug of very dead-looking flowers.

There is also a record sleeve, and on top of it a record broken in pieces. I pick up the sleeve. The title is familiar and the tune is on the tip of my tongue. A tiny phrase suddenly pops into my head, and I can't remember where I know it from. It's right at the back of my memory bank. Something I heard as a child maybe. The same phrase keeps repeating itself, and I suddenly feel like I'm intruding on someone's life here, their memories. I'm not going to hang around. It could be ages before the rain passes, and Lachlan's expecting me to talk to Hector about the other ingredients. I put down the record as close as I can to where it was and step out of the croft, pulling the door shut behind me.

Outside, the rain is easing. Thankfully the stags have moved off the road and are up on the hillside, still locking horns, neither of them prepared to walk away or back down. Why can't they learn to live with each other?! I think of Lachlan and me working together to get the gin made, both travelling in the same direction finally, but for very different reasons.

I set off again, the tune of the broken record running round my head, and I begin to hum it as my feet pound the road. And then the images start to follow. My father, singing the song at Christmas as his after-dinner turn. An old song of the island, he would say, about love, belonging, about

201

home being a feeling that stays with you wherever you go. It was his one song. He'd sing it with tears in his eyes, and when he finished, it was as if he'd put the memories back in the box and closed the lid for another year.

Despite being warm from the running, I can feel the sting of the salty sea air and flecks of rain on my cheeks. I run past the pub, and there outside is Isla, trying to secure the Christmas lights in the increasing wind. I slow down and catch my breath. The run has put me in good spirits.

'Do you need a hand?' I puff, pointing at the lights.

She looks at me, but doesn't smile. Her curly red hair is flying around her face.

'No,' she says flatly. 'I'm fine. Thank you.'

Taken aback, I have no idea what to say. But it's Isla who speaks again.

'So, how's the gin coming on?'

'Slowly, but we're getting there,' I say.

'I've seen the crowdfunding page.'

'Good.' I find myself smiling.

She stops what she's doing and then seems to soften a little.

'I hope it works for you. For you and Lachlan,' she says. 'I hope you'll be happy.'

'Oh, I, we're . . .' She's doesn't know I'm Hector's grand-daughter. She hasn't guessed who I am after all. I thought she might have been suspicious, but she's giving us her blessing. Me and Lachlan. Oh God! I have no idea what to say.

'He's a good man, and he deserves some happiness in his life. Island life isn't for everyone, but I'm glad you're staying,' she says with a smile, and I'm worried she's going to hug me, despite my sweaty, damp state.

'Thank you, Isla. That means a lot,' and then with a smile, I turn and carry on running. I run past the café and shop. I see Lachlan there, probably exchanging goods in return for supplies, or maybe sorting out rotas and shifts. He and the Cruickshank siblings watch me as I run past. I raise a hand and smile, as does he.

'She's still here then?' I hear one of the sisters say.

'Aye,' replies Lachlan.

'It must be true love then,' says the other, and I hear Lachlan cough.

'Taking each day as it comes,' he says, and I'm grateful he hasn't told them who I really am, and find myself smiling even more, feeling a strange connection that I've never felt before. Maybe it's the song running round my head. Maybe it's the gin starting to come together. Maybe it's that I'm enjoying myself. But I'm just passing through, I remind myself, and carry on running back to the house, tears smarting at my eyes, mingling with the salty sea air and the rain.

I try to have a bath, but end up with a cold splash-about in the huge tub, which nevertheless makes me feel surprisingly invigorated after my run. Afterwards, I scoop up my hair and dash down the stairs, adjusting another bit of the worn curtains as I go, humming the tune playing over and over in my head.

I make my way into the living room with my pad and pen. The fire is roaring and Hector is looking through the cupboards.

'Must be here somewhere . . .'

I'm still humming the tune when Lachlan comes in behind me. Hector looks up at me.

'Ah, Miss Rubes.' He smiles, then looks down at his dressing gown. 'One moment, you seem to have caught me unprepared. I'll just get dressed.' And with Lachlan's help he gets to his feet and leaves the room. I raise my eyebrows and smile, delighted that music has made the connection for him once again. I start flicking through the box of records, trying to decide which one we should start with to try and get Hector talking about the other ingredients for the gin. I'm still humming when Lachlan comes back into the room.

'What's that?'

'What?' I turn.

'That song you're humming.' He stands stock still, holding a tray of tea.

'Oh, just a song I've remembered,' I say, wondering whether to tell him about the croft. 'One my dad used to sing to me. Why?'

'It's just . . . I just don't care for it, that's all,' he says gruffly, putting down the tray. 'Not a fan of that old folk stuff.'

'Oh . . . okay,' I say. 'Well, how about this one?' and I pull a record from its sleeve and put it on the record player. 'Better?' I ask, as Billie Holiday starts singing.

He nods, the moment past. 'Much better.'

'Okay, let's see if Hector likes your choice too.'

We smile at each other, and I get that same feeling as I had when running. A feeling of contentment. Could it be a feeling of belonging?

Chapter Twenty-eight

We spend the afternoon in front of the big open fire, the rain sliding down the window panes, the dogs dozing, us drinking tea and playing records and talking to Hector about island life.

'I remember taking Mairead to the pine forest where I proposed. Lots of times. Until she said yes,' he smiles, repeating the story. 'And the day our son was born and the gorse was out in flower everywhere.'

He's talking about my dad, I think. Born in February.

'It lifts your heart to see the yellow flowers over the heath and moorland. It was everywhere when he was born that cold February morning, here at home. The gorse always reminds me of the day we became a family.'

'Gorse? Is gorse something you use in the gin?' I ask, suddenly excited.

'Of course! The flowers brighten even the darkest of winter days here on the island.' He chuckles. 'They say that if the gorse is out of bloom, kissing is out of season! In other words, you can only kiss your beloved when the gorse is in bloom, which is great news, as the gorse is nearly always in bloom!' As his laugh dies down, his eyes fill with memories once more, 'It's always there, the gorse, bringing colour to the island.'

I look at Lachlan and he smiles back at me. So, ingredient number two: gorse. The record comes to an end and I get up and select another one from this amazing collection. Songs from my growing-up. Music from the greats. I'm not sure when I've felt happier.

'And then of course you have the wild juniper.' Hector is on a roll, and our smiles grow even wider. 'Gin isn't gin without juniper. It's the only stipulation. Otherwise it would just be flavoured vodka!' He laughs. 'And the fact that it's wild is what makes it unique to the island. All the best wild juniper is down by the pine forest and the moorland on the other side of the burn, and then over on the dunes and the cliffs on the far side of the island. But you have to be careful not to get swept away by the wind. Nearly had me off my feet once!' He smiles at the memory. 'Always pick them before the frost gets to them, autumn time.'

'Autumn?!' I say.

'And then dry them, or freeze them,' he continues. 'Got stacks in the cupboard in the distillery.' Suddenly all his cupboard-emptying seems to make more sense. 'But everyone knows you need juniper. That's not one of the five special ingredients. Rosehips! That's one! From the hedgerows on the lane around the island. Loved walking the dogs and picking the hips. Used to have four dogs, y'know. Gave one to my son.'

And I remember only too well the black Lab I grew up with when I was young.

'And the others . . . no, can't remember what happened to the others.' He shakes his head, then sinks back into his chair and sips at his tea, spilling drops down his front that he doesn't seem to notice. He looks tired, but very content, and soon drifts off. I stand and take the mug from his hands and pull one of the tartan blankets on the arm of the chair over him. The dogs raise their heads, then lower them again, as contented as their owner.

Lachlan takes the tray of tea things back to the kitchen.

'So it really was the music that unlocked his memories,' he says when he returns to the living room. 'Just goes to show what I know about that stuff!' He smiles, and something in me suddenly ignites, like one of the flames from the fire. A new track starts on the record player and Hector suddenly opens his eyes again.

'Did I tell you about the pine forest where I proposed to Mairead? Kept me waiting for ages, she did!'

We both smile and I go to turn off the record player.

'I think he's exhausted,' Lachlan says. 'Maybe try some more tomorrow. How do you fancy coming down and introducing yourself to Aggie?'

'Aggie?'

'The gin still. Named after Hector's mother, I believe, a fearsome type!' His face lights up. 'And we'll see if we can find those juniper berries. Hector will sleep for a while now. Tomorrow we'll go and find the gorse and rosehips.'

'And the other ingredients,' I say excitedly.

'And the other ingredients.' He nods and smiles as if placating an excited child, and my heart flips over with joy. Simple as that. The joy of just living in the here and now. I push any thoughts of my time here coming to an end out of my head.

Chapter Twenty-nine

The sky outside my window is bright orange, almost red. A long line of it along the horizon, beneath a line of cloud with shafts of red and yellow breaking through like beams of light. It illuminates the other islands in the distance and the rocky shoreline around the bay. It's like there's a fire burning all around me. It's beautiful, and I can't wait to get out and see it from the shoreline.

I pull on my trainers. They're no longer brand new, waiting to be broken in at the vocal retreat. Now they're covered in mud and, frankly, moulded to my feet, and possibly a bit whiffy too from where I've been out running every day now for just over the past three weeks.

Life has fallen into a pattern. I run, Lachlan goes out to see Aggie, the still, and works on trial batches of the gin. There have been tasting sessions too, where we've written notes and tried to think what might be missing. Then we work our way through the record collection, sitting with Hector, looking through old photographs and listening to stories of his life and my father's here on the island. The days out fishing, the winter when the snow came, the big storm that knocked out the electrics at Hogmanay, the parties they threw in the house. And I don't know when I've smiled and laughed as much as I have in these last few weeks, or eaten as well, or slept as well. We've also been checking the crowd-funding page. There's a bit of interest. Not enough, though, and we really need to find a way to get some more. Time is beginning to run out.

I tie the trainers tightly, then put on my scarf and hat, no longer worried about my appearance, and grateful for their warmth. It might look glorious out there, but I've learnt one thing: however it looks, it will be bracing. But although the cold will hurt, it will make me feel like I can take on anything. And today, we need to try to work out the last of the ingredients. We have just over a week left now before the tea party and our crowdfunding deadline, and to get the deposit together for Hector's place at the care home. And although it was great that Hector remembered the first three of the special ingredients, since then, he's been on a loop, like a broken record, recalling the same memories and the same ingredients each time we put on music and start talking. The stories about him and Mairead getting engaged. The day my dad was born. The day they nearly lost the house and business but he went out walking and saw all the juniper berries on the heath and by the dunes and the gin saved them from going under . . . and then, nothing. He doesn't seem to go any further. Why my dad left and never came back. Why I never knew this place or him. Why we can't find the last two ingredients! We can't seem to move forward at all. We're stuck. I don't think we're going to do it, and I have no idea what to do if we don't.

Annoyingly, Lachlan doesn't seem that fazed. 'Take your time. It'll happen,' he tells Hector, but I'm not sure it will, and part of me still thinks he doesn't sense the urgency here. But I do have to leave and go back to my life, back to Joe. And Hector needs to go into the care home, because once I'm gone, it will be only Lachlan looking after him again, and he needs to move on too. Whatever happened between him and Isla, he clearly isn't comfortable around her and Gordan. Getting this gin recipe matters, for everyone's future. Without it, I may never make it to the healing retreat, Lachlan can't leave the island and get away from his past, and Hector . . . well, what will happen to Hector if we can't afford the nursing home? Where will he go?

I run downstairs and outside and nearly get swept off my feet by the vicious wind. It's almost as if it wants to knock me off course, send me retreating inside. But I won't.

I put my best foot forward, and once again am nearly blown over. I take my usual route, down to the edge of the bay and up the hill to the outcrop of rocks to say good morning to the seals. But even they're not out today as the waves crash against the rocks, sending up arcs of salty white spray. The wind stinging my cheeks, I turn away and run towards the heath, where we found gorse for the gin, and on to the pine forest and the craggy mountains and the dunes where the juniper grows and the sea eagles nest. Every bit of this landscape is there in the gin, I think. What are we missing? They have to be here, the last two ingredients!

My feet pound the road, following the burn across the island, full to bursting, bubbling and tumbling as the rain starts to set in and I splash through puddles. I run up through the forest, remembering my treetop climb, and on to the cliffs, where I stop and drag in air whilst looking down at the white horses galloping into battle on the stony shore. A gust of wind suddenly flings itself at me, nearly knocking me off my feet. I feel my lungs filling with fresh, crisp air, making me feel light as a feather on my feet, lifted by the winds as I turn for home.

Home?! Where did that come from? Home is still a dingy flat that I haven't seen in nearly four weeks, and where my poinsettia will most definitely have wilted. Winter Island can never be called home, I tell myself. We have to make the gin so we can sell it and get as much money as we can for Hector and his nursing home.

I wonder what this place is like in the spring. But I'll be gone by then. Candlemas marks the start of spring. A new beginning for us all. Maybe I'll come back, I tell myself. Come back and visit later in the year. *What, when Hector's dead and buried?* I can hear Lachlan's voice in my head and shake it off. My thoughts are as dark and brooding as the sky around me. Somehow right now I can't imagine not seeing Hector again . . . or Lachlan for that matter, I realise. I can't imagine not seeing Lachlan.

I throw myself in through the front door of the house.

'It's blowing a hooley out there!' Lachlan says, pulling on his coat.

'It certainly is!' I say as I stand with my back to the door, soaked to the skin.

'And it's getting worse. I was just coming to look for you.'

I blush, suddenly touched by his concern.

'The power's gone out in the community centre over the

other side of the island. Loads of houses have lost electricity and heat. It's getting worse. Forecast is pretty bad.'

'Oh no, that's terrible!' I say.

'Red sky in the morning, shepherd's warning. It won't be long before the whole island is out,' he says, and with that, the lights flicker and die.

'Oh no! Now what?'

'Plenty of candles in the drawer in the kitchen, and a head torch there too,' says Lachlan. 'Thing is, it's Burns Night, and what with the community centre being out of action, and Teach Mhor having the backup generator . . . I said I'd have to ask you. It's not up to me, and Hector clearly can't make the call on it.'

'On what? Can't make the call on what?' I'm confused.

'Like I say, it's the twenty-fifth of January.'

'I know. We have just a week left on the crowdfunding and to get the gin made. I'm worried, Lachlan, really worried!'

'It's Burns Night,' he repeats. 'The community centre is out, the pub too. There's a backup generator here at Teach Mhor. It's where all the parties used to be held. The locals have asked if we can have the celebrations here instead. I said I'd have to ask you.'

'Me?'

'Well, you are Hector's granddaughter.'

'But they don't know that, do they?'

He shakes his head. 'You have my word, I've said nothing. But it's still your call. If you don't agree, I'll say Hector is . . . unwell.'

I can hear Hector humming in the other room.

'No, it's fine. Um . . . what do you think?'

'I think,' he says with a gentle smile, 'Hector may just like having the house full of people again. And maybe we can get a few more to sign up for the crowdfunding while they're here, by way of payback!'

'Then of course it's fine by me,' I say, feeling very strange about being asked. 'There's a storm, we should do what we can.' I think of people in their homes with no electricity or heat. 'Of course we should.'

'Great. I'll let them know everyone's welcome at the house,' he says, and goes out.

'Be careful!' I call after him as the wind catches the door and bangs it shut.

I find the head torch and start lighting candles, then have a quick tidy-up. I wonder how many guests there will be, and if they'll be staying over if the storm hasn't passed.

To my relief, Lachlan returns shortly afterwards. He opens the back door of the Land Rover and starts pulling out various crates and trays. I hold the door open against the driving rain as he unloads them into the kitchen.

'Haggis and neeps,' he announces. 'Picked up the ingredients from the café. Now all I need to do is remember where I've put my sporran.' And my stomach suddenly flicks like the flames of the candles dotted around the hall.

'Oh, the choir has arrived. Wonderful!' says Hector. 'It wouldn't be Hogmanay without the choir!' I don't bother to correct him and tell him Hogmanay has gone and it's actually Burns Night.

'Is it okay? The power's out!' people ask as they turn up at the door.

'Of course,' I say. 'Come in! We've plenty of room.'

There are candles all the way up the dark staircase along with the dim lighting in the hall and on the big sideboard in the hall. In the front room, Lachlan and I have put tea lights everywhere – along the window ledges and on the mantelpiece to add to the lamplight. Outside, the wind is howling and the rain is throwing itself at the window panes, doing its very worst. I've never felt more frightened yet safe at the same time.

The house begins to fill with people carrying bottles, and the smells from the kitchen drift through to join the chatter and laughter. Fraser is there with his wife, along with Lena, Lexie and Lyle from the shop, and Mrs Broidy, the old housekeeper. Lachlan appears in the kitchen as I'm finding glasses.

'Need a hand?' he says, and I turn and catch my breath. The outline of his broad shoulders is visible under his white shirt, his wild curly hair is as tamed as it can be, and his strong calves are on show below the hem of his kilt. I stand stock still, unable to move for a moment. A knock at the door catapults me out of my transfixed state.

It's Isla and Gordan, carrying a bottle of whisky.

'Thank you for having us all here,' they say, shivering as they come in. 'It's freezing at ours.'

'Come in! The generator's working, and Lachlan's cooking,' and the image of Lachlan in his kilt, freshly showered and smelling heavenly, makes every one of my nerve endings tingle all over again.

I plug in the record player in the big room and put on one of the records from the box, and the house is full of music, chatter and the sounds of the community coming together. Then Gordan brings out his bagpipes and pipes in the haggis, and we all clap. And as Lachlan passes me, carrying the haggis on a silver plate, he gives me a sideways look and a smile, and my stomach flips over and back again and I take a big swig of the whisky that's been handed to me.

When the haggis has been addressed and toasted and everyone has raised their glasses, Lachlan hands round plates of haggis, neeps and tatties and then Gordan plays another tune on the bagpipes. I take a plate of food to Hector and sit by him with my own plate. After some persuasion, Mrs Broidy is persuaded to take to the out-of-tune piano, and the gathered guests begin to join in with her song. As she finishes and everyone applauds, Hector begins to sing quietly, and gradually everyone falls silent. It's the tune from the broken record, the one I was humming, the one I remember my father singing to me, the memory now as clear as anything, and tears fill my eyes. Mrs Broidy and the goat lady, Fraser and the three siblings from the shop join in, filling the room with song. My teary eyes seek out Lachlan, who is looking at Isla and she back at him and then at Gordan. Suddenly Lachlan stands and leaves the room.

I follow him to the kitchen. 'All okay?' I ask.

'Yes. Sure. Just getting the tipsy laird,' he says, sounding choked.

'The what?'

'Tipsy laird! Sherry trifle,' he says, turning round with a huge bowl. There's a cheeseboard with his oatcakes laid out too. I go to pick it up to carry it through to the other room, then pause.

Jo Thomas

'It's her, isn't it? Isla. She's the reason you want to leave.'

He looks up at me, his eyes even more green than usual.

'She's the one I came back for,' he says quietly. 'We'd been childhood sweethearts. But then I went away to the mainland, got my degree and my engineering job. I broke her heart, I suppose. My mother had died before I went to college, and my father wanted me to go and live the best life I could. That's why I left. But then he died too, and I wasn't here. I left it too late to get back. I should have been here. I should never have left. Hector was here for my dad, and then for me. And I realised that here was exactly where I wanted to be; that everything I wanted had been here all along.

'I packed in my job and moved home. I'd got everything ready to ask Isla to marry me. Candles, the fire lit, dinner in the oven. Even had our favourite record playing . . .' He stops and looks at me. 'She turned up to tell me she was marrying Gordan . . . my best friend. She didn't think I was coming back. She'd moved on. I was too late.'

'The broken record at the croft,' I say quietly.

'I thought it was going to be our family home. A new beginning.' He looks at me again. 'You've got it right. You've got a dream and you're going for it. Don't leave it too late. You shouldn't have to live with "what if".' He sighs.

'And if she wanted you back now?' I ask.

'It's a small island. There isn't enough room on it for that kind of hurt. Too many people would end up falling out. The only way for that to happen is to leave and not come back, like your dad did.'

There is a flash and a bang. The storm is blowing up.

'Come on. Bring the cheese,' he says, clearly eager to finish the conversation.

In the living room, Hector is standing in front of the roaring fire, smiling broadly.

'Ah! There you are! Now, are you going to announce the good news or am I?'

Lachlan sets the tipsy laird on the big table and I put down the cheeseboard.

'What news is that, Hector?' Lachlan asks.

'You two, your news! Look at them! Thick as thieves, but we all know what's going on!'

'Oh no . . .' I start to say, and am about to tell him there's nothing going on, then remember that that's why most of the locals think I'm there, as Lachlan's guest.

Lachlan laughs and slings his arm around my shoulders. I look at Isla's face, a smile gently tugging at the corner of her mouth, and I'm not sure if it's regret, or that she's pleased for him, or maybe a bit of both.

The clock strikes midnight.

'Happy New Year!' shouts Hector, throwing his hands up. 'Go on, kiss her, man! It's Hogmanay after all!'

'Oh, I . . .' I blush deeply.

'Remember, go with what he's thinking!' murmurs Lachlan. He looks straight at me, and very tentatively I reach up to him. I'll just give him a peck, I think. Just to help him out of this awkward spot. His lips touch mine, and then I'm sinking into them like I've been waiting for them all my life.

'There you go!' says Hector. 'I mean, if you can't kiss the woman who's having your baby, who can you kiss?'

We fall away from each other.

'What?!' I splutter.

'Um, no . . .' This time it's Lachlan who breaks the rules. 'No, Hector, you must have that wrong.'

'What? Of course not! Don't be shy! Anyone can see she's with child!'

The atmosphere crackles. Lachlan looks at me, mortified, but all I can do is laugh.

Mrs Broidy breaks the awkward moment by playing another song on the piano. And even Lachlan joins in to cover his blushes and the waves of embarrassment that keep bubbling up in both of us, making us giggle. Without realising it, I'm singing too.

'Looks like I'd better keep at the running!' I finally say, smiling.

'It's just Hector . . . he doesn't know what he's saying.'

'I know,' I say, and smile. But I can't help but think about that kiss still sitting on my lips, and the arm around me that he's forgotten to take away.

Finally we start to show everyone their rooms for the night, and those who think they can make it home leave with thanks for a lovely night.

'It's sure blowing a hooley out there!' says Hector as we guide him towards the stairs to bed, the dogs at his heels.

'It sure is, Gran— Hector,' I correct myself. As much as I would love him to know me as his granddaughter, I realise, I don't want to confuse him.

'Be the perfect day for seaweed picking once it passes,' he says.

'Seaweed picking?!' Lachlan and I say as one, standing behind him to make sure he doesn't wobble.

'For the gin. Most important part . . . well, second most important,' he says, and carries on climbing the stairs, singing to himself: 'Seaweed, down at the beach. Perfect for it once the storm has passed.'

Chapter Thirty

The next morning we're both up early. I make endless cups of tea from the big cream kettle on the range, and Lachlan serves pancakes, then together we see people off, standing in the big doorway. The power should be back on later in the day.

'But if not, come back. We have plenty of room!' I call.

'Thank you,' says Lena from the shop, 'and if the tea party is half as much fun as that, it'll be a great night! We've signed up for it.'

'Looks like we got ourselves some crowdfunding supporters,' Lachlan says, waving them off.

'Let's check the total when they've all gone.' I raise a worried smile, hoping we've drummed up enough interest.

I turn to see Isla behind us, about to leave.

'Thank you, for everything,' she says to me. 'I know . . .' Gordan puts his hand on her shoulder. 'I don't think I was very welcoming to you when you first arrived, but I can see that you make Lachlan happy, and that's what counts. I just don't want to see him hurt . . . again.'

I'm taken aback. 'Oh, that whole baby thing? It's not true!' I wave a hand in the area of my stomach. 'A misunderstanding!' I laugh, very loudly. 'It was all a misunderstanding . . . I'm not, we're not . . .'

Isla laughs too. 'Shame, or we could have been celebrating having our babies together.' She gently rubs her well-wrapped-up belly.

'You're pregnant?' I say with surprise, suddenly feeling for Lachlan standing behind me. There's never going to be a chance that she'll come back to him now. I get the feeling that he thought if he waited long enough, she might change her mind. But there is no way that's going to happen. She's made her decision and she's sticking by it. She and Gordan are moving on with their lives. It's Lachlan who can't. And I can feel him behind me, as if the wind has been knocked out of his sails. Like all the air has left his body, hitting me in a warm blast on the back of my neck, making me shiver.

For a moment, no one says anything.

'Well, congratulations!' I say, going into autopilot.

'Yes, congratulations,' Lachlan echoes, and shakes both Gordan and Isla by the hand, then we bid them goodbye and finally shut the front door.

'I know what you're thinking, and it's not true,' he says, turning and walking down the wide wooden-panelled corridor, now strewn with glasses from last night. I follow him, both of us collecting glasses as we go, and join him at the glazed Belfast sink in the kitchen, which he starts filling with water. 'At least the well should be full after that deluge.'

'The what?'

'Where we get our water from. The rainwater collects in the big well.'

'And don't change the subject on me,' I say. 'What am I thinking?'

He squirts in washing-up liquid, not looking at me, and

221

sighs. 'That I'll be upset because Isla and Gordan are having a baby. You think I'm still in love with her after what I told you last night.'

'Well you are, aren't you? She was the one you came back for. The reason you haven't left.'

He turns to look at me, and sighs again. 'Everything changes. Just because I came back doesn't mean I still love her.' He dries his hands. 'It came as a shock, but only because it made me realise that it really is over. They're settled. A family. It's time to move on. It's time for everyone to move on,' and he looks straight at me, making me feel like my insides are shifting, like something in me has moved on too. I just don't know what it is. But I do know that that kiss has changed something in me. It's somewhere I want to go back to but know I've got to leave behind when I get on that ferry in a week's time.

'Now, let's look at this crowdfunding page, see if we're going to be able to get you to Tenerife!' he says with a smile and growl that is actually really attractive, I realise.

In a week's time, this will all be in the past, I think with a strange sense of sadness, almost melancholy. I wonder what I'll miss the most: my early-morning runs past the seals and the sea eagles? The sound of the burn as it makes its journey from the hills where we picked the gorse, through the pine forest, across the heath where the juniper grows, beside the country road where the rosehips come from and finally to the sea? Or will it be Lachlan's growling voice, deep, thick and layered with meaning and humour? And Hector too, I realise. He may not know who I am, but I have enjoyed getting to know him, hearing the stories of my dad's childhood, and sharing stories of my own about our life before Dad died.

'Your father sounds like a lovely man. With good taste too! He obviously inherited good genes!' Hector said one evening when I'd been reminiscing.

'He was, and he did!' I replied with a lump in my throat.

'I will come back,' I suddenly tell Lachlan. 'For a visit.' Before Hector's funeral, I add silently.

Lachlan has the computer open and is looking at the page.

'And?' I ask expectantly, and he shakes his head.

'Not as much as we need yet.' He shows me our total to date.

I look at him. 'We're not going to make it, are we? What if we don't make it? We need something to really get us noticed, otherwise Teach Mhor and its gin and Hector's legacy will be lost forever.'

And I suddenly realise that it's not about me leaving, or Lachlan leaving, or even the place at the care home. It's about Hector and making his life's work count.

'Come on, get your kit on, we've got gin to make!' he says.

'First man who's ever told me to get my kit *on*!' I find myself joking. 'Mind you, if Hector's opinion counts, it's obviously good advice.' I laugh again at last night's embarrassing moment, and we both smile and look at each other and seem to hold each other's gaze. And it's not Hector's announcement that's making me blush, I realise; it's the memory of that kiss, those surprisingly soft lips that made me feel like I'd fallen into warm sand, and the waves washing up through me, building, full of excitement and expectation.

I try to remember how Joe's kisses make me feel, and realise with a deep sadness that I can't. And if I can't remember that, what else is there? What's left?

'Okay, let's get going,' I say, breaking away from what I really want to happen next, which is to taste those sweet lips on mine again . . . and that will never lead to any good!

'I'll bring the camera, get some shots of the shore. Maybe that'll tempt in some more investors. Once they see how beautiful this place is, they'll be flocking in!' he says, and we both know that if they don't, we're in real trouble.

'Lachlan?' I say as we're about to leave. 'You knew, didn't you? You knew it was seaweed. The fourth ingredient?'

For a moment he says nothing, then, 'I had a good idea. I've been foraging around these parts long enough.'

'Why didn't you say?' I suddenly feel cross with him.

'Let's just say I thought it would benefit you both,' he nods at Hector, 'to take some time working it out.'

I stare at him. He didn't say! On purpose! And I can't decide whether I'm furious or pleased. Discovering the island and rediscovering the music I grew up with really has been wonderful.

'And the final ingredient? The fifth?'

'Now that one, I have no idea!' He shakes his head. 'And if we don't get enough crowdfunding, we're sunk anyway.'

We're going to need a miracle to pull this off now, I think.

Chapter Thirty-one

'Seaweed! Loads of seaweed!' Lachlan says as he wanders along the wet sand and over the rocks, still sodden from their soaking last night.

'Ah!' says Hector, holding out his arms and breathing in deeply.

Although the storm has passed, the sea breeze is still rolling gently in with the waves, buffeting our cheeks and blowing away any cobwebs. Hector might not remember why we're here, but he's clearly happy that we are. The dogs sniff around in the grassy dunes, then wander down to stand next to him as he steps down unsteadily onto the beach; the beach where Lachlan and I sat on Christmas Day and ate oysters and drank gin from oyster shells. Back where it all began; where we made a pact to work together to find the gin recipe. And now we're nearly done, I think with a mixture of joy and sadness. I hold out a hand to help Hector, but he doesn't take it. Proud to the last, I think with a smile.

Lachlan is inspecting glistening clumps of what I presume must be seaweed. 'The thing is,' he says, 'it's not the best time of year to be harvesting. It's usually left to rest over the winter and harvested later in the year. But if we take what we need, carefully, and from places where there's plenty, we should be able to get enough for this limited edition batch, and then we . . .' he stands up, 'or whoever owns Teach Mhor gin next, can come back and harvest what they need in the spring. They can dry it or even freeze it,' he adds. 'Harvesting when there's plenty and then freezing the ingredients could be the best way forward. These are things to look at . . .' and suddenly he stops talking, 'for the new owners,' he finishes flatly.

I stand and look at him. 'We're doing this for Hector,' I say, reminding myself as much as him.

'Quite right,' he answers, and gets back to collecting the seaweed.

Hector is strolling cheerfully up and down the shoreline, and I begin to scour the area for driftwood, just like Lachlan did on Christmas Day. I pull my scarf around my neck and let the clean, crisp air wind its way around me, and focus on the sand beneath my feet, somehow feeling anchored there, part of the landscape. I look up briefly at Lachlan and Hector, both content in what they're doing, then look down again, and find myself thinking about the night before, the house full of music and laughter.

My life in the city with Joe seems so far away. I feel like I'm living in some kind of parallel universe. There are hardly any cars on Winter Island, no buses or sirens, all the things that used to connect me with life and living. Out here there's just the seals, bobbing up to say good morning as if asking if we survived the night okay. The eagles no doubt will be circling the clifftops, and I can see the deer covering the golden heath. I bend to pick up another piece of wood and breathe in deeply, so it fills my whole body. Then, without even noticing I'm doing it, I start to sing, the tune that has been playing in my head since I found the record in the croft, making me feel like my soul has grown wings and taken off. I carry on singing, I can't stop: the songs we played on the record player last night, the songs I heard when I was growing up with my dad. The songs that I realise now were his connection with this place and that have now in some way connected me too. I look out across the bay, holding back my hair from my face and singing as if no one is listening. I have never felt more alive.

I turn to see Lachlan with his phone held up, photographing me. He lowers it and looks at me. 'You sing beautifully,' he says as he walks towards me.

'Thank you.' I blush. 'I didn't know I was . . . or if I could . . . I mean, I joined in last night. But that was different. My voice, it's taken on a whole new tone. Something about this place just made me want to sing.'

'I know,' he says quietly. 'Sometimes we don't know what we want until we stop thinking about it.'

'I . . . I can't believe how good that felt.' I'm suddenly beaming, feeling like I've just crossed the finishing line in the Olympics and broken a world record. 'And you really thought it sounded okay?'

He raises an eyebrow. 'Ah, y'know me . . . what would I know, tone deaf!' he laughs, but suddenly what he thinks really matters to me. 'You sing beautifully,' he repeats. 'Here . . .' And he shows me the phone.

'You videoed me!' I say, surprised. I don't usually like seeing myself on film, but something in me is delighted to hear the song back. He smiles down at me.

'It just seemed right. You don't mind?'

'I . . . love it!' I say. I look up at him, feeling excited, alive. I want to throw my arms around him and hug him. Because he made this happen, I realise. Spending time in this place made this happen. Seeing something of the past, the present and maybe thinking about my future. I feel like me, but not like the old me. A different me! A freer, happier me, living in the moment! I think about that kiss, and how I long to feel his lips on mine again, taste the clean, salty sea-filled air on them. But why?! Why would I think that? Because I'm grateful for what he's done, or because those lips feel a lot like home right now and they are within touching distance? But there's no way I can start to fall for Lachlan. I just can't. That would be far too complicated. There are so many reasons . . . There's Joe, for starters! Joe who thinks I'm at a vocal retreat and is waiting for me to come home! We have to make the gin and move on!

'It was here, here that he told me he was leaving.' I hear Hector's voice and turn away from Lachlan to face him. Lachlan stands behind me, right behind me, and puts his hand on my shoulder. Hector is looking out across the bay.

'Are you okay, Hector?' Lachlan asks.

But the old man looks pale, as though he's seen a ghost.

Chapter Thirty-two

'Let's get this fire lit, shall we? Hector, you sit down. Here, have a nip.' Lachlan guides Hector to the big log and hands him a battered silver hip flask from his jacket pocket. His kindness makes me smile, and my heart beats just a bit faster too.

I smile warmly at Hector, but his expression doesn't alter. Something is troubling him. He wobbles as he goes to sit on the log, and we both reach out to catch him, making sure he doesn't fall. It's what we've come to do, the three of us: make sure none of us falls. We help Hector to sit down. And then Lachlan begins to build the fire.

'Ruby will sing for us again, won't you, Rubes?' he says.

'Was that you singing, Miss Rubes? Very good. Brought it all back to me,' he says, his eyes filling like pools of water. Suddenly tears spring to my own eyes, seeing the pain in his, and a huge lump bobs up in my throat. Is he about to tell me? Is he about to tell me what I've been wanting to hear? Why he and my father never spoke? Why I was never a part of this place?

I look at his face. When I arrived, it shocked me at how familiar it was, yet I knew nothing about this man. Now . . . well, I know him for who he is now, not who he used to be.

The Hector who is forever emptying cupboards looking for the recipe. The Hector who forgets to dress and forgets how many dogs he has. Who loves a boiled egg cooked 'just so' and who has forgotten that his wife and son have died and lives as if they were still here.

'What . . .' my voice is tight, 'what did it bring back?'

He gazes out across the water. 'Um . . .' He looks round at me. Lachlan is building a sort of washing line for the seaweed close to the fire. 'Oh . . . my son. It was here he told me he was leaving.' He looks out at the water again. 'We had a terrible row.' He shakes his head as if wanting to forget the memory. And I don't want to cause him any pain, but I do want to know.

'What did you row about?'

He puts a hand on each of the dogs.

'We said some dreadful things—'

Suddenly there's a clatter behind me, making me jump. I turn and see the stags, up on the rise where we watch the seals, about to do battle once again. Only this time the older stag is looking tired, less up for the fight. Lachlan stands and shoos them away. The younger stag struts off, his head held high, but the older one dips his head, looking defeated. I turn back to Hector, who looks defeated too.

'Someone needs to give in,' says Lachlan. 'No good will come of it. Looks like the old man is seeing sense.'

'Pride comes before a fall,' says Hector shakily. 'Maybe I could learn from that.' He looks at me. 'It was here he told me he wanted to leave the island,' he says, and I feel a shiver up and down my spine like someone is walking over my grave. This is it. He's telling me what happened, and all of a sudden I'm not sure I want to hear it. I've loved the last few weeks getting to know this place, and Hector too. I don't want that spoilt. I'm not ready, I think. I thought I was, but I want more time to get to know him and the island before that bubble is burst. But time is the one thing we haven't got.

'We came here for a walk, with the dogs. I think we had three at the time . . . or was it four?' His mind wanders. The fire begins to crackle and I can feel its heat. Lachlan smiles at me reassuringly.

'And you came here with your son, Hector. What was his name?'

'Campbell. Campbell Hector Macquarrie,' he says carefully.

Even hearing his name brings back the grief I felt when he died. The grief I've tried to shut out for many years. I can see his face so clearly. He wasn't one of those funny, make-you-laugh dads. But he was always there for me. Unlike my mum, who was always chasing the next fun idea, the next group of friends, hoping that what she was looking for was round the corner. It still isn't.

'That's right, I remember Campbell,' says Lachlan, and I'm enjoying hearing his name again. I'd like to join in and help prompt, but there's a huge ball still stuck in my throat.

'There was a storm brewing. We walked down here and he told me he wanted to leave the island. I was . . . well, devastated.' Hector looks up, and a single fat tear drops from his eye and splashes onto one of the Labradors at his feet. The dog doesn't flinch. 'I didn't know what to do. The business was going well, really well. We were shipping out gin, far more than the whisky. Much to my father's disgust. He thought gin was an English drink!' He manages a deep chuckle. 'But the whisky business was in trouble. We were going under. We had to diversify.

'It was walking the island, taking in the sights and sounds, that gave me the idea for the gin, a drink that told the story of this place in a mouthful.' Tears start to trickle down my cheeks. 'A drink that told people how beautiful it was, how clean the air was, how refreshing the sea mist could be. A taste of the world that I loved, right there in a bottle.' He looks down, as if imagining the bottle. 'It was a hard time. The distillery was losing money. We had to make the most of what we had. Luckily, what we have here on this island is pretty special. Even in winter!' he says, and I find myself agreeing. It really is special. And I realise I want to tell everyone about it.

One of the dogs raises its head, looks around, then puts it down again. I remember the bottle, holding it up to the light and thinking it was exactly the colour of the sky and water around the island.

'And what happened when you suggested the gin to your dad?' Lachlan feeds the fire and tends the seaweed on the drying rack. Then he takes the hip flask from Hector, wipes the top and offers it to me. I smile and take a swig, hoping it will shift the lump in my throat.

'Oh, he didn't like the idea at all! But after a bit of butting heads, he told me to try. He didn't really have any other option. The business was going to close unless we could think of something.'

'And it worked!' I say.

'Yes! It grew and grew. We took on more people from the island, and it saved the business and the house. People came to help for nothing to start with, and in the end we took them all on. It's good to look after your workers, because they look after you.' He smiles a watery smile, and I think of the parties they held at the house, their way of saying thank you to the community.

'And Campbell, was he part of it?'

He nods. 'He was . . . for a while.' He looks down at the dogs, and for a moment my heart plummets and I wonder if that's it . . . if he's lost his train of thought. If transmission has been broken. I glance at Lachlan, who nods encouragingly, and I swallow to clear my throat and begin to sing, the very song that Lachlan finds it so hard to hear. Then Hector joins in with me, quietly but beautifully, and the tears fall all over again. When we finish, I reach out and put my hand over his. It doesn't matter if he can't remember, I tell myself. This is what matters. But he starts to talk again.

'He'd met a woman, he told me. Well, we all knew that. He'd been with his girlfriend for a couple of years by then, a girl from a family from the other side of the island. We were waiting for an engagement. And that's what I thought he was going to tell me. Instead he said that he'd fallen in love with a visitor to the island. He was absolutely smitten. He told me that he was leaving and going with her back to England! Not even Scotland . . . England!'

'What was her name? Was it Stella?' I manage to ask.

'That was it! She was a singer. Here visiting a friend who had come to the island to write some music. All very glamorous, it was. We had a terrible row. Said terrible things.

I told him he had to stay. There was no one else to take over the business after me. I was depending on him. The island was depending on him!' He sniffs. 'And he told me that he had to leave, that he was in love. More like under her spell, I told him. That was it. He stayed a few more weeks to help finish up orders for the gin, but we hardly spoke. I just hoped he'd change his mind and see sense. He had a good life here, but he wanted more.'

The flames flick-flack in the wind and I pull my coat around me.

'But the day came. He packed up his belongings and stood waiting by the ferry. And then he told us there was to be a baby. His mother was in tears. I stupidly told him that if he went, he shouldn't come back. He had to choose between us and leaving with Stella and the dreams she'd filled his head with. He told me they were to marry. I said it wouldn't last the year. We haven't heard from him since. We just . . .' he looks up, 'we locked horns and neither of us would step back. Stubborn, like the stags. I should have just let him go. Let him find it out for himself.'

'They separated just after I was born,' I say almost to myself. 'I lived most of my early life with my father. After he died, I went to live full time with my mum. But it was never in the same place for very long.'

'What's that?' He looks at me, confused, and I realise he hasn't heard me.

'Oh, er . . .' I look at Lachlan.

'She says she's sure he'll be back,' Lachlan says.

'Oh yes, I don't doubt it.' Hector lifts his chin a little. 'He'll come back soon, the baby too no doubt. My grandchild.

And I'll be here when they do, welcoming them home with open arms!' He beams and sniffs at the same time.

I stare at his lined face. My grandfather, waiting for me with open arms, and for my father too. There was always a place for me here, but I never knew it. Both of them too stubborn to back down. But I know it now, and it's not too late, for me at least. I just hope it's not too late for Hector.

There's no way we can let the gin fail at this stage. There's no way Hector can be let down again. The weather turns and the rain comes in, and we gather up the seaweed, Hector and the dogs and Lachlan and I move as fast as we can, laughing as we get caught in a huge shower, all the way back to the big house to dry the seaweed in front of the range. *Back home*, I find myself thinking, and wishing I hadn't. Unless we can get the gin recipe sorted, this will be no one's home. It will be sold off; who knows, maybe even knocked down, given its current state, and the past will be lost forever.

Chapter Thirty-three

I switch on my phone the next morning to get an update on the crowdfunding and see nineteen missed calls, mostly from Joe, but some from Jess too, as well as several voice messages. And then the phone jumps to life in my hand and starts ringing.

'Hey, Rubes!'

'Jess!' I reply excitedly. Then I check the time. Jess never rings anyone in the morning. We just aren't morning people. We work late, then stay up late to unwind, and mornings are catch-up-on-sleep time. Or they were until I came here. 'Is everything okay? What's happened?' All sorts of scenarios are running through my head, first and foremost: who's died?

'Everything's fine,' she says with a deep early-morning huskiness to her voice. I let out a sigh of relief, then check myself. There has to be a reason for her ringing this early; before nine a.m. is more like the middle of the night for her. Ah, maybe she hasn't been to bed! That makes sense! This is Jess in after-show party mode.

'How have the gigs been?' I ask.

'Great. Lulu did great. I mean . . .' she corrects herself, 'not as great as you would have done, but great.' Strangely, I don't feel a thing. A few weeks ago, I was terrified of this young woman taking my place in the band, taking my place in my world. But now, something has shifted and I'm pleased for her. Really pleased.

'That's great. She's worked hard. She deserves a shot in the limelight.'

There's a silence at the other end of the phone that I read as shocked.

'Jess?'

'But what about you? That's why I'm ringing!'

'Me? I'm . . . fine. I'm . . .' What am I? 'Well, the storm did some serious damage, brought down some trees, but the villagers have been out clearing the road. Did I tell you there's just one road around the island, and there's this stream, the burn they call it, that I follow on my runs, all the way across the island, up to this waterfall—'

'Ruby!' She cuts across me.

'Yes?'

'I mean, how are you? How's your voice? You're supposed to be in Tenerife. Where are you? When are we getting you back? Joe seems a bit confused about your plans!'

I suddenly feel like I've been tripped up, and I think about the missed calls.

'Look, I don't know what's going on, Rubes, but there's a big gig next week. The first of February. It's being recorded for BBC radio. One of the other acts has dropped out. There'll be loads of coverage. It's a really big deal. We could do with you back here for that!'

'Wow! That's massive! Network radio!' my mouth is saying. That's the day before the tea party, is what I'm thinking.

'Yes!' shrieks Jess. 'And now you're back on track . . . well,

I say that; *are* you back on track?' It seems she takes my silence as a yes. 'Amazing! Now you're back, we're going to knock it out of the park!'

'I, er . . .' Oh God! She wants me to come back and do the gig, but it's the day before our crowdfunding deadline to try and save Teach Mhor! I can't believe I'm doing this, but I can't leave before the tea party. I just can't. 'I don't think my voice will be back in time, Jess. It needs more rest.'

There is silence again at the other end of the phone.

'What's going on, Rubes?' she says eventually. 'Are you leaving us?'

'What? No!' Leaving the band is the last thing I want to do. 'No, I'm not leaving you. That's why I'm . . . away. Getting better. I want this more than ever. I want to be back singing!'

'Really?' says Jess. I look out of the window and check the weather for my run, and find myself wondering if the seals will be out.

'Of course,' I say. I'm thrilled to hear from Jess, but I'm also keen to get outside and take in the air. 'Look, why don't we catch up later? I need to do some exercise . . . vocal exercises. But I want to hear all the news, how everyone is.' I find myself telling a small white lie. 'Let's talk this evening, when . . . when my voice is feeling stronger.'

'Really?' says Jess, suddenly sounding a lot less enthusiastic.

'Look, I know you'd like me to be back for the gig, and if I could, I would.' I can feel myself digging a deeper and deeper hole. 'You know I would. The band is everything to me.'

'Really?' she repeats.

'Yes, Jess. I just want to get my voice back to how it was,' which is true.

'Well,' says Jess, a little frostily, 'from what I've seen, your voice is fully back to how it was. In fact, better than I've ever heard you!'

'What? What do you mean?' I'm confused.

'Rubes, if you're going to put stuff up online, you should realise that everyone is going to see it. That *is* what you were hoping, isn't it, that everyone would see it? But I get it, you think Lulu's doing a great job. You don't want to come back for the gig. Just let me know by the end of the month what you want to do, whether you still want to be a part of this band.'

And that's it: she hangs up and I feel like I've been slapped in the face. I look down at my phone, and with shaking hands access my voicemail. Joe's voice barks in my ear.

'Unless you get back to me immediately and tell me what's going on and where you are, Rubes, that's it! I don't know what's going on, with you, with you and me, but I can't believe you've made me look such a fool! I mean it. Call me. We need to work out how to sort this mess out! If I don't hear from you by the end of the day, if you're not back as soon as you can, it's over. You're making an idiot out of me.'

He knows I'm not in Tenerife. I have no idea how, but he knows. He knows I lied to him. I feel terrible. I need to ring him and explain. But first I need to work out exactly what I'm going to say. I need to tell him how I feel. I have to be honest with him. I also need to know how he found out I'm not in Tenerife.

Chapter Thirty-four

'You knew, didn't you! You knew I was trying to keep it quiet about me being here. You knew I was scared about whether I could sing again. You knew . . . everything! And yet you went ahead and did it without asking me!' I say as I march towards Lachlan.

'Ah, there you are, Mairead. Now there's no need to go getting all hot and bothered. We're just going to walk the dogs. Check the stags . . .' Hector is pointing around with his stick, and then loses his train of thought.

I look back at Lachlan.

'So you've seen it?' His eyes light up and he smiles one of his rare smiles.

'Seen it?! How could you? How could you do that without asking me?' I fume. 'I trusted you! Sing as if no one is listening, you kept saying.'

'Exactly! And it worked!' Lachlan smiles again, his cheeks ruddy in the cold morning air. He bangs his gloved hands together and swings his arms to keep warm. 'You're singing again . . . without any trips to Tenerife and your healing thingy.'

'But that's not the point, is it?!'

Lachlan throws his hands up and turns away, clearly not

wanting to talk about this. Hector wanders back into the house.

'Ah, good walk,' he says, taking off his hat and coat.

'No, wait, Hector,' I say, looking after him. But he's taken himself off to his chair.

'Now see what you've done!' says Lachlan.

'What I've done?! You're the one who's done this, not me!'

'I was just trying to help, that's all.' He lets out a long exasperated sigh. 'You wanted to sing again. You wanted to "get back to where you were".' He uses two fingers for speech marks. 'You needed to get back to your band and try and get a record deal.'

'Yes, all those things!' I say.

'So what's the problem? Don't you think you sound good enough?'

'Yes . . .' I say, grappling to find the words to tell him why I'm right and he isn't. 'I think I sound better than I've ever sounded, in fact,' I say reluctantly.

'Well then.' He throws his hands up in the air again. 'Now, are we going for this walk or not? I have a trial batch of gin distilling that I need to get back for.'

'Without the final ingredient?' I ask, distracted.

He shrugs. 'I thought I'd try. I've already had one go. It's what I do: try and make things work. They don't always turn out quite right, though.' He looks at me, and I feel a buzz of excitement leap up and down my body. 'I'm sorry. I was just trying to create some interest. I thought you sang beautifully, and I thought it might bring in some more investors.'

I sigh. 'We're not going to make it, are we?'

'I don't think so, no.' He shakes his head. And all of a sudden I want to hug him, and for him to hug me back. Everything we've worked so hard for . . . 'We're just not getting enough investors, and even if we were, we can't do what we promised. We can't give them an exclusive bottle of original Teach Mhor gin. We haven't got all the ingredients!'

He reaches forward and puts his hand around the back of my neck and draws me to him. I resist at first. I can't let myself fall for this man. I'm going soon. But where to? Joe clearly feels I've betrayed him, and yet . . . I feel I've finally been true to myself. I need to speak to him.

I look up. 'Where will you go?' I ask. 'When you leave here?'

'To the mainland, like I said.'

'But what about a job?'

'I'll find something. The care home have offered me some gardening work. Might suit me fine. They said there'd be a job for you too if you wanted to spend some time singing with the residents.'

'Ha, I might just take them up on that!' I try and laugh through the sniffing and the tears that have started to roll. Tears of frustration and sadness. 'Joe knows I didn't go to Tenerife. He knows I've lied to him. He says I have to go back now, or it's over.' Everything I've known for the past four years, over. Lachlan pulls me closer, and this time I don't resist; I let myself fall against his big chest and his soft knitted jumper, breathing in the aroma of woodsmoke and what smells a lot like home right now.

'Come on,' he says finally, as I stand up straight and he

pulls off his gloves and wipes the tears from beneath my eyes. 'Let's see if there are any kippers left.'

We turn towards the house. It's a magnificent building. Despite its sorry state inside, it is as proud as its owner on the outside. Smart and upright and brave in the face of adversity. We start walking towards it, and Lachlan keeps his arm around my shoulders.

'I'll take down the video of you singing. Like I say, I just thought it would attract some attention on the crowdfunding page. I thought it did exactly what you said we should do, show off the island at its best.'

I look up at him. 'Did you?'

'I did, yes. But I'll take it down now. I'm sorry I didn't ask you.'

'It's got me into a bit of bother. Joe's given me this ultimatum and I'm in trouble with the band, with Jess.'

'I should've thought. I'm sorry. I just saw it and thought how beautiful you looked in it, how beautifully you sang and how you were everything this island is. You're a part of it as much as any of us. This is your home too.'

The tears well up again and I drop my head as we walk back into the house and towards the big kitchen, where my old laptop is sitting on the table.

In the doorway, I turn to Lachlan.

'I'm sorry again,' he says. 'I really didn't mean to cause trouble for you. I just felt . . . well . . . I just thought it was beautiful. I didn't think.'

'It's fine, really,' I say, looking up at him.

He smiles back, that familiar smile, and just for moment I look at his lips and he looks at mine, and I feel myself drawn to him, but he suddenly turns and goes in to Hector and throws another log on the fire there. I blush. Was I going to kiss him because I feel bad and let down by Joe, or because I'm actually falling for him? I can't let myself be confused by the two things. Thank goodness he pulled away first, otherwise I could have made a big mistake. I seem to have made a few of those recently.

I open the computer and click through to the crowdfunding page. There's the video. Jess must have seen it before me. And now she thinks I've lied to her and that it's over for us as a band as well as for Joe and me. Even if I do go back, will she and the others want me after this? Can you be a band if you don't have trust? Has all this been for nothing? We're going to lose the gin, the house, everything. And Hector will end up who knows where. A long way from everything he knows and loves.

I look at the video and play it. Like I say, I usually hate to watch myself, but somehow, this time, it makes me smile. I'm there with my hair being blown by the wind, collecting firewood on the beach, gazing out across the water. It's everything I will remember when I leave this place. It's everything that was there in the gin.

'Here, I'll take it down,' says Lachlan, leaning over me, making my nerve endings stand to attention again. He takes hold of the mouse. Hector has wandered into the kitchen, clearly having heard the singing.

'It was back on the beach, that's where it started . . .' And he launches once more into the story of the day my father left. '. . . But he'll be back. With the baby . . .' and I can't help but smile again, knowing that Hector was here waiting for me. There was always a place for me in the heart of this home, and in his heart too.

'Wait,' says Lachlan, the cursor hovering over the delete button. 'I think you should probably see this first.' And he points to the screen.

'I can't look!' I say. I close my eyes and put my hands over my face.

Chapter Thirty-five

'Take your hands away, look!' I hear him say, but I can't. Then I feel his hands on mine, gently guiding them from my face until they're on the wooden table in front of me. 'Now open your eyes,' he tells me. 'Go on!' he urges. He's standing right behind me and I can feel his warm breath next to my ear. Excitement and fear are building in me, and I don't know if it's because of what he wants to show me on the screen, or something else.

Slowly I open my eyes. What if investors have pulled out? Changed their minds? I know we haven't made the target yet, nowhere near in fact, and the tea party is under a week away. This is my fault, or it feels like it anyway. I sigh deeply, resigning myself to the fact that we're going to have to cancel. I raise my gaze to the screen, then blink and look again. I turn round to Lachlan, who's smiling widely, creases forming in his cheeks, his flecked green eyes sparkling.

'Looks like they're investing in you!' he says. 'They love you!' The smile on his face is mirrored in his voice.

'Oh my God! People are paying! They're really putting up money!' I look at the figure on the screen again. 'Aren't they?' He is still beaming and nodding, watching the total, which has just changed and gone up again. 'Oh!' My hands shoot to my face. 'A new investor!'

Lachlan leans in over my shoulder, making my heart pick up its pace as I smell his now familiar aroma of woodsmoke and pine. 'Look, it's the care home. The Island View. It says the residents have had a whip-round and want to be Teach Mhor investors. And they want to know if you'll come back and visit again soon.' He points. 'And there are loads of comments about your singing. Looks like it's you they've fallen in love with. "A slice of island life", someone's written.'

Transported me straight there, can't wait to taste the gin! I read another comment. *Enchanting and magical. Felt like I was there! Who is this woman?!* And then many more wanting to know who I am and where they can hear more of my music.

'The number of shares and likes it's getting is going up and up. People are reposting it all over the place! And look at the total, it's amazing!'

I stare at the number in astonishment, not believing it's the same page we closed the computer lid on last night, thinking this was never going to happen, that we'd blown it.

I turn to Lachlan once again, tears in my eyes, but this time they are tears of joy at the happiness I seem to have shared by being happy myself. He looks at me, his face close to mine, and I study its now familiar lines and curves, a map of the journey life has taken him on, just like Hector's well-worn and weathered face.

'Do you still want me to take it down?' he asks.

I shake my head. 'No, leave it there. Thank you. It's lovely. It'll be a lovely memento of my time here,' I say, my mouth suddenly dry. 'And other people seem to like it too, which is what counts,' I add quickly. Teach Mhor's Winter Gin appears to be gathering an expectant audience. 'Maybe this is how I finally helped!' I realise I've said that last bit out loud, and I feel my cheeks pink.

'Without you and your love of music, we'd never have found the recipe,' Lachlan gently reminds me.

'But without you, the gin will never be made.'

'Well in that case, as I've told you, we make a good team.' He smiles. 'Who'd've thought it?!'

I can't help but smile back. Who indeed?

I look back at the screen.

'But even if we do make the target, we still haven't found the final ingredient. We still have to deliver a special edition bottle of Teach Mhor Winter Gin, A Taste of the Wild Side to each of these bidders, or we don't get our money. We won't be able to deliver!'

Lachlan nods thoughtfully. 'There's less than a week to go. Even if we start now, we're pushing it to get the gin ready for the weekend. We're going to have to go ahead without the final ingredient.'

'But what if someone notices that it's not the same? That we haven't brought back Teach Mhor gin? That's what you promised Hector you'd do. Besides, we've said on the crowd-funding page that it has five special ingredients gathered from the island. We've shown the first four . . . look, people are waiting to hear what the fifth one is!' I point to the screen and the comments there.

Hector wanders into the kitchen with the dogs at his heels.

'Hello, Hector. We're just watching all the orders come in for Teach Mhor's Winter Gin.'

'Always was popular!' He smiles and sits in the rocking chair by the range, the dogs at his feet. And then the younger of the two dogs, Douglas, stands and comes to sit by mine. Rhona stays put. 'Wish I could find the recipe. Can't think where I've put it. Lovely singing, by the way. Heard it from the other room. Was it Mairead singing?'

Lachlan and I look at each other and smile.

'I think it was, Hector.'

'Beautiful voice has Mairead. Always did have. She's probably getting ready to go out. I'll wait for her here,' and he rocks back and forth in the chair, humming gently to himself. 'I think that's why Campbell fell for a woman who could sing. He loved hearing his mother sing. Loved the house being full of music.' He closes his eyes. 'I proposed to her in the pine forest, you know. Where we pick the pine needles for the gin. It's what gave me the idea. Always loved the smell of pine. That and the smell of the sea. This place runs on water. It's who we are. We wouldn't be the island we are without it.'

'You know,' Lachlan says quietly, 'they say that in brain function tests, they can't find where the memories are . . . that they're not actually stored in the brain.'

'So where are they stored?' I tip my head and look up at him.

'Some would say in the heart,' Lachlan says, fetching two glasses and pouring two shots of his tester gin. 'And when we have nothing else, we'll still have memories, so we'd better make them good ones.'

We chink our glasses together and sip. I can see the island, taste it . . . but there is something missing. What is it?!

'I have an idea, if we really want to get more crowdfunders,' he says.

'What is it?'

'We offer an intimate gig, with you, at the tea party. They obviously love your voice. You sing, and by the sounds of it, they'll come.'

Could I? Could I get back up there and sing again?

'Actually . . .' he continues, 'look, don't be cross at me again, but I've already said you will.'

'What? Why?'

The screen pings again and another investor is added to the list. I know one thing for sure: I can't go home now. Not yet.

'Excuse me, but I have to make a call,' I say, and I step outside to ring Joe. I know exactly what I'm going to say, and why.

Chapter Thirty-six

Much later that night, or maybe early the following morning, we finally close the computer and wearily but happily make our way upstairs. We guide Hector to his bedroom, where Lachlan helps him into bed. The rain is hammering down outside and the wind is rattling the window frames, just like the first night I arrived here. I look at the fire in my room. It's dead. Since I agreed to stay on and help find the gin recipe, it's been lit every night, and a hot-water bottle in my bed too.

There's a knock at my door. Lachlan's head appears.

'I haven't lit the fire,' he says, concerned.

'Oh, it's fine, I'm going straight to bed,' I say, and wave a hand at it.

He looks at me for a moment.

'Goodnight, Ruby,'

'Goodnight, Lachlan.'

He hesitates. 'You okay? Joe, your boyfriend? Has he forgiven you?'

I look up at him, seeing the concern on his face. Then I take a deep breath and let it out as I say flatly, 'We finished.'

'Oh God, Rubes, I'm sorry, I didn't mean for—'

'It's fine. It was the right thing. Ever since I got here, I've

251

realised how little we have in common. I mean, we have "the plan".' I use my fingers to do inverted commas. 'Getting the contract, buying the flat, et cetera, et cetera. But actually, what I came to understand is that he's all about life plans and not about living. I could never have seen him fitting in here. Joe likes his smart shoes and tailored suits. You'd never have got him in a pair of second-hand wellies!' And we both give a small laugh.

'You're sure you're okay?' says Lachlan.

'I may not be right now, but I'm sure I will be,' I say, and smile.

'Goodnight then,' he says.

'Goodnight, Lachlan,' and I shut the door and listen to his footsteps as they walk slowly away and up the stairs.

I get into bed and push the hot-water bottle down to my feet, almost scalding them. I shiver and pull the covers around me, listening to the sounds of Lachlan moving around overhead. But even once it's quiet, I can't fall asleep. I think about the video, how singing on the beach made me feel. I think about the crowdfunding page. I think about Jess asking if I still want to be in the band. I think about the silence in our band group chat. I haven't heard from any of them in a while. Have they made another group without me? Has the space I used to fill been filled by someone else? And then I think about Joe telling me we're over unless I go straight home. I think about our conversation earlier this evening.

'I'm not coming back yet, Joe,' I told him. 'I have to finish what I started. I have to do this for Hector, but for me too. I need to be here to . . . well, to find the missing piece of me, I suppose.'

'I have no idea what you're talking about. You've lied to me, Rubes! Made me look an idiot in front of everyone – the band, my family. We had a plan. You just had to stick to it and we'd have had it all.'

'No,' I said quietly. '*You* had a plan, Joe. You had it all mapped out. You had my life mapped out.'

'And you were happy with that!' he shouted.

'But now I'm taking the scenic route, and I realise that there's so much more out there.'

'I meant what I said, Rubes. If you and I are going to get back to where we were, you need to come home, now!'

I took a deep breath. 'No, Joe, I won't be coming home yet.'

'You're not . . .' he spluttered. 'I mean it, Rubes. You can't get anywhere in life without drive. Maybe you should take a leaf out of Lulu's book. She's going to do really well.'

I know he meant to hurt me, but instead I just felt pleased for her.

'I'm glad to hear that, Joe. And I hope it brings her happiness. Happiness is so much more than waiting for what's around the corner. It's enjoying what's happening right now. And I'm living in the now, not for what might happen tomorrow.'

'Well . . .' he spluttered again. 'That won't be with me, then!' And he ended the call, as if slamming the door shut on four years of my life.

It's over. Joe and me are over. It's sad, but I know it's the right thing. We were never going to grow old together. We were never going to last the distance once my band days were finished. I realised that the day Hector told us about proposing to Mairead. Joe never proposed to me; it was more like a business plan. But love and marriage isn't a business plan; it's about the memories you make together. I couldn't conjure up any of the memories Joe and I had made, only the plans for when I got the record deal. I couldn't even remember how his kiss felt. But I know I'll never forget the kiss I shared with Lachlan, or the oysters and gin on the beach.

I listen to the rain against the window pane, feeling very much like I'm living in the moment, and feel a strange sense of relief wash over me. It's over. I think about texting the band group chat, but have no idea what to say, what GIF to send to explain how I feel.

'This place runs on water,' I hear Hector saying, and I try to retrace my early-morning runs in my head, following the path of the burn across the island, from the sea, over the moorland, through the forest and up into the hills to the waterfall. I remember the time Hector went missing. The waterfall, I think as I slowly drift off to sleep.

The next morning, my eyes open with a ping. The waterfall! *This place runs on water. It's who we are. We wouldn't be the island we are without it.* It's the water. I was running the wrong way round. The burn starts at the waterfall and flows across the island, picking up flavour and scents from every part of it, finishing in the sea . . .

It starts at the waterfall! It's the water that makes the gin so special.

Chapter Thirty-seven

I throw on my clothes over my pyjamas – well, a tracksuit that has doubled as pyjamas whilst I've been here. I pull on my trainers over my thick socks, jumping from one foot to the other, trying to hop towards the door whilst putting them on. It doesn't work, and I trip and stumble, eventually grabbing hold of the end of the bed to steady myself. I scoop up my hoodie and pull it on, and run out of the room, over the threadbare rug and the bare floorboards, launching myself towards the door to the attic.

'Lachlan!' I shout. I don't wait for a reply, but run up the narrow wooden stairs, around the turn on the tapered steps and up towards the light from the window on the landing.

'Argh!'

'Argh!'

We meet at the top of the stairs. He's just a silhouette in front of the window there, while I look like some kind of monster from the lagoon. It's just like the first time we met.

'What's up? Is it Hector?' He's pulling on his jumper, his T-shirt pyjama top lifting to reveal his stomach, and my own stomach flips over and back again.

'No, no, it's not Hector,' I say. He drops his arms with relief. 'It's . . .' I suddenly smile up at him, wishing I'd

Jo Thomas

stopped to brush my hair and tidy myself up, all of a sudden
feeling very self-conscious about my dishevelled state. But
why? This is Lachlan! It's not like I . . . I look at him standing
in front of the window, his bed hair standing on end. It's not
like I fancy him, I tell myself slowly as I realise just how
fanciable he looks in his soft pyjama bottoms and thick
knitted sweater, rubbing his sleepy eyes.

'What then?' he laughs, throwing out his arms and letting
them fall by his sides.

'It's, it's . . .' I suddenly feel dizzy with excitement, and I
don't know if it's the news I'm about to tell him or Lachlan
himself that's making me feel like that. 'It's the gin!' I finally
say, my smile widening as I do. 'I think I know the final
ingredient!'

'Whaaaa!' he says. 'What is it?'

'It's the water!' My cheeks are pink and my smile is as
wide as it can be. 'The water from the waterfall! Remember,
that's where Hector went that night he went missing. And
he's always saying it's the water that makes the island what it
is.'

Lachlan smacks his open palm to his forehead. 'I can't
believe I didn't see it! Where the water is filtered through the
rock. It's some of the oldest on the planet, the purest water
you can get.'

'It's where the story begins,' I say. 'We found the end of
the story, the seaweed, at the beach. We just had to work
backwards, across the cliffs for the gorse . . .'

'. . . the forest for the pine and the hedgerows for the
rosehips,' he joins in.

'And finally the mountain spring!'

'The story of the island!' he says, smiling and nodding.

'It's the burn. I was told when I first got here that I couldn't get lost if I followed the burn. It takes you right across the island.'

'The story of the island and of Teach Mhor gin. You did it, Ruby Macquarrie . . . you did it!'

No one ever calls me Macquarrie, I think. But that's how I feel, like a Macquarrie. And then he takes my face in his hands and very gently moves in to kiss me, his eyes darting from my lips to my eyes, and it tastes just like it did that night of the storm, when Hector thought it was Hogmanay and told everyone I was pregnant.

Suddenly there's a banging from out on the landing.

'Mairead? Mairead? Are they here? Is Campbell here? Is the baby with him?'

Our eyes ping open and we fall apart, smiling.

'Sounds like someone's been having happy dreams,' I say.

'They're on their way, Hector,' Lachlan calls. 'On their way,' and he looks at me. 'It's all about living in the present,' he says quietly, and we both laugh, the moment broken but not forgotten as we head back downstairs, wrapped up against the weather, with Hector and the dogs in tow; a laughing, happy trio heading out to the Land Rover and loading the boot with water barrels to fill.

Chapter Thirty-eight

'We're going to need help, all the help we can get,' I tell Lachlan as he hands me one of the full water barrels from his precarious position by the waterfall edge.

'Agreed,' he says, holding out another barrel, and I take it from him and put it on the bank, feeling like a contestant in the final of *I'm a Celebrity . . . Get Me Out of Here!* Only I'm not a celebrity, and weirdly, right now, getting out of here feels like the last thing on my mind. Getting this gin made is what matters and meeting the crowdfunding target.

He hands me the last barrel, full of cold, clear, mountain-fresh rock-filtered water, then turns to make his way back to the bank before stopping and bending down.

'Here,' he says, and scoops up a handful of what must be freezing water and offers it to me. 'Quick!' he laughs as I hesitate and the water trickles through his fingers. I quickly step forward and take his hands in mine, and sip. I don't know what's more invigorating, holding his hands, or the water itself. Whatever, I feel myself feeling excited and very much alive. I can feel my eyes sparkling and my body tingling.

'Right, let's get this gin made!' he beams.

I put the back of my hand to my lips and brush away any

moisture left there, then roll my bottom lip in, still feeling the taste of the water.

'Hector, open the back door of the Land Rover,' I call out as we head down the slope to the track, both of us with a barrel in each hand.

Hector does as he's asked, with a big smile on his face.

The three of us get in the car with the dogs, although Douglas insists on sitting up front with me, and we head back, via the village, the pub and the shop.

'I'll go to the pub; you see who's in the café,' I tell Lachlan. We need as many hands as we can find to get this batch made in time for the tea party.

Everyone I speak to is happy to come and help out, by way of a thank you for the night of the storm, and our journey back to the house is cheerful and excited, singing along to the crackly radio. As we reach the end of the drive, we all stop singing when we see a car waiting outside the front door.

'Anyone expecting visitors?' asks Lachlan, glancing at me, and I shake my head.

'Someone's beaten us here,' I say, but I find it hard to believe.

'It'll be Campbell and the baby!' says Hector.

Lachlan and I look at each other and smile sadly.

Chapter Thirty-nine

'Ah, good, just the person.' It's Fraser, the solicitor. Suddenly our good mood evaporates.

'Is everything all right?' I ask. 'We're not due to meet, are we? We're hoping to have everything ready for the house to go on the market after our crowdfunding event.'

'Yes, indeed . . . and looking forward to the tea party we are too, as investors!' He smiles.

'Well that's fantastic, we'll see you then.' I pick up one of the barrels of water Lachlan has unloaded.

'Hector!' says Fraser. 'Good to see you!' He shakes Hector's hand.

'Good to see you too,' says Hector. He turns and walks towards the door. 'Who's that?' I hear him asking Lachlan loudly. 'Must get on,' he calls over his shoulder. 'My son and grandchild are coming home!'

I watch his back as he disappears into the house. He's looking tired. Yet I can't help but wonder: did my dad mean to come home before he died? Was that ever a plan? Did they make it up with each other?

Fraser smiles. 'He's looking better than I've seen him in a long time. Your stay here must have done him some good.'

'Thank you,' I say, 'but actually, I really have to get on.

We have a batch of gin to get made for the tea party.'

'Actually, about that . . .'

'What, the tea party?'

'Uh huh. I've brought someone with me,' he says.

'Oh?' I look at him quizzically.

'I'm going to the distillery,' says Lachlan, watching as several battered trucks come down the drive. 'Unless you need me?' He raises an eyebrow.

'No, no, you go on. I'll catch you up. Just follow Lachlan, everyone,' I say as the locals pour out of the trucks.

'Come to help, Fraser?' says Isla as he passes us.

'Hopefully!' He beams as a passenger gets out of his car. A smart young man, half Fraser's age, doing up his suit jacket button beneath his smart knee-length woollen coat. I wonder for a moment if it's one of Fraser's family, brought as reinforcements.

'This is Jack Drummond. From Drummond's Spirits.' Fraser looks at me. 'On the mainland,' he adds, as if I should know what he's talking about. Seeing that I don't, he carries on. 'Drummond's is a very big company, making a range of spirits.'

'Oh, right.' I nod, a lot, not quite sure why he's here. 'Well, we make just the one gin,' I laugh, and can hear that I sound slightly hysterical. And we won't make one at all if we can't get on with this batch, I think.

'At the moment.' Jack Drummond smiles, a bright, attractive smile, and I realise that he may be interested in becoming a crowdfunder, which would be brilliant.

'Yes, just one, very special gin,' I say with pride. 'Made with foraged botanicals from the island. We're making an exclusive limited edition batch as we speak, whilst we're crowdfunding to get the business back on its feet . . .' I deliberate on how to put it, 'after a few years on the back burner.'

'So I hear,' he says, and I'm not sure what he's referring to: the crowdfunding, the limited edition batch, or the fact that the business has been on the back burner . . . or more like dead in the water. 'I know of Teach Mhor gin, of course.'

'I, er . . . well, if you're interested in investing, we'd be delighted. We still have a little way to go to meet our target,' I say, clapping my hands together and smiling. Today really is getting better and better.

'You're the woman singing on the crowdfunding page, aren't you?' he says, flashing me an even brighter smile.

'I am.' I find myself blushing.

'You were great. Really gave a sense of what this place feels like.' He looks around him, then up at the house. 'Like it has a real sense of identity.'

'Oh, it does.' I smile. 'It's a very special place indeed. Now, if you'll excuse me, I have to get on. But we'd love to see you at the tea party if you're interested in investing.' I pick up another barrel of water.

'Oh, I'm not interested in investing.' He smiles his killer smile again. 'I'm interested in . . .'

Isla appears at the front door. 'Lachlan says have you got that water?' she says good-naturedly, and turns to go back to the distillery just as Jack finishes his sentence.

'I'm interested in buying the place, the whole lot. Lock, stock and barrel.'

'You're what?!' says Isla quietly and steadily from behind

me, and I spin round. She has stopped in her tracks and turned to glare at Jack, and then at me. 'Does Lachlan know about this? Or Hector, for that matter? Do they know you're planning to sell Hector's home from under him?' She is clearly appalled. 'Is this why you're here? When you said you were helping with the business, is this what you meant: that you're here to sell it to the highest bidder?'

I look at Isla's furious expression and have no idea where to start explaining who I am or why I'm here or that everything seems to have changed and leaving is the very last thing I want to do. She turns, her face like thunder, and stalks off.

'Er, great! Take a look around,' I say, waving a hand at Jack and Fraser, and run after Isla.

'Look, it's not what you think,' I say when I catch up with her. I reach out for her arm in the wood-panelled hall, but she shrugs me off.

'Oh really? You turn up here and make out you're with Lachlan and that you're helping bring the gin back, but really you just want to sell off Hector's home.' Her eyes are flashing.

'Actually, I never said that Lachlan and I were—'

'Does Lachlan know? He'd never let this happen!' She cuts me off, and again I struggle to find the words.

'Actually,' says a familiar and very welcome voice behind me, 'he does.' I turn to see Lachlan standing in the hall. Outside, Fraser and Jack Drummond are looking at the building's facade and I can hear Drummond's voice. We all can.

'It's got a great vibe. Nothing has been spoilt with updating. You can just see the tartan and the log fires. You can feel the heritage of the place. We want to celebrate its history.'

'Except the history and heritage will be gone!' Isla says.

'Look,' I say. 'Fraser asked me to come here and we discussed selling the house so Hector could go into a care home. I'm his only remaining relative. His son's daughter. His . . . granddaughter.' And again I wonder why Fraser called me in the first place. He didn't need me to agree. I didn't even know Hector. But I've learnt a lot about my past since being here, and maybe a bit about living in the present too. I've spent my life chasing career goals, yet here, I live every day for what it brings. The seals, the stags, the changing weather. You go with what life throws at you on the day.

Joe has stuck to his word and cut off all communication with me, bar a message saying he'll send on a box of my belongings from his flat and do I want any of the towel set we bought together. But I don't want any of it. My life back there seems a million miles away right now. I have no idea what the future holds for me. I only know I have to get this gin made and organise the tea party. That's as far as it goes right now. The last thing I need is to cause any upset before I leave.

'The hospital thought it best, after his last fall, what with the way he is now,' Lachlan is explaining.

'But the house couldn't be sold with a sitting tenant.' I try and help out.

'And the money's needed to pay his care home fees.' Lachlan and I seem to be working in sync to explain everything.

'But Lachlan had promised Hector he'd find the missing recipe for the gin and bring the distillery back to life. He wanted to repay him for everything he'd done for him, taking him in after . . . after he returned to the island.'

'Letting me stay on in the croft after Dad died. Even though I couldn't stand the thought of being there after . . .' He looks at Isla.

'After you asked me to marry you. But I was already engaged,' she finishes for him.

'Yes,' he says. 'After that. But time has moved on, and so have I. Hector let me stay with him while I found my feet again, and now I'm repaying him. He wants to know the gin business is up and running again before he . . . It's his last wish.' He swallows, and I do too. 'I couldn't find the recipe. It was Ruby who unlocked the secret. She's the one who realised it was all in his head and it was the music that made him remember.'

'So we made a deal to get the distillery up and running and then sell the place. We had to crowdfund it to get the money to pay for his place. His legacy will still be here,' I try and explain.

'And then what?' Isla says.

'It's time I moved on,' Lachlan says. 'Moved out. Left the island again. It's time I let you get on with your own life.'

For a moment, neither of them says anything, then Isla nods sadly, as if finally letting him go.

'And you?' She turns her gaze on me.

'I . . .' I feel choked.

'Ruby has her singing career to get back on track,' Lachlan says. 'This way, we all get what we want, and the gin business will provide jobs for the islanders, just like Hector wants. Please, Isla, don't say anything to anyone else. It's for the best: for the island, for everyone.'

She looks at him with soft tears in her eyes. 'For everyone?'

He nods. 'Like I say, we all get what we want this way. Jobs for the locals, a new start for you and Gordan without me moping around . . .'

'As long as selling to some big mainland company doesn't mean we'll be swallowed up. I couldn't be a part of that. Forgetting what makes us and this place special.'

'We won't let that happen,' I say.

'You have to be a part of this place to know what that means,' and Isla turns and walks away.

Lachlan and I look at each other. We both got what we wanted, didn't we? says a voice in my head. Well, nearly.

Chapter Forty

'So each distillation can be divided into three parts,' Lachlan tells everyone. 'We need to separate out the heads and the tails, the bits that we don't want to flavour the gin and spoil it, and keep only the heart.' He looks at me as he says it, and I swallow. Stripping life back to leave just the heart seems to be exactly what being on the island has taught me. To live for now and for the people that matter. But in no time at all, I'm going to be leaving, and I have a feeling I will be leaving my heart behind.

For the next seventy-two hours, Aggie, the big old still, does her thing and everyone helps, following Lachlan's instructions. The place is buzzing. We barely sleep. Lachlan takes catnaps in the distillery and I stay in the house with Hector to keep an eye on him. Despite the obvious pleasure he's getting from seeing the distillery coming back to life, he's tired, and much quieter than when I first arrived.

The night before the tea party, we get the baking organised, and then the gin is bottled and boxed and ready to go. The sun sets in a blaze of red and orange, reflecting across the still sea. It's cold, much colder, and still, a hush over the island, like an audience waiting with anticipation for the show to begin. Everyone leaves to go to the pub, and Hector, tired but happy, goes to bed. Once he's asleep, Lachlan leads me down to the shore, lighting lanterns around the dunes and the bonfire there, and then produces a bottle of special edition Teach Mhor Winter Gin from his canvas bag.

'My heart,' he says, and hands it to me. And I have no idea if he means what I hope he might mean, because if he did, I would tell him that he's holding mine too in his hands.

He brings out oysters he's collected, and we open them and drink from them, sipping and licking the salty juice from the shells. Our eyes never leave each other's, lit up by the flames from the fire, and I feel like I've finally come home, that this is indeed the heart of the place, yet at the same time I know that our time together, the three of us, has come to an end.

Chapter Forty-one

The next day, I'm up early. But not as early as Lachlan, it would seem, and as I open my door, I can smell the sweet, warm aroma of baking rising up through the house from the kitchen.

I know we have a busy day ahead, but I want to go for just one more run around the island. After today . . . well, we still have a few more bottles to go to make our crowdfunding target. If we get there, I'll be gone. If not, it looks like Jack Drummond will swoop in and try and get the place at as low a price as he can. Without the gin, the heart of the place, the property is practically worthless. I could only see as far as today, getting the money for Hector to go into the care home; doing my duty and then getting on my way to the voice healing retreat, thinking I was doing the best for everyone. But was I really?

I hurry downstairs, pausing on the landing to rearrange the curtains again. There's so much to do, cleaning, laying up for the tea party and helping Lachlan, not to mention getting the boxes of gin ready to distribute if we make the target . . . if!

I reach over the banister and ease the old gold bauble from the deer's antler, then run down the rest of the stairs. This is it. Today's the day! I go over the list in my head as I straighten a mottled mirror on the wall, then hurry to the kitchen, drawn in by the smell of the freshly baked scones that Lachlan is taking out of the oven.

'Morning,' I say, popping a piece of broken shortbread into my mouth from the batch laid out on the cooling tray, expecting Lachlan to tell me off. But he doesn't.

'So . . .' I clap my hands together. 'Mrs Broidy is due in to clean, and the Cruickshanks are coming over to help set up . . .'

He's looking at me, still wearing the oven gloves.

'Mrs Broidy?' I repeat, and glance at his face. 'She's not coming, is she?' I say slowly.

He shakes his head. 'Rang earlier. Said she had . . .' he hesitates, 'a touch of something and didn't think she should pass it on.'

'And Lena and Lexie?'

Silently he pulls off the oven gloves and puts them on the worn wooden work surface by the sink.

'Got a touch of something?' I raise an eyebrow and hope the tears of frustration gathering in hot pools along my eyelids don't fall.

He nods.

'They've heard, haven't they?'

'It wasn't Isla. Jack Drummond was in the pub last night, asking about life here and the story of the house.'

'They think I'm just here to get rid of the house and push Hector out. They think I'm selling out the island.'

He's silent for a moment, then, 'But we still have other people coming. The ferry's due in at eleven. Maybe we'll still make the target.'

'You've worked so hard to make this happen.' I look at him. 'And now I've gone and blown it.'

'You're just doing what you think is right. And you *are* right. Hector needs more looking after and . . . and I need to move on. I can't stay hiding out here forever, hoping life will come and find me.'

'No, no, I didn't mean that. This is your home.'

'Only it's not,' he says flatly. 'Look, we still need to put on this tea party.'

'Why? What's the point? They're not coming, are they?'

'It . . . we . . .' He pauses. 'We just do,' he says firmly. 'Because it's what we said we'd do. We can't give up now. This is the end of the journey. We owe it to Hector and to ourselves to finish the journey.'

I'm suddenly lost for words. That's why we're doing this. Not for me to go back to my life as I knew it, not for Lachlan to get over his broken heart, but for an old man who locked horns with his son and has spent a lifetime regretting it and hoping to see his family again. For a man who is much loved on this island and shouldn't be forgotten.

I turn. 'Excuse me . . . just going to get some air,' I say, and head to the back door. Douglas is there, offering to be my running partner, to keep me safe within the family. I fling open the door, and despite the cold, cold air and the big white clouds rolling in, I step out, take a deep breath and start to run my familiar course. In the background I swear I hear the front door slam and the sound of the Land Rover starting up.

I run and run, listening to the sound of my feet on the road. And as I do, tiny, light white flakes begin to fall, floating softly from the thick clouds.

Snow, I think. Snow, and I hold my face up to it. I run past the little croft by the bay, closed up as usual, making me feel sad for it all over again. The snow is falling a little more heavily and I wonder whether to stop, but something inside me just keeps pushing me on. The icy flakes feel fresh, almost liberating, as if they're washing away the past and making me feel like today is a new day.

I run on, beside the burn, the burn that follows the island's varying terrain and was ultimately the map for the gin recipe. I push myself hard, and finally, as I reach the pub, my lungs dragging in air and my muscles crying out for a rest, I slow up, seeing Lachlan's dark red Land Rover pulled up at an angle outside the shop and café. I stop and bend over, holding my knees, taking deep breaths, trying to slow my breathing, and as I do, I hear voices coming from the café. My cheeks pink as I realise that the topic of conversation is . . . me!

'She lied to us. Pretending she was here to help get the distillery up and running, get the island back on its feet.'

'Pretending to be your girlfriend . . .' says another voice I recognise as one of the sisters.

'Whoa! Wait!' My heart jumps as I hear Lachlan's voice. 'Just wait a minute,' and the other voices go quiet. 'Ruby didn't pretend to be anything. She came here because she had to. Because it was the right thing to do. Because she's a good person. She could have left a long time ago.'

'Why didn't she then?'

'Because . . . of me.'

'Told you! She's come here, let ya fall for her and now she's buggering off.'

'No, no, it's not like that. She thought she had to come and sign papers to allow the house to be sold. The hospital said that Hector would be better off in a care home on the mainland, with his dementia and no one here to care for him.'

'But you were here.'

'But I'm not his next of kin. Ruby is . . .'

A silence falls over the gathering. I hold my breath.

'You mean . . . she's Hector's . . .'

'Granddaughter. Yes.'

All this time he could have told them, and he hasn't. He kept his word. Now . . . well, it really doesn't matter, I think. If the crowdfunding fails, I will have let everyone down, whoever I am. But somehow, hearing the words 'Hector's granddaughter' fills me with a stirring of pride.

'They'd never met. Her dad . . . well, you all remember Campbell, and you know that he and Hector argued and were both too proud to back down. Ruby never knew her grandparents or this place. When she got here, she realised that to do the best thing for Hector, she had to sell the house, but that meant me leaving it. And until I'd found the gin recipe that Hector could no longer remember, I wasn't budging. Anyway, turns out Ruby's as stubborn as her grandfather. She was determined to find that recipe and get the gin still working, and that's exactly what she's done. Hector's business is up and running again, thanks to her . . . and you. This is what a community does.'

I bite my bottom lip. I want to say that it was him that made it happen. He knew where to go to find the ingredients, how to gather them and prepare them and get the still working. He took the pictures – and the video – that made the crowdfunding page so popular.

'But now she's selling it to that bloke from the mainland and we'll just become an extension of his company.'

'Ruby has tried to do the best for everyone: for Hector, for the island. There are bound to still be jobs. And she knew I needed to move on too.'

Silence falls over the group.

'And all of you, you've benefited from her being here. Jack Drummond and his business partners are staying at the pub. The ferry will be busier than ever today, with any luck; the café too no doubt. When was the last time this island had some hope about what the future might hold?'

'When Hector set up the still,' says Mrs Broidy.

'And now his granddaughter has done the same. And she's back at that house, wondering if anyone is going to turn up this afternoon. After all her work, putting her own life on hold, it looks as if it's all been for nothing. And if it has, what will happen to Hector? Life moves on for everyone. You just have to try and make sure it's in the right direction. If you won't do it for Ruby, or for me, do it for Hector. All of you have had a life on the island, and a good life too, because of him.

'We've all made mistakes. Who here hasn't? Hector certainly did, and not a day went by when he didn't regret not making it up with his son. But we all deserve a second chance. Don't leave it too late. Yes, maybe Ruby should have told you who she was, said what she was doing here. But she did what she did for the best reasons; she followed her heart. And helped put a few back together in the process.'

I take a big breath and lift my face to the gently falling snowflakes, then turn and run back to the house as if my feet have grown wings.

I shower quickly in the big tub and then start collecting up the mismatched vintage cups, saucers and plates we found when clearing out the cupboards, arranging them on the long table in the dining room at the back of the house. I open up the big double doors that connect the room with the living room, where Hector is sitting in his worn wingback chair looking out over the garden towards the distillery through the gently falling snow.

After a while, Lachlan arrives back, without a word about where he's been. He stops and smiles at me.

'Ferry should be in soon,' he says. 'Maybe there'll be guests on it. We'd better get ready just in case.'

I nod, and together we lay out the plates and cake stands for the sponge cakes, shortbread and cheese scones he's made.

'I'll get some gin from the distillery; we can pour it into shot glasses for people to try it neat, and offer tonic for those who don't want it like that. I'll just give the distillery a tidy too,' he says, brushing his curly hair off his face. 'We can give them a tour before tea, and tell them the history of the place.'

If anyone comes, I think, biting my lip. And I'm sure he's thinking the same, but is putting on a brave face.

Suddenly the big bell at the front door rings out, making me jump. I wipe my hands and look around for Lachlan, but he's already outside and heading for the distillery. His happy place, I think, and find myself smiling. And then thinking how sad it's going to be for him to leave it and hand it over

275

to the new owners. But I push that thought away, just for the time being.

I go to the front door and pull it open, hoping to see some of the villagers. And I don't know if I'm disappointed it's not them, or just thrilled to see who it is.

Chapter Forty-two

Jess and the rest of the band are standing in front of me!

'Whaaa!' I say, lost for words.

Jess is pulling off her sunglasses. 'God, that was some journey. I think I left my stomach somewhere back in the middle of that big bit of sea!'

The others all agree. There's Moira, our drummer, Gwilym, keyboards, and Ali, our double bass player. They huddle together for warmth. The sky is darkening and there's a stillness in the air. It's cold and crisp, and Jess is shivering in the snow falling around her.

'What are you all doing here?!' I say with a mix of surprise and delight.

'Come to make sure you actually leave this time!' she says. 'Judging by the video on your crowdfunding page, I'm beginning to think this place is getting right under your skin.'

'And the strange messages in the band group chat . . . all those GIFs and smiley faces!' says Moira.

'What? Of course I'm going to leave!'

'And to see if you're going to come back to the band,' Jess adds. 'I know what I said, but well, I was just, y'know, hurt. And I know you and Joe aren't . . . any more. But that's no reason for us to stop trying to succeed, achieve our goals!' She smiles.

I can't think what to say to her. I think about Joe.

'How is Joe?' I say, my throat tightening.

She shrugs. 'Looks like you weren't the only one keeping secrets. Joe likes to hedge his bets by all accounts. Sorry, Rubes. I should've told you. He and Lulu have been looking fairly close lately.'

'Yeah, he thinks he's found the winning lottery ticket this time!' says Moira, and Gwilym nudges her sharply in the ribs.

'It's fine,' I say, but I realise that's exactly how I felt, like I was Joe's winning lottery ticket. Clearly, when he saw he might not be able to cash in on me, he transferred his attention to Lulu. I should have seen it coming. It was only being here that made me view our relationship more clearly. There was nothing else in it other than my career. And when that looked like it was gone, Joe moved on.

'How long?' I manage to ask.

'Think it started Christmas Eve,' says Ali, and I remember Joe being out on Christmas morning, getting 'a few bits'. I feel angry, but actually relieved too. It hurts, really hurts, but I know it'll get better. I swallow, hard.

'I think,' I say slowly, 'it really is time Joe got a dream of his own.' I gaze out at the snowflakes falling. 'But that's for him to find out.' I look back at Jess, my oldest friend, and the others. 'It's so good to see you!' I say, enveloping them in a group hug. 'It means everything to me that you've come!'

But as I hug them, I see they're not alone. 'Mum?!' I say, looking over Jess's shoulder. My mum is standing there, case by her side, looking around like she's stepped out of the Tardis and gone back in time. 'What are you doing here?'

'Came to see you, darling!'

'More likely you could sniff out the gin!' I laugh, and so does she. It feels so good hearing her laugh.

'Well, this place certainly hasn't changed! Certainly not for the better . . . If anything, it looks like the land that time forgot. Can't imagine why you've got yourself stuck here. I came to see if it really was as I remembered. And to check on you, of course!'

She turns back to me and she too pulls off her sunglasses. What is it with people from the city and sunglasses? I think. You don't get to take in half as much if you're always wearing shades.

'Well, are we just going to stand on the doorstep? This cold will do my voice no good, you know, and I have a cruise show in a week's time! I say a show; actually they want me to run karaoke night, but they'll want me to perform, they always do!' She steps past Jess, balancing her big sunglasses on top of her solid black curly hair, hairsprayed to within an inch of its life, and kisses me lightly on both cheeks, the hairspray catching in the back of my throat and making me cough.

'You should have come to stay with me. You could have come to me on the ship, or we could've stayed with friends in Spain. I'd've done yoga with you on the beach, taken you through your exercises. What's Tenerife got that a few weeks with your own mother wouldn't have solved? In fact, it's given me an idea about setting up a singing centre of my own. Just need to find the backing!' She steps into the hall, clutching her huge handbag over her coat and a sparkly shawl on top of that.

Jess follows, stamping her feet and blowing into her hands, as do the rest of the band.

'We were going to stop and have something to eat at the café, but it was full of a party from an old people's home that came over on the ferry with us.'

Island View! My heart skips a beat. They came! Somebody at least came!

'Well, look, as you're here,' I say, 'there are rooms made up upstairs. We had guests the other night, when there was a big storm. Burns Night, when we piped in the haggis. Dreadful weather. Great night. The weather here can change four times in a day! But it helped fill the mountain spring, where the water for the gin comes from, filtered over some of the oldest rock on the planet.'

Jess, the band and my mum all look at me.

'What?' says Moira.

'Definitely got under your skin!' my mum and Jess say together.

'Definitely time you came home,' adds Jess.

'Come in.' I manage to smile. 'The fire's lit. Just going to do the one here in the hall. And now that you're here, I could really do with a hand. My cleaning help has . . . gone down with something. Actually, she's . . .' I hear my voice start to crack, and I falter.

'What?' says my mum, concerned.

Jess puts her arm around me. 'What is it?'

'I don't think they're coming. I don't think anyone's coming. They think I've let them down.'

'Oh, now if I know anything about this island, it'll all be a storm in a teacup,' says my mum. 'We'll pitch in. Get this place sorted in no time. It'll be fun!' She smiles, making me smile too. She may not have been the most dependable of parents, but she did used to make things fun, and I know she loves me. 'Let's get the radio on and get this party started!' She looks around. 'Might even feel like old times.'

I follow her gaze. It's as if she's drinking in the memories.

'Mum, why have I never been here before?'

'Well, once your dad fell out with his father, that was it. Hector told him if he left to never return. He was dead to him. I don't think he meant it, but the two of them . . .'

'. . . locked horns?'

She looks at me. 'Exactly. And never spoke again. Your dad did plan to bring you here for a visit. But after he died, there didn't seem any reason for me to make contact. You were happy enough. We had our own life. And then we just lost any chance of getting back in contact.'

I nod. I suppose you can only do the best you can in the moment. Regrets won't help. It's living in the now that matters. And right now, I have had the chance to meet Hector, and that seems very special.

'Oh, Hector. Come and say hello.' I guide them down the hall.

'He's here?' says my mum, suddenly apprehensive.

'Of course. Although he may not actually know who you are. But he'd love to say hello, I'm sure. Come on in. Hector, we have guests.'

'Guests? Is it them? Are they here?' He goes to stand from the wheelchair that he's taken to using without complaint over the past few days. 'Is it Campbell and the baby?'

'No, not yet. I'm sure they'll be here soon, though.' I put a steadying hand on his shoulder. 'These are friends, here for the tea party.'

'Oh, right, smashing. Will we have a nip, Mairead?'

'Who's Mairead?' Jess whispers in my ear.

'His wife,' I whisper back.

'What, your grandmother? Ew!'

'Sometimes I'm Mairead, sometimes I'm his personal assistant, Miss Rubes,' I say with a fond smile.

'But never Ruby?' she asks.

'No.' I shake my head. 'He can't seem to remember that part yet. Thinks I'm still a baby.'

'Hello, Hector,' says my mum, putting out a hand. Suddenly all her loud, brash ways seem to have left her. 'We met a long time ago.'

'Did we?' He looks at her with no recognition whatsoever in his frail face. He's lost weight since I got here, despite Lachlan's fabulous cooking. 'You'll have to excuse me. The memory's not quite what it used to be.' He looks out of the window, his mind wandering, and starts to hum gently to himself.

'Seems like all the sad memories have been left in the past,' Mum says. 'That's not a bad place to be in life.' She looks at him. 'I took his son away, and with that, his chance of family life here on the island. I didn't mean to. I just . . . we just fell in love. But it wasn't meant to be.'

'You mean you got bored,' I say, and wish I hadn't, but she just nods sadly.

'I wish your dad could have made it up with his family.'

'Maybe they were about to. Hector seems to think that Dad and the baby were about to visit the island. He's living in hope,' I say.

'Again, not a bad place to be. We should all live in hope.' She smiles. 'Right, let's get this place ready for a tea party, shall we?'

'Oh, and here comes Lachlan,' I say, watching him walking across from the distillery with bottles in his arms.

'Who's Lachlan?!' asks my mum and Jess and the rest of the band at the same time, their eyes widening.

For some unknown reason, I find myself blushing.

'Lachlan, oh he's—'

'He's Miss Rubes' man,' says Hector, suddenly stirring. 'She's having his baby, you know!'

'So let me get this right,' says my mum, holding her hands round a cup of tea, laced with something stronger, I suspect, and leaning against the old range to warm her behind. 'You're Miss Rubes . . . but you're not having a baby.'

'No.' Lachlan and I both laugh, and my insides flip at the memory of the kiss on Burns Night.

'So you two aren't . . .' Jess points between us.

'No!'

'Good God, no!' says Lachlan at the same time. 'We can barely stand the sight of each other!' He smiles at me and I tingle all over. 'And, um, there was no one else on the ferry?' he asks. 'Just you guys and the care home party?'

'That's it,' says Jess. 'I mean, who else would be mad enough?'

Lachlan and I look at her.

'What? I mean, it's not . . .'

'Tenerife?' says Lachlan, with a smile in the corner of his mouth. And I wonder who else Lachlan was expecting?

I think about all the effort he's put in to get to today, finding the ingredients, making batch after batch of gin until it's just like we remember it from that Christmas Day on the beach and again last night, when everything was, well, just perfect. Every time I shut my eyes I can taste it. It's a taste I will take with me when I leave. And every time I think of it, I'll be able to see the island as clearly as if I was back here. I swallow, wondering how it'll feel to be back in my own bed, back in my own little flat, closing my eyes and tasting and seeing the island in my head.

'Right, let's crack on,' says Lachlan. 'Let's make this the best tea party we can . . . whoever turns up. Let's do it for Hector. Jess, you help Ruby. And . . . Stella, is it? You can help me.' My mum beams. 'The rest of you, follow me.'

'We'll get Hector holding the bag of drawing pins when we put the bunting up,' I tell Jess, who is looking at me totally bemused.

'Ruby? What's going on?' she says as she follows me into the dining room.

'What do you mean?'

'You, this place . . .' she nods her head, 'Lachlan!'

'Oh, there's nothing going on with Lachlan.' My mouth is dry, and I realise that more than anything I'd love to say there *was* something going on with him, but even if he is feeling the attraction like I am – and judging by the way he looked at me last night when he gave me the bottle of gin, I think he is – we both know nothing can come of it. We'll be leaving the island after today.

'So now that it looks like you don't need to go to Tenerife, we can get straight back to gigging. There's plenty booked in for the band, especially after the big gig yesterday. Loads of interest! And I've had a call asking if you're available for saloon singing sessions. They have lots of slots if you want them. And . . . the big news!' She claps her hands together. 'I finally got hold of the A&R woman. She said she'd try and see us again. So with you sounding so great, the sooner we get back out there, the sooner we could get seen.'

We're draping bunting between the curtain poles, Jess holding it, me reaching and draping.

'That's great news!' I say.

'So you'll come back?'

'Of course.'

'When?'

'Well, if all goes according to plan today, the house and the gin business will be sold and Hector will move into the care home. There'll be no reason for me to be here after that,' I say, whilst my heart says otherwise. Because I love it here, and because Lachlan is still here!

'This is some house.' Jess looks around. 'It'll probably be turned into a boutique hotel, with a Michelin-starred chef and its own distillery.'

'It is beautiful, isn't it?' I look out across the bay as the snowflakes fall like glitter and wonder if the seals are out, and whether they'll appear for the guests when Lachlan walks them down there.

'It's got to be worth a bit, what with the gin business as

well. Even with paying for Hector's care home, there'll be quite a pot of money once you've sold it. You know, it would pay for us to take the band on tour. A European tour, do the festivals, really get our name out there.'

'Jess!'

'What? I'm just saying. If and when anything happens to the old . . . to Hector, you'll be in line for whatever's left, being the next of kin and all that.'

I shake my head. I don't even want to think about it. 'There's no way I'm financing a European tour with Hector's money!'

Jess shrugs. 'I'm just saying think about it. I bet he'd want you to do something with the money.'

'Well, he's doing just fine and that's not going to be an option.'

Jess shrugs again and Hector coughs from the other room.

'Come on, Hector. Come and hold this bag of drawing pins for me,' I call. Right now, Hector not being around is the last thing I want to think about. I've only just found him, and I feel I'm only just finding me too. I don't want that to stop.

'We'll put some music on,' I say, and climb down from the chair. It'll put us all in the right mood. This is supposed to be a celebration, after all.

Chapter Forty-three

By five to three, the house is looking amazing. My mum is pulling off rubber gloves, and I'm pretty sure that's the first time she's ever come into contact with a loo brush.

'That Lachlan! He's a hard taskmaster!' she says, tossing the gloves into a cleaning bucket that Lachlan picks up and puts in the scullery. She shakes out her hair. It still doesn't move.

'Right, time for a drink, everyone,' Lachlan says, pouring gin into glasses on a tray and carrying it into the living room where Hector and the others are.

'Ah, Miss Rubes!' Hector says, but he doesn't stand as he usually does. He may have been asleep.

The rest of us gather around the roaring fire where he's sitting. The dogs are dozing in front of it. The crackle from the logs is the only sound other than the tick of the clock. Slowly, very slowly, the big hand eases its way around to three o'clock. And as it hits the hour with a chime, I hold my breath.

The bell at the front door rings, making me jump, as usual. Hector looks up.

'Visitors. Lovely,' he says with a smile that seems to take all his energy.

'Show time,' says my mum. 'Just like the old days.'

Chapter Forty-four

The dining room is buzzing. The whole of the island seems to have turned out, along with the residents from the care home, Fraser and his extended family and Jack Drummond and his business partners. The visitors have been on a tour of the distillery, and those that could manage it have taken a walk to see the seals. Lachlan has shown them a glimpse of the places we've gathered the botanicals from, the ingredients that give the gin its taste of wild and rugged island life. Now a record is playing, and everyone is enjoying the tea, having a really fun time by the looks of it.

'All okay?' I hear Lachlan's voice behind me, making my nerve endings stand to attention.

I nod. 'You?' I ask.

'Uh huh.' He's not looking at me but gazing out of the window across the lawn, as if he's looking for someone. 'Seems to be going well,' he says. Isla is glancing over at him anxiously, and I have no idea what's going on between them. I thought they'd sorted things out. Moved on. It would break Gordan's heart if anything were to happen between them. Not to mention what it would do to mine.

I look at my mum, who's holding a teapot and looking

out of the big French doors along the back wall of the wood-panelled dining room.

'You okay, Mum?'

'Yes, darling. Just . . . you know, being back here. Makes me remember how I felt when I first fell in love with your dad. And sad, too, looking back at how things turned out. I should never have let it happen. I didn't think about the consequences for him. Just took what I wanted at the time.'

'It all makes sense now, though.'

'What does?'

'Dad. His funny ways. He's just like Hector. I can see now that he longed to be back here, as if he'd left a part of him behind.'

Mum smiles and puts her spare arm around me, hugging me.

'Your dad loved it here. Always did. That's why it broke his heart to leave. He should have come back. I told him to. But he was too stubborn, just like Hector. Once they've decided on something, they stick to it and make sure it happens. Like someone else I know.' She smiles at me and looks around the room. White tablecloths that I found in a suitcase cover every table we have in the place. 'I'm really proud of you,' she says, tears filling her made-up eyes.

'I'm glad you came, Mum.'

'So am I,' she says. 'Maybe I'm finally growing up. Maybe it's time I stopped chasing the next exciting adventure, settled down a bit.' She looks around the room. 'You know, this place, with work . . . you could sell it on when Hector, y'know . . .'

'Mum!'

'I'm just saying. Then you could come into business with me. We could set up a yoga retreat in Spain. Work together. Mother and daughter. What do you think?'

'I think you'd probably get bored of the idea and want to move on after about six months!' I smile affectionately at her. 'Besides, this house isn't mine and isn't ever going to be. It needs to be sold,' I swallow, 'to pay for Hector's care home. And soon.' I look over at Flora, who is cutting up a scone for one of the old ladies, her napkin tucked into her front.

'We're neither of us getting any younger, and the music industry is so brutal these days,' my mum says.

'Excuse me, I'm just going to put on a different record,' I say, glad of the excuse to get away as the speaker begins to crackle. I look around for Lachlan. I should do my singing spot really. He did promise them. We need to crack on before it's time for the ferry to leave.

'Lachlan, I think I should sing now,' I tell him.

'Soon, soon,' he says, and I have no idea why he's suddenly so reluctant. He moves away, offering refills of gin to the guests and passing on the information he's learnt from Hector. 'Gin and tonic was developed to prevent malaria,' I hear him saying. Let's hope that by the end of the tea party we've got a few more orders to meet our crowdfunding target, and can get the bottles sent out to those who have pledged money. Not that I'll be here by then, I think with a pang.

I take the record off and slide another one from its sleeve, lining up the needle. The crackle begins again and then the music starts to play, and as it does, there's another noise, a strange whooshing and dipping sound. I look at the disc revolving on the turntable and wonder if it's warped. But it doesn't look warped. The noise seems to be getting louder, and the chatter in the room seems to be growing too. But the room's getting darker, very quickly. Is it thunder? Another storm rolling in without warning? A snowstorm? The days have been so calm and cold, with fiery red skies in the morning, purple sunsets, and a sugar frosting covering the fields, sand dunes, heathland and forests like a Christmas card. A storm now would certainly be out of nowhere, but nothing is impossible here, I've come to learn. I've come to learn a lot about this place since I've been here, I think suddenly with a twist in my heart.

I look round, and everyone seems to be standing at the windows, staring out. Lachlan is standing next to Isla and smiling. My heart gives a further wrench. The sky is getting much darker and the rumbling is almost deafening. What on earth is going on?

Chapter Forty-five

I push up against the window in between my mother and Jess, and follow their gaze upwards. The record player is all but drowned out now by the noise and the light practically obliterated by the helicopter descending from the sky, landing on the lawn. My mouth drops a bit.

'You look like you're catching flies, darling,' says my mother.

'Who's that?' says Jess.

'I have no idea,' I reply.

'You must have some idea; it's got to be one of your crowdfunders,' Jess says, not taking her eyes off the settling helicopter and its swirling blades.

But as I look around, everyone I was expecting is here. Even Jack Drummond, who is looking very interested in the new arrival.

'Maybe it's landed here by mistake,' I say, 'what with the snow.' But the snow is only just starting to settle. I turn and see Lachlan and Isla grinning at each other and high-fiving, and I can't help but feel totally bewildered.

'Who is it?'

Everyone shrugs. Lachlan finally walks over to me, grinning. Oh God, what if this is how he and Isla are leaving, making a dramatic exit like my mum and dad did. His work here practically done. But not quite.

'We haven't reached our target, not yet,' I blurt out, and he looks momentarily confused. Then he smiles again as the door of the helicopter opens.

'What, did you think I was off the moment we hit the crowdfunding target?' he laughs.

'Well, aren't you?'

He looks at me. 'That was the deal. But not by helicopter.' He nods as a pair of legs emerges from the door and a man in sunglasses gets out, followed by . . . I catch my breath.

'The A&R woman! What's she doing here?!'

And Jess squeals.

I stare up at Lachlan and can't even manage the words to ask how this has happened.

'The video,' he says. 'It just got shared and shared. You saw what happened to the crowdfunding after I put it up.'

He looks out at the two figures ducking under the blades and making their way to the French doors.

'They messaged the page. Asked if you'd be singing here today.'

'I didn't see that,' I say, trying to recall it.

'That's because I replied. I knew that if you knew about it, you'd worry. As it is, you just have a room full of old people, locals, friends and family to entertain.' He shrugs and smiles. 'And a passing A&R person and record producer.'

'So you're not leaving?'

'Not yet. I made a promise, didn't I? Not until the distillery is up and running.'

He smiles at me again, and suddenly I realise that the

very last thing I want right now is for him to leave and never to see him again.

'I . . .'

I want to tell him, but as I try to speak, the French doors are flung open and a huge blast of cold air comes in, together with a few flakes of snow and the two new arrivals. The man rubs his leather-gloved hands together.

'I hear there's some gin to try.' He beams a very white smile. 'And as I'm not driving . . .'

My mother shoots forward and hands them both drinks.

'Thank you, and you are . . . ?'

'Stella. Stella Macquarrie,' she says, using her married name rather than her stage name!

'Are you part of the band?' he asks.

'Oh, er, no, I'm . . .'

He sips the gin and then looks at it. All his focus now on the glass. 'This is good,' he says, 'really good.'

'Made here on the island with local botanicals, including seaweed from the beach just over there.' I find myself going into autopilot. He nods.

'And you are?'

'Ruby Mac,' I reply, my mouth going dry. 'And this is Jess. She's our band manager and songwriter.'

Jess is behind me, putting out a hand. 'If only we'd known you were coming. The band, I'm mean, we're not set up,' she says, excited and pained all at the same time.

The man smiles. And then the A&R woman speaks.

'It's okay, Jess. It's Ruby we've come to hear. We heard she was going to be singing here this afternoon.'

'Oh,' says Jess, and I feel her spirits plummet.

'Did you . . . ?' She points at me and at the new guests, her eyes hurt.

'No, I did,' says Lachlan, introducing himself to the A&R woman. 'Local forager and apprentice distiller,' he adds.

'Well if you made this, I'd say they'd better make you the head distiller!' says the record producer, and Jack Drummond steps forward.

'That's a conversation we should have,' he says, and suddenly my heart lifts. What if he wants to take Lachlan on as head distiller? That would be perfect! I smile. Today suddenly got better!

'I'm not singing what I usually sing with the band,' I tell Jess quickly. Somehow I feel I want it to be okay with her.

'Do what you have to do, Ruby,' she says quietly, and turns away and walks to the other side of the room.

I look at Lachlan, who nods encouragingly. 'Do what you have to do,' he repeats, taking the jug of gin and tonic from my hands.

I look round at the piano, next to the record player.

'They've come to hear the Ruby they saw on the video,' he reminds me, just in case I'm in any doubt. 'The song you sang at the beach.'

I think about the song, one that has meant so much to him over the years. Will this finally mend the broken pieces of the record between him and Isla?

'Sing it like you sang it then,' he says.

I nod.

'Okay, everyone, as promised, we have the fantastic Ruby Mac to sing for you.' Lachlan holds out his hand and everyone starts to applaud. I take a deep breath. I'm going to do this just the way I planned it, and not change a thing just because the record producer is here. I'm going to do it my way. Sing it from the heart. And with that, I walk over to Hector, who is sitting in his wheelchair. I whisper to him, then wheel him over to the piano.

'Mrs Broidy? Would you?'

She nods and hurries forward to where I'm standing, Hector sitting in his wheelchair next to me. The Cruickshanks from the shop shuffle in beside the piano, just like on Burns Night.

Mrs Broidy looks at me, and I find my hand slipping into Hector's as she begins to play. At once I feel my nerves disappearing, and without thinking, I begin to sing. As I do, Hector gets unsteadily to his feet and joins in, taking my other hand, word perfect. My whole being fills with happiness, and there's a huge smile on my face to match his, and tears in my eyes. The small choir joins in gently behind us, but it's mine and Hector's voices that can be heard most clearly.

As the song comes to an end, Hector looks straight into my eyes. Then he lets go of my hands and cups my face with his own. Tears are filling the soft skin of the rims of his eyes and finding their way down the crevices and creases of his cheeks, just like the water from the mountain stream.

All around me I can hear clapping, but it's muted, as if far away. All I can see is Hector, looking straight into my eyes.

'You came!' he says shakily, and I nod. 'My granddaughter! You came!'

'Hello, Grandad,' I say, and the words catch in my throat. 'I knew you'd come . . . one day.' And he plants a wet, teary kiss on my cheek. 'I always knew you'd come!' he repeats. I help him back into his wheelchair and towards his favourite seat looking out over the lawn. 'Not sure about your mode of transport, though!' He nods to the helicopter on the lawn, and laughs.

Then Mrs Broidy plays again and we all join in. 'Looks like the island choir is back together,' she smiles, and I suddenly wonder if they'll keep going once I'm gone.

We sing a rousing rendition of 'The Bonnie Banks o' Loch Lomond' and finish with 'Auld Lang Syne'. Hector looks happy but exhausted from the exertion. Lachlan comes over with a cup of tea and a cheese scone for him, but he doesn't really respond. He seems to be thinking deeply as he looks out beyond the helicopter on the lawn.

'You were brilliant, fantastic,' says Lachlan, suddenly hugging me.

Over his shoulder I see Isla, who smiles at me. When he puts me down, I say, 'So, you and Isla . . .'

'She was the only one who knew about these guys coming. I knew I couldn't tell anyone else, but I couldn't keep it to myself either. I saw her in the café today.'

'So you're not . . . ?' I raise my eyebrows.

'No, Ruby. It's over. She and Gordan are having a baby. They deserve to be happy without me moping around making them feel bad. I need to find some happiness of my own now.'

Just as I go to reply, the producer and the A&R woman come over.

'Is there somewhere we could talk?'

'Um, sure,' I say, looking at Lachlan, who nods his head

towards the kitchen with an encouraging smile.

I lead them through the small crowd, who all stop me to tell me how beautiful the song was, many of them with tears in their eyes. My mum is now wearing her sunglasses, and is dabbing at the corners of her eyes. I'm not sure I've ever seen my mum cry. A song that hasn't been heard on the island in a long time, brought back to life; a song that I remember my father singing to me, and that his father must have sung to him. A song from the sea.

Jess is standing by the door. I look at her, feeling like I've betrayed her, like I've stolen the most precious thing from her.

'It's okay, Rubes.' She smiles like we're two lovers who realise they have fallen out of love and are walking different paths in life but will stay cherished friends. 'Do what you have to do.' She gently squeezes my arm.

I turn towards the hallway and lead the two visitors into the kitchen, wondering what my dad would've made of today, and whether we'll ever see another day like it here.

Chapter Forty-six

Holding the contract in my shaking hand, I look at them both.

'So it's a record deal, you sign to us,' says the producer.

'Just me?' I confirm.

'Just you. Doing what you did out there today and on the video. The girl from the island.'

'Oh, but I'm not . . .' I stop myself. Because suddenly I feel very much a part of this island, and I want to make them all proud. I suddenly feel very hot. 'Could you give me a moment?' I say. 'I just need some air.'

The producer looks at his watch. 'We don't have long,' he says. 'By the way, that gin . . . how much more did you need to sell to make your crowdfunding target?'

'Just another case and we're there.'

'In that case, I'll take a case!'

I turn and head out into the hall, where Lachlan is waiting.

'We've just sold the last case! We did it!' I whisper with excitement.

'We did it!' he beams. 'What's that?' He looks down at the brown envelope in my hand.

'Just something I need to think about,' I say. 'I'll only be a minute.'

I turn to the big front door, remembering how I pushed it open that first night in the storm. And now the fire is lit in the hall and the fairy lights and lanterns are shining one last time before we take them down tomorrow. Everything will look very different then. I slip outside and take some deep, deep breaths, breathing from my butt once more, trying for some semblance of control. And look what happened last time I tried to control what was happening: I ended up here and just let life take me where it thought I should go. I think of the mountain burn and my early-morning runs. I'd give anything to be out on one of those runs right now.

I breathe in deeply again.

'Hello!'

I jump about a mile in the air. It's Jack Drummond, from the drinks company.

'Sorry, I didn't mean to scare you,' he says. 'Just thought I'd take a moment to look around.'

'It's beautiful, isn't it?' As I speak, my breath comes out like smoke from a fiery dragon. The snow is falling more heavily now, and my teeth are chattering.

'It is. And you sang beautifully too, if I may say so.' He smiles.

'Thank you.'

'You have your orders in?'

'We do! We've just met our crowdfunding target, so the gin run can happen.'

'Excellent! Now that you have, I take it you'd like to sell this place with the distillery?'

'That's the plan!' I try and sound happy.

'Well, then we at Drummond's would very much like to

buy it. Let's talk figures over the next few days. I'm sure we can come to an agreement. Like I say, we're very keen to buy, before anyone else gets the chance.'

I bite my lip. This is everything we could have hoped for, I think, and wish I could feel over the moon. Maybe I'm just in shock. Or it's the cold.

I look at the brown envelope in my hand.

'So, will you be offering Lachlan a job too, as head distiller?' I say, unable to resist.

He nods.

'Lachlan will be carrying on making Teach Mhor gin? That is excellent!' And this time I do feel a surge of excitement. 'I want to know everything that's going on and when it will be launched! I could sing at the launch . . . if you want me to,' I add hastily.

'That would be wonderful. Though I don't know if he's taking the job yet. He said he had to think about it.'

'Think about it? What's there to think about? He's brilliant at it!'

'Exactly. And he said he had to move to the mainland anyway, so it makes sense.'

'Perfect,' I say, then pull myself up short. 'Sorry, did you say the mainland?'

'Uh huh, we're based just outside Edinburgh. You must come and visit our set-up there. Bit bigger than this.' He smiles.

I frown. 'But the gin, it'll be made here?' I confirm. And he shakes his head.

'We'll make it at our base. Much easier. It'll still be branded Teach Mhor gin, though. We'll do some lovely labelling with a picture of the house, maybe an old photograph. List the ingredients, maybe use a map of the island to show where they're usually found.'

'Usually found?'

'Yes, once we've got the recipe, we can use our own suppliers. I mean, water's water, right?' He laughs.

'No, not right,' I find myself saying. 'The water comes from the waterfall up the mountain. It runs into a burn that flows across the island and the flavours are gathered on its journey out to sea. That's the point!'

'Excellent story, excellent story!' He nods.

'It's not just a story,' I say, suddenly horrified. And right there, I see the future of this place. 'It's about Winter Island. So you can shut your eyes and taste the place. What about the crowdfunders? The people who have supported us? Jobs and business for the island?'

'We'll make sure everyone who's bought into the crowdfunding gets their gin, and then we'll buy them out with a gift of goodwill.'

Someone clears their throat behind us. I turn to see Lachlan standing at the front door.

'The ferry's leaving soon. People have to go,' he says.

I turn back to Jack Drummond. 'It's much more than an excellent story!' I say, my hands and my voice shaking.

Chapter Forty-seven

I walk slowly back into the busy dining room, where Mum and Jess are serving more gin. Hector is in his chair still, looking out over the bay, his tea and scone untouched.

I walk up to the microphone. Jess's voice is in my head: *Do what you have to do.*

'Thank you, everyone, for coming today.' The room falls silent. 'Thank you to all those who dug deep and helped us reach our crowdfunding target!' A small cheer goes up. I take a huge breath, pulling up my chest and my backside. 'Many of you know that I came here for one reason and one reason only . . . to sell Teach Mhor.' There's a ripple around the room. 'As Hector's next of kin, I had to agree to sell the house so he could move into the care home.' I see Fraser in the audience and a small smile tugs at the corner of his mouth.

'Away from the island,' shouts one of the Cruickshank sisters, and I nod.

'But in order for that to happen, the gin business needed to be revived and the recipe had to be recovered. Today, we've done that. And I have got exactly what I have dreamt of and worked towards for the past fifteen years, right here . . .' I look down at the envelope in my hand. 'But I know it wouldn't have happened if I hadn't come here and met . . .' I look at Lachlan, unable to say it out loud, 'if I hadn't met Hector, my grandfather. I realise that he and my father were just like the stags out there locking horns, and I only wish they'd seen sense a long time ago. Before it was too late.'

'Ruby, we have to go,' says the A&R woman. 'The contract?'

I glance down, then hold the envelope out to her. 'Thank you, but no thank you. Being here on Winter Island has brought my voice back. It has taught me why I love singing and how it makes me feel. How it makes others feel. The memories it makes.'

I look over at Hector's chair.

'But I won't be signing the contract, or leaving the island, and neither will my grandfather. Teach Mhor and its distillery isn't for sale.'

A cheer goes up.

'I'm going to stay and look after him, make sure he has the care he needs and oversee the gin business with the help of its shareholders here on the island. The island is at the heart of that business, and at mine too. So I'm sorry, but like I say, I won't be signing with you.'

'Okay,' says the A&R woman slowly. 'Well, if you change your mind . . .' She smiles. 'Though I can see you won't.'

'I may, however, set up the island choir again and collaborate with the care home to show how music can help people with dementia. Perhaps your record company would like to support that project to help raise awareness of music and dementia?' I look at the producer.

'Now that could be interesting,' he says.

'A Christmas single, recorded right here on the island?' I say, and beam. 'In the distillery. "Gingle Bells", a Christmas medley!'

'I'll send over the paperwork,' he says with a grin, and with that the two of them leave through the French doors and the helicopter blades start up again, blowing up the settling snow.

Everyone is crowding around me and congratulating me. I look around for Lachlan, but can't see him.

'Are you sure about this?' says my mum.

'Never more so,' I tell her.

'You don't fancy the yoga retreat idea then?'

'No, Mum. I'm staying put right here.'

'Well, I know your dad would have been happy about that,' she says, and smiles as far as her Botox will let her. 'I have to go. The minibus is going to give us a lift to the ferry.'

'Don't leave it another thirty-five years before you come back and visit.'

'I won't. I'm very proud of you,' she says quietly, and tears spring to my eyes once more.

'Jess?' I turn to her, and she hugs me.

'Looks like I'm a band member down, and those are blooming big boots to fill!'

'You don't mind?'

'I told you, you have to do what's right for you.'

'Yeah,' the others agree.

'You've got to follow your heart,' Moira adds, and I suddenly realise she is looking longingly at Gwilym and he back at her. This place really does make you see what's right in front of you!

'As long as we can come along as the support band when you record "Gingle Bells"!' Jess says.

'Deal!' and we all hug again.

The care home people are getting ready to go, busy saying goodbye.

'Um, has anyone seen Lachlan?' I look around.

'Talking of doing what feels right for you . . .' Jess raises an eyebrow. 'I saw him leave, just after the helicopter took off.'

I turn and run up to the attic, but it's empty. All his belongings are gone. He must have been packed already.

He thinks he has to go now! I realise. Now that the distillery's up and running. I have to stop him! I turn and hurtle back down the stairs.

Chapter Forty-eight

Hector is fast asleep in his chair, and I'm not surprised after all that singing and excitement. I slip on the first pair of wellingtons I can see by the back door, and Douglas is up and beside me. Rhona stays close to Hector's chair.

'Good girl!' I tell her, and she looks at me as if letting me know she's there to keep watch over him.

I pull the back door open. There are still locals milling around in the dining room, and the gin is flowing just the way Hector would want it to be. Everyone is in celebratory mood. Everyone except me, it seems. None of this seems right without Lachlan here as a part of it. Tears fill my eyes, and running is made twice as hard by my blurry vision and the whiteness outside. The snow is falling heavily now, the wind picking up and starting to swirl it. I stumble to the distillery to see if he's there in his usual place, looking over the big still. I throw the door open hoping with all my heart to see him checking on his creation.

'Lachlan!' I call out, but the place is empty and dark. I know he's not there. He's gone. He couldn't bear to stay another moment; like ripping off a plaster, the quicker he did it, the quicker the hurt would pass. I dip out of the distillery and close the heavy door, as heavy as my heart. The one person who should be here to celebrate is him. I'm not sure I can even do this without him.

I turn to look at the bay and hold my face to the cold, feeling the sting of snowflakes on my cheeks and lips. I put my head down and run to the harbour, back to where I arrived only six weeks ago, just in time to see the ferry leaving in a wash of white horses. I put my hand up.

'Stop! Lachlan! Come back!' I shout as the snow falls all around me. 'I can't do this without you! I love you!' But no one is listening.

The ferry gives a cheery toot on its horn and many of the old folk wave back at me as it powers off towards the mainland. Slowly I lower my hand and watch it go, Douglas sitting at my side.

Then, with the snow swirling, twisting and tumbling all around me, I turn and set off again. I'm stumbling and tripping but I can't stop; I need to keep moving. I take my usual route around the island, following the burn, running as fast as the thick layer of snow on the ground will let me, trying to escape the voice in my head telling me how I've messed up. I should have told him when I first realised how I felt about him. I should have told him I didn't want him to go!

I run faster, tears falling from my eyes as I see the croft in the distance and wonder what will happen to it now. This was Lachlan's family home. I draw closer, then pause. My vision is blurred with tears and snowflakes, but it looks like . . . I squint to try and see better . . . it looks like . . . and my heart suddenly leaps and twists all at the same time. It looks like the door is open.

Chapter Forty-nine

As I put my hand to the wooden door and push it open further, my heart pounds like it's going to burst from my chest. And then practically explodes as I see Lachlan standing there in front of me, holding the pieces of the broken record. He looks up at me uncertainly.

'I thought you'd gone,' I say, my mouth dry.

'Thought I should take a look at this place.' He glances around. It's the first time he's been in here since he moved back, I know. 'See how it's been after all this time. I grew up here, you know. I can still see my parents here.' He smiles.

'And Isla?' I ask tentatively.

He shakes his head. 'I can't see her here any more,' he says. 'She's happy and I'm happy for them both.' He looks at me. 'I could always . . .'

'I don't want you to . . .' I say at the same time. We're as nervous as each other.

'I said I'd move out when the gin was made. I didn't say where to.' He smiles. 'This is a good house. I could move in here. Then if you needed help . . .'

'I don't want you to go anywhere!' I say suddenly. 'Teach Mhor is about more than just Hector; it's about you too. It's your home, and you're as much a part of the business as I am. I can't do it without you.'

'You could. Just like you sang again. You followed your instincts.'

'I don't *want* to do it without you. I don't want you to go anywhere. Please say you'll stay. Stay in the house. Be the head distiller. Stay! The three of us together.'

He looks at me. Then he steps forward so that he's standing right in front of me and kisses me, and I know I'm finally home. Any doubts about my new life disappear completely. Everything I want is right here, right now, and my heart sings louder than it ever has before.

Eventually he pulls back and looks at me, and I wonder whether we could just excuse ourselves from the last of the party, light the fire and spend the night together here.

'Maybe we should go and see what Hector thinks.' He smiles. 'Tell him the news. See if he'll let us both stay. He may get that wedding party he's been hoping for!'

As we pull the door to, our arms wrapped around each other and Douglas by our feet, I look at the croft.

'You know, it would make a lovely home . . . but it would also be perfect for foraging holidays. You could teach people about foraging and run gin-making workshops.'

He nods. 'Or a recording studio?'

'Oh no, I'm going to do that in the attic!' I laugh. So does he.

'Looks like I'm going to have to move rooms then!' He raises his eyebrows and stops to kiss me again, the snow falling on my cheeks. And as I feel myself melt into his body, I know that tonight can't come soon enough.

'Come on, let's go and talk to Hector,' he says, his arm around me, steadying me in my oversized boots, laughing as we go.

When we reach the back door, Rhona is standing by it barking, slowly, like a metronome.

'All right, good girl. We're back,' I tell her, and rub her head. 'It's okay, I found him. We're all here now.'

We take off our coats and I step out of the wellies, still smiling. There's laughter coming from the dining room, and it looks like Jess and the rest of the band are going to the pub with the locals. Coats and hats are being pulled on.

'We'll meet you down there!' Lachlan tells them.

'Don't be too long!' Jess waves a finger and gives us a knowing look, and we laugh. Rhona is still barking, slowly and methodically, and I rub her head again, then step into the warm living room, where Hector is still sitting looking out of the window, his tea and scone still untouched.

'Hector,' I say, walking over to him. Lachlan stops to put another log on the fire. 'Hector,' I say again, thinking he hasn't heard me and beaming from ear to ear. 'Have you heard the news? I'm not leaving, and neither is Lachlan. In fact we're . . .'

I pause and look at him, and straight away, I know.

Chapter Fifty

'Do you think he knew?' I swallow. Outside, it's snowing hard now. I don't know why, but I put an extra blanket over Hector's cold body.

'Judging by the smile on his face, I'd say he knew everything,' says Lachlan, his arm around me. He passes me a cup of tea and I can smell the whisky in it. 'For the shock,' he tells me.

'So you'll stay?'

He nods. 'I'm going nowhere. Why would I leave when everything I want is right here? You don't always have to go away to find what you're looking for. Sometimes you just have to go back.' He smiles at me, then looks at Hector's peaceful face. 'I'd say Hector was right back where he wanted to be. The house full of people, the gin business up and running and his family here at Teach Mhor.'

'And I'm not going anywhere either. This is where I found me again. You helped me find my voice. You made me remember why I love singing; what singing can do for me, not what I can do with singing. I may not have grown up here, but it's where my heart is, definitely.'

'Sure?'

'Couldn't be surer.' I smile, and then look back at Hector.

'And I think Fraser might have had an idea about that when he asked me up here.'

'Doctor and funeral director are on their way,' Mrs Broidy says from the doorway.

'What will happen to him?' I look at Lachlan.

'He'll be cremated and the ashes scattered on the water down at the bay. If that's okay with you. You are the next of kin after all.'

'You were the one who knew what he wanted. You were the one who knew he didn't want to leave the island. He wanted to end his days here.'

'Looks like we managed to give him his last wish. I think that was granted when he realised his granddaughter had come back home. His family together again,' says Lachlan.

And then he kisses me all over again, as the snow falls heavily and silently, and I have never felt more at home. I know that my life is here on Winter Island with Lachlan, and that the songs in my heart will never leave me, nor will the memories I made here with Hector, my grandfather. Right here is my past, my future and my present.

Epilogue

It's August 30th and the sun is setting bright red and orange in the sky. Lachlan has lit a bonfire on the beach as the heat goes out of the day. It's been a busy summer, welcoming visitors to the distillery, giving tours and making up the gin orders. The pub has opened up rooms to rent again and the café has taken on a full-time manager, Fraser Gillies' daughter, who has returned to the island for good. Once the fire is going strong, we all stand around it and I hand out glasses and fill them with gin. Everyone from the island is there, everyone except two people ... well, three now, actually.

Lachlan calls for our attention. 'First of all, I'd like you to raise your glasses to Hector.'

We all hold our gin aloft and chorus, 'To Hector!'

'And secondly – and I know Hector will be raising a glass wherever he is too, with Mairead – to Isla and Gordan and baby Murray! Mother and baby are doing fine, I'm told. A healthy, bouncing nine-pound baby boy. Gordan and Isla cannot wait to leave hospital and bring him home to the island.'

'To Murray,' we all cheer, and sip the clear spirit. I watch as everyone looks down at their glasses and then up at Lachlan.

'Ah,' he says. 'A little surprise for you all,' and I beam with pride. 'This is our new seasonal gin, made with summer botanicals from the island.'

'What's in it?' asks Lyle.

'I couldn't possibly divulge the recipe. But I think, if you all agree, we should call it The Island's Song, to remind us of the importance of music, and the memories it makes.' Lachlan's eyes are suddenly damp, and I step forward and wrap my arm around him.

'And this is just the first of Lachlan's new gins from Macquarrie's,' I say proudly. 'There will be a gin for every season. Four seasons, just like the weather in one day on this island!'

Everyone laughs. Then they all raise their glasses again.

'To Hector, and to baby Murray,' they say, and I go round and top up the glasses as we stand by the fire and watch the orange ball of the sun setting on another day here on the Isle of Geamhradh, where you have no idea what tomorrow might bring, where we celebrate the now, and I know there is nowhere in the world I would rather be.

Acknowledgements

Thank you to Ali Shone, who inspired this book. Ali works with the Strike a Chord stroke choir in Cwmbran and also with dementia patients, working on musical memories. Ali has music running through her veins and her ability is not just in being able to help people sing or play an instrument, it is about a much bigger picture: helping people to live the best life they can with music in their hearts. She has helped young people dealing with anxiety and pressure to face the world learn to breathe and to believe in themselves. Thank you Ali.

With musical memories at the heart of this book, I was also inspired by the settings, dedication and spirit of some of our Scottish Island gins; a particular thank you to Robert Mceachern at The Botanist Gin, made at Bruichladdich distillery on Islay. And James Donaldson, their official forager, for answering my questions about botanicals. Also thank you to the Isle of Harris for your inspiring daily photographs and tempting foodie posts. And to the creators of Lussa Gin on the Isle of Jura for the inspiring story of your island and island life. All of these gins have fabulous websites and tell the stories of the spirit of their island. Please do take a look and order their gin. It's delicious!! And yes, I did have to try them all!

Thanks go as well to Sibling Gin in Cheltenham, for sharing their entrepreneurial spirit and for guiding me through the gin making process and introducing me to the fabulous flavours in their own gins. And of course to Katie Fforde for joining me on this research trip as well as our Scottish island trip, which sparked the idea for Winter Island and The Big Hoose!

And finally, thank you to Jennifer Doyle for her support and faith in my stories and for letting me write the story of Ruby Mac and Winter Island. And to my agent David Headley for always being there!

Discover other books by

Jo Thomas

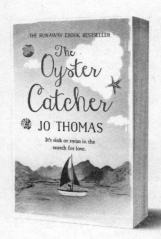

An irresistibly feel-good novel set on the charming coast of Ireland.

'A heart-warming tale full of Celtic charm, set against a beautiful landscape. What more could you wish for?' Ali McNamara

Can love bloom in the olive groves and vineyards of Italy?

'Romantic and funny, this is a great addition to any bookshelf!' *Sun*

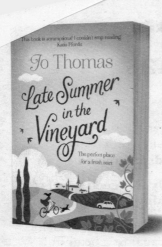

A gorgeous read filled with sunshine and wine in the South of France.

'A fabulous French feast of fun'
Milly Johnson

Let this novel transport you straight to the breath-taking mountains of Crete.

'Perfect escapist magic'
Good Housekeeping

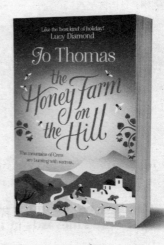

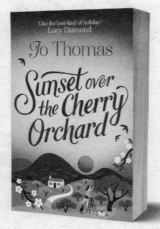

Escape to the sun-drenched hills and cherry orchards of southern Spain.

'Warm, funny, romantic with a terrific sense of place. I loved it!'
Katie Fforde

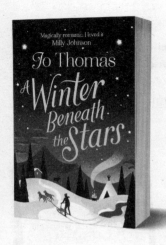

An unforgettable winter story set in the snow-filled world of Swedish Lapland.

'A sparkling, heart-warming hug of a story'
Miranda Dickinson

Could the lemon groves of Sicily be the perfect place to start over?

'A perfect, light holiday read, evoking Italian sunshine, lemon groves and romance'
Woman's Own

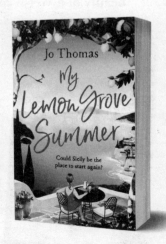

Jo's novels are available in paperback, eBook and audio

Discover the novellas

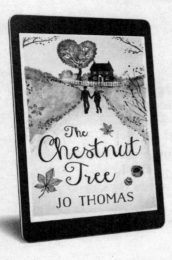

An irresistible romance filled with love and laughter amongst the rolling green of the Kent countryside

A sparkling, feel-good short story set in the picturesque beauty of a Welsh costal village.

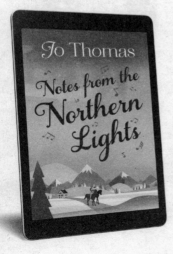

Dive into this gorgeous winter warmer, an irresistible winter tale set in Iceland that will melt the coldest of hearts...

Jo's novellas are available in eBook

Get in Touch

You can find out more about me and my books and
follow my latest adventures on my website:

www.jothomasauthor.com

You can also keep in touch by following me on:

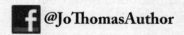 **@JoThomasAuthor**

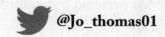 **@Jo_thomas01**

I'd love to hear from you!

Bookends

When one book ends, another begins...

Bookends is a vibrant new reading community to help you ensure you're never without a good book.

You'll find exclusive previews of the brilliant new books from your favourite authors as well as exciting debuts and past classics. Read our blog, check out our recommendations for your reading group, enter great competitions and much more!

Visit our website to see which great books we're recommending this month.

Join the Bookends community:
www.welcometobookends.co.uk

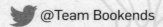 @Team Bookends   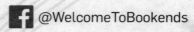 @WelcomeToBookends